DANGEROUS HEARTS

BOOK TWO IN THE SAVAGE HEARTS SERIES

MARY E. TWOMEY

For the people who have walked with me this far,
And for the new ones on the horizon.

And also for cheese. I love you, cheese.
Especially you, Manchego.

DANGEROUS HEARTS

Life in the village isn't as safe as Adelita thought it would be.

With a new family ready to take her in, Adelita still isn't quite sure she belongs, bringing danger ever nearer to her one safe place. Though she's beginning to fall into a rhythm with the three warriors, their protection has some serious setbacks whenever she questions the formidable Cruz.

The Kalku haven't stopped hunting her down. They are determined to steal her strength at any cost. When Adelita realizes the protection the village offers might be at risk, she knows that even though she wants to remain with them, if she wants to keep them safe, she has to leave them all...

...Even the ones who have stolen her heart.

THINGS I CANNOT UNDO
CRUZ

My sister's greeting at our return to the tribe has been slightly lackluster. "You're an absolute idiot," Eva says, folding her arms with a frown.

I cast Eva a glower but she never cowers under the weight of my frustration. "Not helping." Normally everyone in the house finds an excuse to get away from me at the slightest sign of my temper, but Eva regards me as if I'm being annoying.

Only a sister can get away with that.

She taps her foot as she stares me down. "You tell father you're bringing home a rescue and that you're setting them up in our home. Quite the convenient omission of a pronoun. Then lo and behold, you come home with an actual woman, carrying her like she's a fainted bride over the threshold. Beautiful as the day is long. What did you expect?"

"Santos was shaking too badly to carry her and Rafi's pissed about something so I *had* to carry her."

Me. Rafi's pissed at me because I was too rough with Adelita when I tried to train her to stand up to the Kalku. Addy is the strongest person I've ever come across but learning how to be strategic and agile in your fighting is still a necessity when you're a beautiful woman with a target on your back.

But I leave all those details out so I don't have to soak in another layer of my sister's wrath. Eva's got a mouth on her when she gets worked up. Why can't she be wary of me, like everyone else in the village?

Eva starts pacing in front of the kitchen's long island. "Her. Her. Who is she? Does she have a name? Dad's already announced to the tribe that you've brought home a woman to live in your house. Do you know how that sounds?"

I hold back a groan of frustration. "It sounds like a marriage announcement he had no right making. He can have fun prying his foot from his mouth. I certainly didn't do anything to encourage this."

Eva glances up at the ceiling as if praying for patience. "It's like you want me to yell at you. Do you not understand how long the tribe has been waiting for you to choose a bride so you can continue the family line? Everyone assumed you'd..."

I know what she's going to say. She's not wrong. I'm supposed to end up alone. That's the point of La Sayona's curse.

I roll my shoulders and avoid Eva's needling. "How does me bringing home a random survivor equal out to a wedding?"

Her glare cuts to me, her hands on her hips. She's only an inch shorter than me, which is taller than most of the men in the village. She wears her height like it gives her an extra boost of authority, which I can't imagine she needs. She has sheer volume, birthright and tenacity on her side. The height is just overkill.

Arms akimbo, she lowers her voice to properly scold me. "It does when you're next in line to produce an heir the whole tribe is counting on. You know how the villagers feel about outsiders."

"I think the giant border wall around our tribe speaks for itself." I cannot believe I'm letting Eva bait me, but apparently, I can't help myself. Adelita's earlier criticism of our wall stuck in my brain. "I know the gig. We rescue victims from the Kalku. Sometimes we even let them into the village for our healers to get them back on their feet. Then we pat ourselves on the back for what compassionate heroes we are, but really everyone in Cáceres is counting the seconds until the newcomers are out of here. The second the outsiders enter the village, they're treated like lepers. Can't have the purity of the tribe infected by too many foreigners."

Eva rears back at my blunt assessment, but recovers coolly, as she always finds a way to do. "Survivors usually are sent to the healer's home, not the chief's home, and then they're placed outside of the village once they're recovered from whatever the Kalku put them through. They don't take up residence in the village, much less the chief's home."

"Santos did."

She narrows her eyes at me, her sarcasm flaring. "Yes. I'm sure if you married Santos, even that would be an improvement to your current state."

I grab an apple from the teal-painted pottery bowl in the center of the kitchen's island, rubbing it on my shirt before taking a bite. Man, I miss fresh food. Weeks of gas station grabs and takeout is the worst. "You're just mad because if I had brought home a wife, the heat would be off of you to find a husband."

She lets out a long exhale like she's purging the air from a tire. "That would be a bonus, yes. Dad set me up with another one of his selections while you were away. As if that's all it takes."

"Let me guess: A decorated warrior who hasn't cracked a smile since he was a toddler."

"It's almost like you've heard me complain about this before."

"One or two hundred times, yes."

The bickering cools between us, since we're in the same boat. She wants to continue to sit in on policy meetings with Dad, but if she gets married, that spot will go to her husband. Our tribe is a pretty strict patriarchy. I'm to rule next, and I couldn't want the job less.

She paces about the beige-tiled kitchen, her teal dress matching the countertops as she turns on her heel and marches back and forth. "I'm not sure how much clearer I can be that I have no desire to marry a warrior. My father is the chief who worked his way up from being a warrior himself. My uncle is head of the army. My brother is a highly revered warrior who is completely daft when it comes to women, and who, come to think of it, also hasn't cracked a smile since he was a toddler. I don't want that life. I want to affect change at the highest level."

"And if you ever did get married? If you could have both a position of prominence and a husband?"

Before she speaks, I already know what she's going to say. "I want a poet. I want to laugh and enjoy my marriage, like Mom and Dad do. I don't want to bite my nails for the rest of my life, adding a husband to the list of men I love who I'm constantly afraid might never come home every time they step foot outside this village."

She started out in her usual rant, but it ends on a pained note that hits me right between the ribs. "I missed you too, Eva."

She rolls her eyes at me, though I can see there are tears glistening. "Oh, you're impossible."

When Dad comes in with a grand, "So who's going to

introduce me to my future daughter-in-law?" I groan, and have to explain myself all over again.

It's hard to watch disappointment bloom on my father's face. I do all I can never to catch that look directed at me. I don't know how to avoid it today, though. He looks like me, only jolly and a good thirty pounds overweight. The only way I can picture myself joyful is to look at my father and take away a few years. He's got black hair that hasn't thinned or receded, no matter how much strain the tribe puts on us. He's thick chested, tall and with a stern jawline that I put to better use than he ever could.

Father rarely accesses his disapproval, but I can feel it through the veil of love he wears like a medal of honor.

I scratch the nape of my neck. "I can still introduce you to the newcomer, though. You might want to wait until she's awake. Conversation might be a bit one-sided if you go in now."

Dad recovers as best he can. "Well, I suppose that would be nice. Tell me about this woman."

I shrug. "Name's Adelita."

Addy. I called her "Addy" like she's my playground girl-friend or something. I'm glad she didn't highlight that slip up.

I lean against the counter. "Not much to tell. Actually, you should ask Santos all about her. He could tell you plenty."

Dad's face drains, reminding me that I'm terrible at jokes. "Tell me she wasn't abducted by the Kalku. Tell me you rescued her before they did their damage."

"Nothing like that. I just meant Santos has it bad for her, so he would know better about Adelita than I do."

Father and Eva both gape at me, stunned just as I had been at the prospect. I'm not sure if it was more unbelievable that Santos was capable of something as human as attraction, or if the real shocker was that a woman was showing interest in him.

I grimace at how mean my thoughts sound. Santos is awesome; it's just that the woman in the village are terrified of their resident savage. They don't do well with outsiders, especially ones who lived with the vicious Kalku.

My father doesn't completely regain his composure, but places his hands on the island as his usual smile takes over his features. "Well, that settles it. I must get to know her first thing. I heard her talking while I passed through the hallway."

"Then she's awake now. Knock yourself out."

"If she's awake, why are you out here? She's a rescue, which means you should be with her. Unless..." Eva sees through me, narrowing her eyes while I squirm. "You did something, didn't you."

Darn her for knowing too much when she couldn't possibly know anything about it. I don't want to admit to Eva that I pushed Addy too hard. I'm the one who tore her stitches—twice now. I didn't just toughen her up; I hurt her. Santos had to give her enough sedative for her to pass clean out.

Still, I hate it when Eva's right. She gloats, and I'm not in the mood for it today. "You don't know what you're talking about. I'm not avoiding anything."

She holds up her hands like only the most vexing little sisters can do. "I never said you were avoiding her. But while we're on the subject, why are you avoiding her?"

I run my tongue along the top row of my teeth before speaking. "If you think we're too old for me to throw you into the pond, you're wrong."

"Children," Dad scolds, but it's the most he cares to redirect us. It's all we need to fall in line.

I grab an apple for Adelita, guessing she's probably

hungry since she missed the last meal due to being, well, passed out. I lead them down the many winding corridors toward my room. It's just pragmatic that Adelita is set up in the bedroom next to mine. Santos and I hem her room in, so it's the safest place in the house.

I knock four times in a pattern the three of us know. *Rat rat-a-tat*, letting Santos know it's me.

He's not quick to answer the door. In fact, when it does swing open, it's Rafael. My oldest friend doesn't greet me, but kisses my father and sister on the cheek instead. "Come on in. Good to see you, Dad."

I wish Rafi could take the mantle of keeping the family name going, but the tribe was insistent: just because Dad adopted Rafael and Santos and made them my brothers doesn't mean they can rule. Their children won't be of the royal bloodline.

Shortsighted idiots.

"Good to see you too, Son. I hear we have a new guest in our home. Care to introduce me?" My dad's smile comes easily, though he keeps his voice quiet, as if Addy's a newborn or something.

Adelita. Not Addy.

Rafi gives Dad a sharp nod and a forced smile as he ushers them inside. This room was largely used as our hangout, but upon my call home, Dad and Aarón had the place outfitted with a canopy bed, white linens and gilded fixtures. It truly is a room for a future Tribeswoman.

It's the room that weights me with his silent disappointment more than anything else. I can see his high expectations for me, and how I've never fulfilled that one item on his checklist. He wants me happy, and thinks this is the way to get me there. He also wants me to secure our family's legacy, which is no small responsibility. It's also nearly impossible, given my nightly predicament.

Santos is sitting on the bed, his boots off and his back against the ornate headboard. I groan internally at the wood-carvings that look freshly done, and tell the story of our family's rise to power. Dad tends to go overboard when he's happy. This was meant for my future bride, which Adelita is not.

And there she is, wrapped in a white blanket, cradled on Santos' lap. She's small, all curled up against him with her head on his shoulder. Her nose is pink and her eyes are rimmed in red while Santos brushes his fingers over her raven braids. He's careful with her, like he's stroking glass. The strongest person I've ever met, and he's treating her like it matters when a person breaks.

Adelita will soon learn that it doesn't, and she'll be stronger for it.

"This is our new friend?" Dad asks Santos, sitting gingerly on the edge of the bed. His voice is quiet to match the hushed mood.

Santos nods but doesn't get up to bow and kiss the floor, as he always does when Dad enters the room. Dad's told him a million times that it's not necessary, but it's the only thing Santos has ever been obstinately disobedient about. He reveres the man who welcomed him into his home after he was rescued from the Kalku. Santos adores the father who regards him as a man and not a slave.

Instead of the usual bowing, he holds Adelita tight. It's like he's afraid that if he lets go, she'll come to ruin. In our home. Where there's never been an attack from the Kalku. The other two tribes never bring their turf wars onto our soil, either. Our village is the safest in the world but Santos' hackles are still raised. He coils his arms tighter around her ribs to guard her, even from our dad.

If that's what it's like to be in love, I don't want anything to do with it. I can't imagine feeling the protectiveness I do for my people along with this overwhelming need to make sure a fully capable woman doesn't get her feelings hurt or some nonsense.

I don't want anything like that for myself, but for some reason, I can't look away.

It's an obvious effort for Santos to pry one hand away from her body, but he does so to sign to my father a few details about the woman in his arms. *"This is Adelita. The Kalku want her."* Then he strokes Addy's braids so lovingly, Eva coos, her hand moving over her heart. *"We belong to each other."*

It's the strangest and the most perfect thing I never expected Santos to say. I don't even know if Adelita agrees with it because she can't speak sign. By the way she's molded her body to his, I'm guessing she doesn't have any real reservations about the intensity of their connection.

Dad is careful with his volume and chooses his words slowly. "It's nice to meet you, Adelita. Where are you from?"

She answers, and Dad goes through the litany of questions we always ask when someone's had a run-in with the Kalku.

True to form, Adelita doesn't respond when Dad asks why the Kalku were targeting her. When he looks to me for the truth, I cross my arms over my chest and give him a firm shake of my head. I don't often keep secrets from my dad, but this one doesn't belong to me. It's hers, and I've forced her into too much as it is. I have faith that she'll trust Dad with the truth in time, after he's proven his character enough for her liking.

Besides, the less people know about her ability, the better. If Tio Bruno finds out, he'll draft her into the band of warriors first thing, which would be an utter disaster. She's too gentle for anything like that. Too afraid of herself. I only taught her to fight so she could defend herself if she's snatched at again, and even that was too much.

Or maybe how I taught her was too much. I flinch when her screams replay in my brain.

Dad is kind as he speaks to Santos. "Son, do you want me to call one of our healers for her? You boys have been on the road for a long time. I'm sure you could use a break."

"No, Father José. I am her healer. She will be alright if I'm here. It's only when I step away that she gets hurt."

Dad glances at her fresh bandages with a wince. "Oo. The Kalku really did a number on you."

Rafi moves past me and purposefully knocks my body with his shoulder. It wasn't the Kalku who tore her stitches twice. It was me. *I* did a number on her—this woman who'd just been traumatized and taken from her home forever.

It's never been more clear that I am not ready for a wife. Adelita looks so small and content in Santos' arms; I can't picture her doing that with me. Besides, La Sayona won't leave me alone. Just when I let my guard down, she torments me. Bad enough Adelita was subjected to my screams when La Sayona tortured my mind while we were in the motel. It's good she's on Santos' lap. It's good he kisses her braids. It's good he rests his chin atop her head. I don't want anything like that for myself.

Even if I did, it would be impossible anyway.

Why Dad and Eva assumed I was bringing a woman home for myself is beyond me. The fact that they have hope my curse could one day be lifted is sweet, but foolish.

Dad invites Adelita to dinner at his table once she's feeling better. Instead of looking to me when she doesn't know what to do or who to trust, she looks to Santos, who nods. *"You can trust Father José. He's a good man."*

When she can't read his fingers or lips clearly enough, Rafi translates for her. She can't even understand Santos half the time, since his curse left him mute, and yet they appreciate each other so well.

Dad doesn't comment on the fact that it's a definite barrier that Santos can't speak to the woman he adores without a translator present. Instead his eyes soften, looking on the intensity of their connection with wistful eyes, as if it's the best thing he's seen in years. "Santos, I'm so happy you brought her home to us. Good for you, Son. When she's ready, show her around her new home with us, and take her for a walk in the village. Anything she needs, be sure to let the staff know."

"Staff?" she asks.

"Yes, *hija*. Anything at all, my household is at your disposal. Any friend of Santos is… well, usually is only Cruz and Rafael. You are most welcome here."

She snuggles more securely in Santos' arms, and he accommodates her movements.

Jeez, they're like one body. It's so strange to watch, yet oddly comforting.

"What do you do for a living that you have staff that works in your home? Like, you have a housekeeper?" She glances around the room as if seeing all the trappings for the first time. The gold fixtures, the ornate bed, all of it making it dawn on her that she's not in her old life anymore.

Dad casts me an inquiring look, which I ignore. "You want to know what I do? I would have thought Cruz might say that first thing. I am Chief José, leader of the Cáceres tribe. Cruz didn't tell you any of this?"

Eva breezes by in a flutter of material. "When is the very first possible minute we can spend some time together? All you know of our tribe so far is traveling with three men who have no concept of the finer things."

A smile quirks the corner of Adelita's lips. "What could be finer than motels and gas station food?"

Eva laughs, and for some reason, I exhale. It couldn't possibly matter if my family gets along with Adelita. I mean, for Santos' sake, sure, it makes things less complicated. But it's not like my life would change all that much if Eva and Adelita clashed.

But when Eva takes Adelita's hand and helps her slowly out of the bed, something about the sight feels right. My family likes her. I'm not sure why that matters or even registers, but it does.

Eva doesn't hold back, which is no real surprise. "What are they dressing you in? Santos, honestly. Did you cut her shirt open and retie it?" She closes her eyes as if the whole thing is painful to look at.

I try not to notice the fact that Addy's not wearing a bra.

She has perfectly round, full breasts that lead to a curved waistline and wider hips.

I wet my lips without meaning to and look away.

"The shirt is fine," Adelita lies.

Eva shakes her head, her nose in the air, which is the precursor to her taking over. "Allow me to apologize for my brothers. They've been living on the road for far too long. Santos, take a break. Take a bath. All of you. I've got it from here."

Rafi smirks at my sister. "Good luck getting Santos to let Adelita out of his sight."

Santos does his best to control his anxiety, but it comes out in the rapid and jerky way he signs to Eva. He's careful not to mouth anything so Adelita doesn't catch on. *Do not let her out of your sight, Sister. Please stay in the house. Adelita is injured, so don't let her use her left arm at all. If she needs anything —the smallest thing— I'm to get it for her. I'll be in the kitchen, getting her meal prepared.*

Eva's nose crinkles. "Aarón is serving dinner at the usual time, in like, an hour. Does she have to eat before then?"

"Regular time is fine. I need to make her food. I know Aarón can be trusted, I just... I can't. If Adelita needs something, I will see to it."

I cannot fathom how head over heels a man has to be to have such anxiety over the littlest thing. I mean, Aarón's a fine cook. He's lived with us since before I was born. Santos has never taken issue eating the house chef's food before. He likes Aarón.

It's all too intense for me, so I step out into the hallway and Rafi follows. "How long are we home this time?"

"Just until Santos is stable enough to leave Adelita, so we can go check out the rustling around the curse tree. That's where Tio Bruno wants us." I run my hand over my face. "Man, Santos is so crazy about her. I don't get it. Now he doesn't trust Aarón to cook for her?" I say it like a joke, but I'm truly asking because the whole thing is ridiculous.

Rafi scowls at me, which I gotta say, I'm not a fan of. "It's not Aarón he doesn't trust; it's you. You're the crux of Santos' whole belief system. If Cruz is a good man, other men can be good. Now that Cruz can't be trusted, other men can't be trusted. You really don't get that?" Rafi leans against the wall across from me and kicks his leg up to rest on it. "Look, I get it. You turn into an asshole when you care. I'm under no grand delusion that Cruz the Conqueror has any clue how to deal with real people. But just because Santos and I accept that about you doesn't mean Adelita should. Aside from the fact that you hurt her shoulder twice, you scared Santos. Do you know how hard it is to traumatize a man who survived the Kalku?" Rafi shakes his head and stares up at the ceiling. "I swear, if you take what's good about Santos and break it, you can go on your next mission alone. Adelita is good for him. Lately, you aren't."

Every now and then, I hate that my best friend isn't intimidated by me. Rafi tells me the truth and doesn't feel obligated to hold back. His words smart because they hit too close to the truth. I don't want them to be true, so I ignore them as best I can.

My jaw tightens. "We can stay for a couple days, but then we should get back on the road. Check out the tree."

He fixes me with a steely gaze. "That doesn't sound like an 'I heard you, Rafi. I'll lay off Adelita.'"

I hold up my hands. "Sure. Whatever. Just be ready in a couple days. Santos can sneak in all the kisses he likes with Adelita until then."

Though, to be fair, I've not seen them actually kiss yet.

Rafi levels his gaze at me. "If you ask me, you care a little too much about who she's kissing, Brother." He uses the wall as leverage and kicks himself off it. "I'm staying with Santos until he's okay. If that takes a month, so be it. If you want me along on your missions, you'll fix what you broke before you want to leave for the next job."

He starts to walk away, which makes me brave enough to spout out a mouthy, "Maybe I'll take one of the other warriors who knows how to fall in line."

Rafael laughs at my threat, which irks me. "Typical Cruz. Snarls in the face of the Kalku, but runs like a scared little boy from a conversation with a woman."

Then the bastard starts singing the song the villagers made up about me when I rescued five women from being sacrificed a few years ago. I hate that song, and he friggin' knows it.

I open my mouth to cuss him out, but my words stick in my throat when the door swings open. Eva's arm is threaded through Adelita's, like they've known each other their whole lives. They're giggling about something, but the laughter dies on their lips when they see me standing in their path.

I hate when people do that. I'm not trying to stop people

from laughing, but that's exactly what happens whenever I show up.

Three days. That's how long I can take it before I get itchy and need to be back on the road again. If Rafi's serious about not coming on the next job if I don't work things out with Adelita and Santos in time, I'm screwed. Only Rafi can push me to do something I really don't want to do.

A smile. That's something people like. I catch Adelita's eye and offer up a grin. She freezes and backs up, like I've just told her it's *me* who wants to eat her heart out of her chest, and not the Kalku.

Eva's face pulls in horror. "What is that face for?"

The corners of my mouth fall into my usual grumping. "It's called a smile. Is that not allowed?"

Eva shudders. "If that's what you call a smile, then Brother, you are sorely out of practice."

They leave me standing in the hallway, regretting all the things I can't undo.

2

SILK IN A SEA OF ARMOR
ADELITA

I never had a sister growing up, and I'm only just starting to realize how truly cheated I've been. Eva is incredible. She doesn't talk in half-explanations or whole aggressions, but speaks to me like we've known each other forever. After the week I've had, she's a breath of fresh air, making this strange new place feel like I might actually belong here. The fact that she ordered a bra with removable straps to be brought in for me? Well, that just makes me love her even more.

Eva fishes through her closet, frowning at a pretty garment. "Not this one. It's got sleeves. Rafi said your shoulder needs to be exposed. Something about 'making Cruz see what he's done.'"

I snigger. "Yeah, that sounds like Rafael, alright. Can I borrow a tank top or something? All my things are in storage. One day, when all this is over, you can steal some of my things in return. Though, I'm not sure I own anything as nice as all this. Might not be all that fair a trade."

Her closet is enormous and filled with silks and gauzy

skirts. Her dresses are so nice, I check to make sure my hands are clean before touching them.

Eva's face falls as she sits on her bed. Her teal and pink skirt flows out from her in a gust with the motion. Despite her frown, she is devastatingly beautiful without effort. High cheekbones and perfectly arched eyebrows, Eva carries herself like the daughter of a ruler, indeed. "You assume the mess with the Kalku is going to blow over? I don't think Cruz did all that great a job explaining things if that's where you've landed."

I turn my back to her and leaf through the dresses, searching for something I won't trip over. Eva is a good several inches taller than me, and all of these gowns are floor-length. "I know it won't be overnight, but yeah. One day, I'll be able to go back to my life and get a new job and all that. Isn't that the hope when one goes into battle? That someday the world will be better off?"

"I guess. Maybe. I honestly don't know anymore. It's been too long for hope at this point. I think we've all just grown to accept that the Kalku will always be here. There's nothing we can do but stand our ground and rescue those who get taken as often as we can."

My fingers trill down one of the pink silk gowns. "I think if I believed that, my heart would never stop breaking."

She stares toward the window, taking in the evening sun. "You can learn to live with heartbreak easily enough. In the end, it's the optimism that crushes me. Believing things might get better when they never do. My dad left the tribe on missions all the time when I was little, and now my brother is always gone, doing the same thing. Our tribe produces warriors because that's what nature requires. Anything else is wasted in here."

Her words hit me hard. I study the silks with new appreciation. Eva stands out as a beacon of beauty. It's an act of defiance to the duty that surrounds her. I begin to see what a true gift she is, taking the life that was handed to her and making it something she wants to look at, even if the entire tribe's culture is bent around putting battle at the forefront.

She's surviving. This whole closet is filled with her method of survival. She will seek out beauty even as the world around her calls for blood.

I keep my eyes on the fabrics as I speak. "I think it takes a lot of strength to be silk in a sea of armor."

When a knock sounds at the door, Eva breezes toward it with a sea of fabric floating behind her. She gives a one-noted grunt of a greeting before moving down the hallway, leaving Rafael to meander into the bedroom.

I cast him a smile. "Hey, Rafael. Don't tell me you also wanted to borrow one of Eva's dresses. I might have to fight you for this one." I run my fingers down the smooth material of a red gown.

His smile fights through tension but eventually takes over his face. "Man, do we need you here. Brought you this. I'll have you know I didn't even look inside. I don't need to know that my sweet Adelita wears a pale pink strapless bra with a little heart in the center. I would never look, so don't even try to tempt me."

I narrow my eyes at his dancing eyebrows and take the package. "Your gentlemanly self-control is duly noted."

His face grows serious as his voice lowers. "Did Cruz talk to you yet?"

My mouth draws to the side. "No. About what?"

His shoulders stiffen but he manages to hold on to what I clearly see is a flaring temper. "Nothing important, I guess." Then he covers his frustration so seamlessly, I almost wish he were televised, so I could replay the transition over and over. It's like he doesn't know how to let a negative emotion sit before he has to brush it under the rug with a smile.

"You don't have to do that, you know." I point to his smile, looking up at him from my spot on the edge of the mattress as he stands before me.

"Do what?"

"Look happy when you're not. You don't have to put on a brave face for me. You can be yourself. Remember when we talked about your number on the Enneagram?"

"I'm a seven. It's the best number." Rafi pauses to scratch his head. "But I forget what it means."

"You're the enthusiast. You'll tap-dance and throw a parade to distract from actual pain. You're hard-wired for fun, and run away from things that upset you." I reach out and hold his hand. "My advice? Give yourself a whole minute of feeling the discomfort that comes from negative emotions before you shimmy away from them. The party will still be there, and so will you."

It's a long look he fixes on me before he leans in and kisses my cheek, as if we're the type of people who do that all the time. "I'll try to keep that in mind. If I forget, I want you to kiss me just like that. Maybe it'll bring me back to myself."

I run my hand down his cheek. "It's going to be okay, Rafael."

He dips his chin and lightly pecks my other cheek, spreading a blush over my chest and face. I've never had a friend who kissed me this much. It's sweet in a way that's entirely intimate, yet without being intimidating.

I think I like it.

On the Enneagram—the tool many therapists use to help our clients self-actualize—I'm a six, which is called the loyalist. But for the past two years, I've had no one to commit myself to. I've been aimless and, let's face it, depressed since my mama died.

But Rafael's sweet kisses reawaken my six nature, tethering me to this family in ways I worry might be permanent.

Rafael makes a contented "mm" sound before he glances over my shoulder and postures. "Eva? What's wrong?"

My intake of breath isn't quiet when I spot Eva's wet eyes as she comes back into the room. "Oh, what happened? We were talking and now you're upset. Did I say something?"

She waves off my concern with a watery smile and plops down on the side of the mattress next to me. "I'm alright."

Rafi crouches before Eva, who's sitting on the bed in a pile of expensive fabrics. He's cute like that, all sweet and concerned for her. I'm a sucker for a big man on his knees. "What's wrong, Evita?"

She sniffs as she searches for a tissue. "Nothing. A million things. I don't know. Adelita and I were talking and... No one's ever put things like that to me before."

"Like what?" I go back over our conversation to search for anything damning.

"You said I was silk. That I'm brave because I'm silk in a world full of armor. Most of the time I feel silly being me, but that... Thank you. I think I needed to hear that."

Rafi casts a wry grin my way. "That's how women talk to each other? Call me burlap, *viento*. Tell me I'm rough and gravelly against your skin. I'll be dewy-eyed for sure." Rafi jokes, but then pulls a bandana from his back pocket. He grumbles that it's pretty dirty, but still, he offers it to Eva, and she dries her eyes with it.

"Thank you." She makes to hand it back to him, but he shakes his head.

"Keep it. It's pretty much ruined, anyway. It's stained with the blood of the enemy and all that war stuff you don't like to hear about. I was going to throw it away."

She glowers up at him when he rises, and I don't blame

her for it. I don't know why he took a perfectly sweet gesture and dumbed it down so it's completely unrecognizable as a nice deed.

I cast him a curious look but he brushes it off, like he does so many things. Rafi straightens. "Santos and Aarón are nearly done with dinner. I'm to escort you fine ladies."

Eva snorts. "Escort us to dinner? Since when is that a thing?"

He jerks his thumb at me. "Since this one came into the picture. Frankly, I'm surprised Santos has stayed away this long."

"Alright. Give us a minute. I've got to get changed." I wave him off as Eva strolls into the massive closet.

Rafi leans in and speaks quietly with mischief dancing in his eyes. "Don't hold back on my account. I've already *not* seen your pale pink strapless bra with the little heart in the center. I wouldn't mind not seeing a little bit more."

Maybe that would be off-putting from someone else, but Rafi's a goof, and I find it doesn't bother me one bit. "Yeah, yeah. Out you go, burlap." I palm his grin and back him through the door.

I almost have him out the room when he pauses, gripping the doorjamb before I can shove him through the exit. "Wait. I just remembered something." He waits until I remove my hand from his face. "Santos needed to know if you're allergic to anything. He's upset he didn't ask you before."

"Nothing. Tell him he's a sweetheart to ask."

"I'll be sure to tell him exactly that. Be right back to provide the escort, so if you have a preference on whether or not you're dressed, you've got five minutes to make that happen."

"I've been properly warned."

Then Rafi leans in to bless my lips with a quick peck

before he leaves, as if that's a thing we do now, which I guess it sort of is.

I feel my heart attaching to this goofball, to this adorably loveable friend.

I don't belong here, but I'm not sure I have it in me to leave.

3

CRUZ'S DIMPLES

ADELITA

I shut the door and lean against it. "I'm going to leave my wardrobe to you tonight, Eva. I've never had this many options to choose from; it's stumping me."

"It's not that many."

"To put it in perspective, your closet is the size of my entire bedroom back at my apartment. And your accessories corner is the size of my kitchen."

She winces at the comparison but takes my plea for help in stride, and stands to rifle through with more precision than I have the skill for. I'm grateful for Eva, since getting undressed one-handed is a feat of endurance. I can't even work out how I would fasten my new bra without being able to move my shoulder or use my left arm.

"Give me a week, and I'll have your closet so stocked, you won't have enough days in the month to wear it all."

"I really don't need…"

"It's not about need," she snaps, though not rudely. It's as if she's determined to indulge me in a better life so she has someone to share in the scandal of silk. "It's about happiness."

I tilt my head to the side. "And are you happy?"

That was too much. As soon as the sentence slips out, I can feel my misstep. That was my therapist self talking, which she did not ask for.

Eva swallows hard. "I have no reason not to be happy." She answers my totally pushy question, but at the same time, deflects it without actually telling me the truth. She swallows down her voice, like she's well aware of the damage a woman can do if she's honest about who she is and what she wants.

The whole thing breaks my heart.

But it's not my business. She's not my patient.

She dresses me with careful fingers, fanning the gauzy sky-blue material out over my hips as she ties the ribbon in a crisscross down my back.

The straps are thin, but the whole gown is so light and airy that it has no trouble staying in place. The trim waistline makes me more aware of my body. It feels like my curves are something to be proud of. My injuries clash horribly with the elegance and fairy-like qualities of this ethereal gown. Eva even compensates for my lack of height by tightening the straps to raise the hemline just enough so I don't trip.

Then she leans down and fits me with the softest gold slippers I've ever worn.

Time with Eva is so very different than the jeans and black t-shirt life on the road with the guys.

"I think I like it here," I admit. "I've never worn anything so beautiful."

If only Mama could see me now. She made a big deal when I wore the yellow sundress I got special for my college graduation. She acted like the queen had come to town just to build me up. It worked, let me tell you. There were far fancier dresses worn that day, but I felt like I actually belonged for once, instead of sticking out like a sore working-class thumb.

Eva refastens my sling and taps the underside of my chin with her fingertips. "Tonight, you are not being chased by the Kalku. You are not sleeping in some disgusting motel." Her spine straightens, reminding me to do the same. "You are the friend of a Tribesdaughter."

I hug her gently, afraid of creasing the delicate material, but Eva's embrace is tight and filled with the loneliness that comes from not having a sister to confide in.

I know that loneliness well, so I tighten my grip on her and kiss her cheek.

Again, my six nature on the Enneagram clicks into place, reminding me that I was built for connection, and I've isolated myself for too long. This hug feels right.

It feels like coming home.

At Rafael's knock, Eva straightens her own gown and opens the door, curtsying as he bows. Rafael grins at her. "Your escort, m'lady."

"Why, thank you. I don't how I'd find my way to my own dining room without you to show me." She fans herself while Rafi sniggers.

"That's the thing about having a penis. You know far more than anyone else," Rafi jokes, pinking Eva's cheeks. His crass humor makes me laugh every time. "*Linda*, you back there?"

I come out into the hallway, smiling when Rafi's mouth drops open. His eyes bug out not too cartoonishly, so I hope at least some of his reaction is genuine.

It's when his eyes roll back, his knees buckle and he collapses that I shriek.

I drop down at his side and slap his cheek. "Rafi! Wake up! Oh, honey. What happened?"

Boots thunder in my direction, and Cruz stops short. "Holy..." He gapes at me and then shakes himself back to the problem at hand. "What happened to him?"

"I don't know! He fainted out of nowhere. Can you get him some juice or something? Is it a blood sugar thing? Get Santos!" I lift Rafi's upper half and hold his head to my chest, cradling him as best I can with one functioning arm. "Rafael, can you hear me?"

Cruz's shoulders loosen. "He's fine. Get up, Rafi, or I'll kick you straight in the balls."

Rafi's eyes open and he sits up, totally coherent. "Come on, man. I had a beautiful woman's arm around me."

I guffaw, completely taken aback that he tricked me so thoroughly. It's only then that I realize Eva is still standing, and didn't fall for the ruse at all.

She rolls her eyes at him. "Don't pay attention to Rafi's theatrics unless you see the knife sticking out of him. Even then, it might be a prank."

Rafael stands, making like he's coming out of a stupor. "I don't know what came over me. I was just standing there, and two visions of loveliness appeared before me. I think my heart up and stopped for a second."

Instantly I forgive him for worrying me. He bends down to help me stand, and we share a smile. It's nice to know that even after all the running and fighting, life can still possess moments of sheer ridiculousness.

It's then I begin to appreciate Rafael for the gift he is. To find reason to laugh and give laughter in the face of all he's been through is a strength most people disregard as foolishness. But I see him finding a way to survive, to live his life, rather than merely survive it.

That gives me hope, and I'm so grateful for the gift of it all.

Rafael kisses my cheek and thumbs at my lower lip. He ignores Cruz's intake of breath at our closeness, and then moves to Eva, extending his elbow to her. "May I? Cruz is going to escort the lovely Adelita, which means I get you all to myself." Then he shoots Cruz a look of stern warning that has more than a hint of deadliness to it.

"Lucky me," Eva deadpans, though I can see she doesn't mind this one bit.

My face falls that I've been stuck with Cruz. Neither of us has it in us to pretend that I need an escort, so we walk with a healthy two feet of space between us.

"Am I supposed to comment on your dress?" Cruz asks stupidly, as if he's never been allowed to socialize before today.

"I think us not talking about anything might be best." I'm not trying to be cold but I had a nice moment with Eva, and I don't want him to ruin it with his aggressive nature.

"Rafi said I'm supposed to apologize for tearing your stitches while we were training."

I wait for Cruz to continue but he goes mute. "Are you working your way up to it?"

"No. That was it."

My mouth is in a taut line of irritation. I knew any trace of a smile would vanish if conversation happened between us. "Awesome. I suppose I'm to forgive you, then."

He shoots me a goading look. "Are you working your way up to it?"

"No." And it's true. I don't forgive him. "I told you when we were sparring that it was too much, and you didn't listen."

Truthfully, I'm not even sure I'm mad at him. It was exhilarating, pushing myself beyond my breaking point.

All the same, he should have listened to me. Yet, even so, I accept that this is who Cruz is. He does what he feels he has to so the job gets done.

Forgiveness isn't the same as trust, though. That will take more than a conversation about hypothetical apologies.

When Rafael and Eva round the corner and disappear from view, Cruz quickly moves to block my path, his face all serious. "Look, we don't have to get along or even like each other. But it's going to tear Santos up if we can't coexist. Santos matters to me. He's important enough for me to say whatever you need to hear to make sure we don't fight in front of him."

I weigh the logic of his words and wish it wasn't easy to see. A stubborn part of me doesn't like it when Cruz is right, but my more mature side concedes.

My shoulder slumps as I wave my white flag. "Okay." I turn and lean against the wall, doing my best to organize my thoughts. "I get what you're trying to do, and part of me appreciates that you want to train me so I stay alive and whatnot. I'm not opposed to that. But I haven't known you a whole month yet. Maybe let my shoulder heal before we go at it again." I lower my voice, gearing up to address the time he tore into my shoulder to extract information, rather than to train me to be a better fighter. "And perhaps the next time you suspect I am keeping a secret from you, understand that it is none of your business. Trust goes a lot farther than torture, as far as currency. I feel like I shouldn't have to say that to a grown man."

Maybe that was too long a lecture, but it had to be said.

Cruz runs his tongue along his top row of teeth before responding. "Alright. I can lay off until you're healed. You're really okay with more sparring?"

"Consensual sparring? Yes. But you have to listen to my limits." My chin lowers as I battle with anxiety. The guys told me the Kalku capture women with extraordinary abilities and tear out their hearts so they can boil them and drink the broth, imbibing the woman's power. The thought still churns my stomach. "I... I don't want the Kalku to take me."

I don't expect Cruz to hook his finger under my chin, but I let him control the tilt of my head until I'm staring up into the darkness of his eyes. "I will not let them take you, Adelita. I will keep you safe."

My chin quivers, but I do what I can not to let moisture well in my eyes. I don't trust myself to speak, so I simply nod.

When Cruz steps back and clears his throat to shake off the moment, it's an effort to regain my composure.

I hold up my hand, pushing my luck. "One more thing."

His eyes lift toward the ceiling in exasperation, ever the drama queen. "I knew that was too easy. What?"

"Twice you ripped open my stitches." He glowers at me but I ignore his temper. "I want two free punches. Whenever I want, no explanation needed. I think that's only fair. Then we can move on and be cool."

He raises his eyebrow, amused that this is my sticking point. "You want to punch me twice? That's fair. Sure. Go ahead." He leans in and presents his chin to me.

I pat the sharp edge of Cruz's freshly-shaved jawline a few times, like we're old friends given to such affections.

I retract my hand quickly. I just smooched Rafael's lips a few times, but touching Cruz's cheek feels far too intimate.

I compromise and flick his nose. "What's the fun if you know when it's coming? Could be tonight. Could be next week. Could be three years from now. Enjoy the wait."

And there they are, those perfect, mostly unexercised dimples. Cruz chuckles at me, and I can tell he likes this game, the masochist. He's handsome like this. Not like it matters. It's an utter waste that he doesn't smile more often.

Cruz moves to my good side and pops his elbow out to me. When I take the gentlemanly offer and cuff his bicep, he smirks, covering my hand with his larger mitt.

He holds my gaze for a few seconds more than he usually does.

I can't put my finger on the war that comes to life inside of me. It shouldn't be so tumultuous a thing to make eye contact with a man who's got you on his arm. And yet, I'm worried the racing thrum of my heartbeat might turn audible and alert him to my nerves.

"I think this will work," Cruz says as he walks me down the hallway to the dining room.

I, however, am dubious.

4

AT THE TABLE
ADELITA

The look on Santos' face is priceless. I can't tell if he's more shocked that Cruz and I are getting along, or if it's the dress that's bowled him over. I remind myself to thank Eva again later.

Santos beelines to me, his arms extending to wrap me in a hug I desperately long for. But before we make contact, he stops short. Taking a few steps back, he bows his head apologetically, motioning that he'd like to wash his hands before he touches me.

They don't look dirty to me, but I don't begrudge him the ritual if he needs it. "Okay."

When my eyes flick to the grand table with spotless white linens and gold utensils, my stomach tightens. Despite my degree, I am a housekeeper. Our table was clean but never fancy. I'm immediately worried I will spill something the moment I get near the opulent display.

There are taper candles in golden candleholders. I am definitely out of my element here.

Santos turns to leave, but I stop him with a low whisper

laced with nerves. "Santos, when you come back, will you sit with me? I'm a little out of place here."

He nods with a smile that's so precious; I can't believe I haven't kissed him yet. It's all I keep thinking about whenever he comes near. He's got this intensity that cuts my breath short, and a sharpness to his angular features and wider jaw that makes it hard to look away.

He vanishes into where I assume is the kitchen, making me wish he was near.

The dining room is the size of the entire therapy clinic, with a table big enough to seat at least twenty.

Rafael and Eva are already seated, whispering and giggling like mischievous teenagers while the chief looks up at us from the head of the table. "Ah, Adelita. How good of you to join us. I see my daughter's gotten ahold of you and shown you her closet. Lovely, dear. Simply lovely."

I don't think I've ever received a compliment from an adult man before. Maybe a few times on a term paper, the professor would hold it up and tell me how great a job I did on it. That counted, for sure. But the paternal affection this man oozes melts into the sadder crevices of my heart, spackling over old wounds that come from being raised fatherless. "Thank you, sir."

Chief José's black hair is thick, and peppered with brushes of silver. His face looks like he's smiling, even though his lips aren't tilted upward at the corners. Must be his natural disposition, which I find calming and pleasant.

Chief José fixes his gaze on me. "Inside the house, I'm Dad. Out in the village, you can call me Chief or Don José."

I trip over my own two feet. Cruz has the grace to steady me. I have no idea what to say to that. I mean, I'm a perfect stranger to him. Not just that, but I have never used that word on a man before. It will sound unnatural and weird coming from me, I'm sure of it.

My inner six on the Enneagram longs for this connection, but I'm too timid to trust it will last.

Instead of testing out the new word, I chicken out and murmur a humble, "Thank you."

"Now, now. Out in the village, you're *Mighty* Chief José. Don't sell yourself short." A woman with a low, sultry voice strides into the dining room from behind us and pauses to touch Cruz's shoulder. "What a good day this is. Tell me who is this stunning creature on your arm, Cruz. There's been much excitement that you brought home a woman to stay with us."

Cruz gives the woman a tight nod, which I guess is supposed to be some mixture of "hello," "good to see you," and "don't touch my shoulder." He doesn't flash his dimple, which is an absolute waste. "This is our new houseguest, Adelita. Adelita, this is Consuela, my father's wife."

The distinct avoidance of the word "mother" rings through the hall like a gong of awkwardness.

"Very nice to meet you," I offer. My therapist brain is going into hyperdrive, studying the sudden stiffness of Cruz's form beside mine. "You have a lovely home, from what I've seen of it so far."

Her laugh is loud and so high-pitched, it startles me. Rafael catches my eye from his place at the table behind her, his eyebrows dancing at the family joke they all share about her strange laugh. "Oh, you should've seen the place before I got here. Everything was beige. Beige, beige, beige. I'm a big fan of bold colors, so every time you see something teal, feel free to tell me how much you love it."

Maybe Cruz doesn't like Consuela, but I think she's great. Her eyes laugh, and even though she's clearly closer in age to Cruz than her husband, it seems fitting that Chief José would choose a wife who smiles so easily.

Consuela has brown hair in two long braids down the

sides of her head and a smattering of freckles across her wider nose. She looks to be no more than a handful of years older than me.

"Mama, I'm hungry!" comes the voice of a little boy. Sure enough, a short-haired boy wearing jeans and a black t-shirt bounds into the dining room. He's got a wooden sword tucked in his belt.

When his eyes fall on Cruz, he stops running and sticks out his chest. I'm immediately in love with this… I'm guessing seven-year-old. He is clearly dressed as Cruz.

On his heel scampers in a round-cheeked little girl who can't be older than two. She reaches for her mother with all the feigned helplessness of a beggar. "Mama!"

Consuela scoops up her toddler and smooches her cheeks loudly. "To the table, ruffians! Adelita, this is Mira and Roberto. Cordelia just turned eleven last month, and she'll be joining us shortly. Children, this is Cruz's future bride. She's going to be living here with us!" She raises her fist in the air to celebrate in time with the blood draining from my face.

Then again, why wouldn't she assume I'm Cruz's girl-friend? I'm still holding onto his arm, and am freshly moved into his home. "No, no. I'm Cruz's friend," I correct her. Though truly, "friend" is a generous assessment, if not an outright lie.

Consuela stops short, setting Mira in her highchair on one side next to the foot of the table before she takes her seat there, all the way across from José. "Oh, I just assumed that when a woman finally moved into the house, it would be because Cruz found a bride. Friends? I didn't know our son had any of those who weren't Rafi and Santos. You're sure?"

Cruz's tone is gruff. "That we're not dating? Yeah, I'm sure, Consuela." He drops his arm from mine and shakes off my touch, like the mere thought of being near me is disgusting. Like it was me who asked for his arm, instead of him offering it. "Get off me."

My mouth tightens before sarcasm flings out. "But if you don't let me hang on you, how will I walk? I mean, without the Great Cruz around to keep me from smacking into walls, how will I survive?"

Consuela laughs again, and though I've just heard it a minute ago, the shrill sound still makes me jump. Yet a smile from Consuela calms my indignation towards Cruz.

Cruz is not amused. He yanks back his chair and plops down next to Rafael. "I'm sure you'll manage. Stop aggravating me, woman."

I slide into the seat beside him that he kicks out for me. I take care not to scrape the wood of the chair across the beige tiles. "But that's the only thing on my to-do list today. I can't handle more than one item at a time. Not if you're not there to help me figure the rest out."

He mimes laughing and makes a show of turning his back on me.

Roberto is in the seat across from Cruz and mirrors his body language. Roberto sets his elbows on the table and turns his nose up as he makes a show of angling his head away from me. It's too cute to be insulting, which I know it's supposed to be. Roberto even looks down at his bicep to make sure it's flexed.

An overwhelming urge to pinch Roberto's cheeks comes over me but I fight it back.

"Was your table this big growing up?" Eva asks over Rafi and Cruz. "I like it full like this, but not when there are two *idiotas* between us."

I grin at her. "Nothing like this. It was just Mama and me." Rafael catches my eye and winks because that's just who he is. "How about you, Rafael? How many brothers and sisters did you have?"

The table goes from lively chatter to total silence. I shrink, realizing I said something horribly inappropriate. I retrace my steps. I know he was stolen as a baby, but liberated when he was five and brought back to the village. Maybe his family died, and I just brought it up. I mean, he was adopted by the chief for a reason.

I'm so stupid. I'm not in a therapy session. I'm at the dinner table.

Cruz scowls at me. "Santos and I are Rafi's brothers. Eva is his sister. That's all that matters." Then, as if remembering the others at the table, he motions to Roberto. "And I guess Roberto, Mira and Cordelia, too." He says it all like the younger siblings are a nuisance and an afterthought, which makes me want to shove him.

"It's okay, Cruz. She's allowed to ask questions." Rafael swallows hard and brushes a brave smile across his lips. The expression is meant to come off casual, but I can tell it's strained. "You know about my abduction by the Kalku when I was a baby. The person who does that particular job is called La Cucuy. When I was liberated by Tio Bruno and his men at the age of five, my parents wouldn't let me back in their home. So technically I have four blood brothers, but they don't speak to me."

This is a conversation for a private setting, but I can't hold myself back. "You were five years old! Why wouldn't they let you in?"

I want to kiss the faked smile off his face, but I'm guessing that wouldn't be appropriate, given our audience.

Instead I touch my lips with two fingers. Catching my eye, he does the same motion, kissing me from afar to remind himself that some things don't need to be dressed up with a smile. Some things are simply terrible.

He shrugs, as if it's all no big deal. "Some things can't be undone. Once you're taken by the Kalku, it's assumed you're partially one of them. Even though I was born part of the Cáceres tribe, my time away made me an outsider. Dangerous. Plus, there's the whole half-dragon thing. That's one magical step too far. To them, I'm ruined for life." His eyes lift to a spot near the entrance. "But as our dear Santos and I have proven, that couldn't be farther from the truth." He waves and starts signing. "Hey, man. Cruz is trying to steal your girlfriend right out from under you. Lucky I was here to stop him."

When I turn, just the sight of Santos puts me at ease, even though I've made a complete wreck of the casual dinner conversation. His brows are raised in surprise, but then fall to disbelief with an eyeroll at the notion that Cruz and I could ever be interested in each other.

He's carrying a plate, which he sets down in front of me, stealing a moment to kiss the back of my hand. It's so sweet. So civilized. I love it, and I don't mind at all that everyone is watching me blush for him. "I'm glad you're here," I admit.

Santos' eyes dart around warily before he takes the empty seat to my right. Everyone's quiet, but it's not until then that I realize they are not focused on my conversational faux pas anymore, but are gaping at Santos.

"Finally!" Eva exclaims, her hands lifting to the heavens as if in praise. "You're really eating with us? It's only been two years you've lived here. Adelita, I wish you'd found your way to us sooner. This is nice."

"I told you all to start without me." A man's deep voice fills the room. Now it's Cruz who sits up straight. He watches the tall, solid male who enters with the confidence and grace of a true Alpha.

I don't like him—whoever this man is. I don't usually jump to such snap decisions, but my reaction is spinal and unquestionable.

Cruz tracks the man's movements with the same hopefulness Roberto uses to study him. The man stops in his tracks, stunned at the sight of Santos. "You're eating with the family now?"

I can't decide if he's approving or hates the idea. Santos lowers his head beside me in response. The muscles in his neck are tensed, and I immediately want to shield him from whatever it is that's upsetting him.

Don José speaks up, since the guys have gone mute. "Of course, Bruno. Santos has always been welcome at the family table. Apparently he didn't feel himself worthy to sit with us until today."

Eva turns and smiles at Santos, who won't look up from the table. "Good for you, Santos. I like my brothers at the table with me."

Don José leans forward and taps the side of his beer stein to garner Santos' attention. "Son, look at me."

Santos doesn't have it in him to disobey.

There's a Santa Claus-like kindness in Don José's eyes that not only melts my heart, but breathes a gust of self-esteem into Santos I can tell he desperately needs. "You are always the thing my heart needs. You belong here, Santos. Do you protect the tribe?"

Santos nods firmly.

"Do you make sure Cruz and Rafael come home to me in one piece?"

Again, a determined nod.

"Am I your father?"

Santos hesitates, but finally nods.

"Then from now on, there will be no more of you eating in the kitchen. You're to dine at the family table as often as you're home." Then Don José turns his focus to me. "Thank you, Adelita. You gave me a part of my boy we've all been hoping he'd one day grant us."

"What's that?" Roberto asks.

José's eyes twinkle as they flicker between Santos' insecurity and Roberto's innocence. "Just you. That's all we've ever wanted. Nothing more. Nothing less. Each of you belong here, just as you are."

I don't know much about the tribe or this hidden world that's been operating in the shadows outside of my mundane existence, but I decide, just as surely as I know I will not like Bruno, that I might always trust Don José.

5

EATING WITH THE FAMILY
SANTOS

*I*t's strange to eat with them all. I know I'm doing it wrong. We weren't given forks and spoons in the cave. Knives were for hunting and eating. What you couldn't do with a knife, you figured out with your fingers.

Chef Aarón lets me eat on the floor under the table in the kitchen, where I'm comfortably out of sight. Last year, he taught me how to use a fork and a spoon, but he only makes me use them at dinner, and far away from public view. It's his constant battle between leaving me to be the savage I am, and prying me from the ways of the Kalku, even if it can only be done in small steps.

I can't mess this up. If I do, Adelita will know how very beneath her I am, and maybe she will go off and marry someone like Cruz. That would make sense. No one is more shocked than I am when she gazes at me like I matter.

Adelita is so beautiful; I can hardly look at her. It's too much—this dress, this woman. I'm afraid to touch her, for fear of dirtying something so perfect. I scrubbed my hands and arms, but deep down, I know I am savage, and she is cultured and demure.

People pay money to talk to her. That's how Rafi explained her job to me. I'm sure, given the option, nearly everyone in the tribe would pay money to never have to talk to me.

I'm holding my fork wrong. When Aarón comes out to set the food on the table, he covertly signs for me to loosen my chokehold on the utensil and to sit up straight.

I like eating under the chef's table. No one looks at me. If I spill something, it's not a big deal because the floor is already messy from meal prep.

Roberto is regaling Cruz with his latest swordfight, but Cruz is barely listening. Cruz is more focused on Tio Bruno, who eyes Adelita as if she is a tool he hasn't yet figured out how to use. Tio Bruno is coming to the conclusion, as we did early on, that the Kalku don't have the motivation to chase down a random woman twice. He knows something is off that they've pursued her over such great lengths.

I don't like it. I don't like Tio Bruno. But Cruz idolizes him, so that's where we're at.

Cordelia comes to the table only after Consuela goes and gets her. Even then, the preteen sulks as she eats, as if her privileged life is so vexing.

I cannot imagine the luxury involved in pouting. I was not raised with choices like those.

Cordelia blushes when Rafael greets her with a huge grin. Consuela calls it a "schoolgirl crush." Whatever that means. Rafael eats up the attention, which only adds to the poor child's infatuation.

Cordelia cuts her meat while drinking in Rafael's smile. "Did you do anything cool while you were out?"

Tio Bruno frowns at Cordelia's question. "What does 'cool' have to do with any of it? Cruz, Rafael and Santos are to defend civilians and the tribe against the Kalku. That is all."

Father José feigns a pout. "Hey, I happen to think that's pretty cool."

The ruling brothers couldn't be more different. Tio Bruno is all about domination and protection of the tribe. If the conversation isn't about that, he's not interested. Father José is focused more on quality of life inside the tribe, making sure everyone knows their role and serves the tribe with a smile.

The brothers both have height and build similar to Cruz, but Father José has the starting of a belly, and Tio Bruno is far more muscular than strictly necessary. His neck is so thick, sometimes he has to turn his shoulders just to turn his head. He commands the warriors with unswerving confidence that they will be the best, or else. The Kalku were about muscle, sure, but they coupled that with flexibility and agility training, which I know Tio Bruno doesn't value.

Rafael takes the stage Cordelia presents him and runs with it, his eyes dancing in his haste to entertain his captive audience. "Cordelia, I'm so glad you asked. It was a battle so harrowing, I'm certain they'll be writing songs about it to sing at the next feasting day."

Rafi stands up and grabs Adelita's shoulders from behind, ducking down to hide. I tense until I see he's barely touching her injured side.

"First we stalked the Kalku because we knew—we just knew—they were up to no good." Then he pops up. "How did we know which ones to follow? Well, Cordelia darling, we're just that good. Your big, scary brother wanted to wait until they pounced on whatever prey they were stalking. Wise, that one. Oh, so wise. Cruz the Conqueror indeed!"

He jumps behind Cruz and reaches down to steal the roll off his plate, which I'll admit, makes me smile.

Cruz harrumphs while Rafael munches on the roll.

Cordelia is enthralled that this whole reenactment is happening just for her.

Consuela keeps laughing, which makes Rafael harder to hear, but not impossible.

Father José is shouting "boo" and "hooray" at the right moments, putting Rafael in his element—which is at the center of a captive audience.

He crouches down behind Cruz's chair. "Then, just when we thought the Kalku would lead us to nowhere, they show up in a parking lot where this young lovely is just getting out of work. They attack her friend."

Rafi jumps up and snarls, throwing the bitten-into roll at Cordelia, who catches it and throws it back with a wide grin.

Mira claps her chubby hands and throws her roll at Roberto, thinking it all a marvelous game.

Roberto takes his lead from Cruz, who is never amused. The two share a scowl because Roberto would be thrilled to share anything with his big brother.

Adelita's giggle is the best sound in the world. I never put much stock in laughter until the chance of hearing Adelita's sweet happiness became an option.

"They stab her with their mortal blade before we can intervene." Rafi pulls Adelita up from her seat and spins her around in a circle before he pins her spine to his chest, his arm across her throat. He mimes stabbing her in the shoulder with his fist, and she plays along for the children's benefit.

Because she's fun.

I'm not fun. I'm the savage. I have no idea what to do with the idea of fun, but Adelita does. She lets loose a quiet shriek and goes limp in his arms.

"Cruz and I fight off the Kalku with our bare hands while Santos swoops in and takes the girl for himself, the greedy bastard. He sweeps her off her feet and carries her off into the sunset."

Rafael whaps me upside the head, making it clear that I will involve myself, or the antics will only get worse.

I do my best to play the game, standing and flexing my muscles for the kids, though I'm certain I only manage to scare them. Cordelia is floored that I'm here at the table at all, her mouth dropping open when I go for broke and sweep Adelita off her feet. It is the greatest feeling in the world, cradling my treasure in my arms.

Adelita laughs and rests her hand on my chest, unaware of just how far outside my comfort zone I'm operating right now.

But I play the game—being the man who sweeps her—and my reward is bountiful. Adelita leans her head against my shoulder and coos, "My hero."

Maybe I shouldn't kiss her forehead in public like this, but I can't not. It's a safer option than kissing her lips for the first time in front of the guys, the family and Aarón, who's gaping at me from the doorway. The gap between his teeth is that much more obvious with his mouth hanging open like a fish.

Cordelia screams in fright when my lips touch on Adelita's forehead. I freeze, knowing I've gone too far. It's one thing for Rafael to do as he pleases but I forgot myself. I wasn't careful. I'm not the funny guy who everyone loves to see. I'm the wicked heart-eater they avoid, for fear of me ripping out their innards to feast upon.

As if I could ever harm this angel in my arms, who is confused as to what the upset is all about. It's then she realizes how shocked everyone is, even Tio Bruno, who usually dons only one militant expression, no matter the occasion.

She's sees it clearly, how very wrong I am for her. Everyone knows it.

I need to get out of here. I knew this was a bad idea. I belong under the table in the kitchen, not sitting at the chief's grand dining table with silverware, a family and the most beautiful woman in the world. Obviously, this is all wrong.

I gently set Adelita's feet on the floor and pull her chair out for her before I beeline for the exit. Rafael calls my name but I don't listen.

Chef Aarón stands in the doorway, his arms crossed to block my path. We both know I could easily throw him to the ground, but Aarón knows me enough to guess that I wouldn't dare. He's one of the few who doesn't think I'm savage, so occasionally I remember not to be. Aarón is a good man, but he looks angry with me now. He knows I shouldn't have picked up Adelita. He sees how wrong I am in this setting.

But when he speaks, it is with a firm command I don't understand. "Go back to your seat, Santos. You eat at the family table now."

I sign to him that I want to eat under the chef's table in the kitchen, but he doesn't move.

Father José calls my name, but I don't turn around. I don't want to see his disapproval at my behavior.

It's not until Adelita squeaks out an indignant, "Stop it!" that I spin around to deal with whatever it is that's upset her.

Before I know what I'm doing, my feet are running toward her, taking in the clear droplets she's smearing across her face.

She's scowling at Cruz, who munches his chorizo without looking at her. "I just flicked her with water, is all. You weren't going to come back unless you thought she might need you. Problem solved."

My napkin finds its way into my hand and dabs at her face until the offending drips are gone. I check her stitches for good measure and touch her wrist to feel her pulse. It's jumping, but it's healthy.

When she looks up into my eyes, I see that she's anxious. Her eyes are plagued with worry. She holds onto my hand as if she is afraid to let go. "I don't understand what just happened. Did I do something wrong? I'm sorry, Santos."

My shoulders deflate. It baffles me that she thinks anything she does is wrong. That she could ever be imperfect. It's laughable, because she's brilliant. I shake my head and point to myself, indicating it's me who is very, very mistaken in thinking I belong here.

Her voice is quiet but everyone else is completely silent, so her words travel to both ends of the table. "Will you stay with me? I'm nervous."

And just like that, I'm taking the empty seat beside her, disregarding every instinct that tells me to run. I slide her chair closer to mine so the wooden sides are touching. I wrap my arm around her shoulder in a half-hug I can tell she wholly needs.

Her eyes close in relief—actual relief—and she leans her temple to rest on my neck. She leaves it there for only a beat, but it's the best feeling in the world.

I'm her comfort, not her savage.

I place her free hand atop my thigh so we can remain connected while I cut her meat. I know she can't do that one-handed, and she's much too embarrassed to ask for help.

"You don't have to do that for me."

I shoot her a dubious look, silently asking her how she expected to eat the chunk without being able to cut it.

"Well, okay, you sort of did. Thank you." She motions to Rafael's plate. "I have different food than everyone else. Did you want to try some? The corn is really good."

It's problematic that I can't speak aloud and she doesn't

understand sign. I try to tell her that I made it for her, but she only furrows her brows at me in confusion.

Rafael translates for me. "Santos made your meal, *linda*."

"Oh, really? That's so sweet. Thank you. Rafael mentioned you were helping in the kitchen."

I tell her of course I made her meal. It's got extra iron to compensate for her blood loss. It wasn't cooked too long, so it's denser in nutrients. There's no salt, so she doesn't dehydrate. No one poisoned her food. I made sure of it.

Rafael runs his hand over his face. "I'm not translating that last bit. You're only going to scare her."

That there *isn't* poison in her food? Why would that be scary?

She takes a bite and I hold my breath until she makes this tiny "mm" noise. The sound goes straight through my body and settles in my chest, which swells with pride.

"This is delicious. I didn't know you were such a good cook."

"I only cook for you."

She shakes her head and turns in her chair to face me more fully. "Slower, Santos. Teach me how to listen to you. Whatever your voice sounds or looks like, I want to know it."

I stop moving, stunned by the beauty in her words. Of course they would be heartwarming; they came from her. Adelita Corazon. Her last name means "heart", which is fitting, because she cares even about someone as lowly as me.

I close my eyes so I can soak in her request. This woman wants to hear me. *Me.* Santos the Savage.

I sign slower and make sure she can read my lips. Her fingers twitch, and I can see her frustration peaking. "I can't do it! I only have one working arm. This sucks!"

I'm just bold enough to take her hand and sandwich it between mine, giving her knuckles a kiss before I show her an amended version of the sentence, which requires only one hand.

I love the blush in her cheeks from my lips briefly touching her fingers. I did that to her. She's all business, though, doing the motions over and over until she's committed it to memory.

Consuela dabs at her eyes with her napkin, reminding us that we're not alone. "That's the sweetest thing I've ever seen." Then she throws her roll clear across the table, aiming to smack it on Father José's chest.

I intercept it, because even though it is only a piece of bread, Don José is my father now, which means I am to protect him with my life. Even from bread.

José laughs at the scandal but Consuela is indignant. "How come you've never cooked for me? Do you see how precious they are?"

"Okay, so when do *I* get to cook for *you*?" Adelita asks quietly when the others start to splinter off into pockets of conversation. "Have you ever had churros with lime zest?" When I shake my head, she waves her hand to excuse my lack of worldliness. "I'll teach you how."

I smile at her moxie. *"I can't wait."* And I mean it. She repeats the sign a few times, and I'm utterly enamored of her for the effort.

Tio Bruno is talking with Cruz and Father José about the border wall while Roberto does his best to chime in with anything relevant to impress the important men. Eva and Rafael are bickering about who knows what while Cordelia tries to regain Rafael's attention. Consuela is bargaining with Mira about eating the next bite.

But none of that matters. The outside of Adelita's thigh is touching mine. It's like a little secret we wear in plain sight. She eats the entire meal I made for her, down to the last kernel. When she makes that "mm" noise again, it's the best sound in my life. I did it. I made the beautiful woman happy.

After she finishes, she holds my hand under the table while I polish off my meal. Her shoulder touches mine and she yawns.

I wonder if this is what I've been missing out on all this time. I kept myself under the table in the kitchen because I knew I didn't belong, but sitting here now, I'm content. If they mind me joining them, they don't say it. In fact, Father José even makes it a point to draw me in to a few exchanges that have nothing to do with the tribe or the Kalku.

Though everyone is done eating, Father José doesn't want it all to end. He's in high spirits tonight, and insists we all have drinks by the fire in the grand family room.

I don't drink alcohol, but sip my water while Adelita and I take one of the large oval seats for ourselves. They're cushioned on the bottom and the back, curving in a half-circle I never fully appreciated until I was able to share one with her. They're built for two, and as she cuddles into my side, I realize how wonderful the design of these chairs truly is. She so easily fits against me. My arm drapes around behind her as the outside of our thighs touch. It's the best feeling in the world, and she grants it freely to me, as if I'm deserving of something so decadent as her touch.

There are tall plants everywhere in this room, making it feel like we're both outdoors and indoors as the stars blink at us from the enormous floor-to-ceiling windows. We're two stories above the rest of the village, looking down on them as they turn in for the night.

Chef Aarón brings out tumblers of mezcal and a platter of lime and orange wedges, along with a dipping bowl of salt.

Rafael grins at me while he bounces Mira on his lap to give Consuela a break. "Are you finally going to try alcohol, Santos? First sugar, next liquor."

Tio Bruno notices everything but says little unless it involves battle. At this, however, he speaks up. "Santos ate sugar? When?"

I cast Rafael a simpering look. *"It's not that big a deal."*

Rafael plops a lime in his drink. "Ever had mezcal before, Adelita?"

She shakes her head. "I don't drink all that much. Is it good?" She takes a glass and a lime wedge, watching Rafael to mirror his actions.

I want to sniff the liquid first to make sure it hasn't been poisoned, but she sips it before I can.

Her face pulls in an immediate grimace. "Oh, that's strong."

The fire crackles in the enormous hearth. It's wider than I am tall, and Aarón stokes it to make it that much hotter.

Eva gets up and grabs a blanket from the basket near the hearth. Instead of wrapping herself in it, she unfolds it and drapes it over our laps. Eva's never done anything like that for me before, but when she kisses Adelita's forehead, I see that it's for us, not for me.

Eva grips my hand for a brief moment, meeting my eyes with real emotion that she's doing a terrible job of holding back. "I am so glad you ate with us." Her eyes flick to Adelita. "Both of you."

"Tio Bruno, tell Adelita about the time the Mendez tribe was under attack, and we came to their aid."

Adelita sips on her drink while Tio Bruno regales us of a war story too boring to really be called a story. No one dies. Near misses. Barely any clash to begin with. Still, it serves as entertainment mostly because Adelita deems it so. And any tale that doesn't end in the slaughter of our village I guess is a good one. Though the Kalku elders never would've wasted their breath retelling a story that ends so tamely.

The story is enough to put anyone to sleep. Coupled with hefty doses of mezcal, Adelita's eyes begin to droop.

This might be the best feeling in the world—having Adelita in my arms, resting like she's not afraid of her own dreams. She's not completely out, but she's headed there.

After the usual hemming and hawing, Cordelia consents to putting Roberto and Mira to bed, so Consuela can sit in one of the oval seats with Father José. Tio Bruno's story is still tiresome but no one minds, since we're all content and the alcohol is kicking in.

The fire crackles in a low hum that makes me miss my twin brother's face. Santiago had this way of blowing on the flames at just the right time to make the fire last longer than I ever could. I wonder how the elders are making do without us there to torment. I touch the scars on my face, as I often do when I miss my twin.

"You're sad," Adelita observes in a whisper, alerting me to the fact that she is still fighting for wakefulness.

I'm ungrateful, is what I am. I'm dwelling on tragedy when I have a woman too lovely for words in my arm. Santiago has been gone two and a half years.

The corners of my mouth lift to convince her that I'm fine, but the pucker between her eyebrows tell me she's not buying it.

When she drains her glass, I set it on the round table in the center for her and settle her more comfortably in my arms. True warmth fills me from the fire, the blanket and her. Just when I think it can't get any better, she rests her head on my shoulder.

It's no surprise that Tio Bruno's story puts her to sleep. Eva's nearly there herself. The mezcal brewed inside the village is quite strong, from what I've heard.

I sign one-handed to Cruz that I'm taking Adelita to her

bedroom, and can he please do a tour of the grounds tonight so I don't have to leave her unguarded.

"She's safe, Santos." Then Cruz gives me a look of pure sadness. "*You're* safe. We're in the village. We have our border walls. You can relax here, brother. Adelita being here might make this a good time for you to learn that."

I can't imagine anything I want to learn less. Adelita being here means everything should be better taken care of, more closely watched. I sign as much to him.

Rafael puts his drink down, only half-finished. "I understand. I'll do a check of the grounds. Would you like it better if I did two rounds, just in case?"

I exhale tension I didn't realize I had in me and nod. *"Thank you."*

Rafi stands and says goodnight to everyone, knowing I won't be able to relax if her safety isn't taken seriously.

I don't want to wake Adelita, but even though I'm careful as I slide her onto my lap and stand, her eyelids crack open halfway. "Where are we going?"

"Santos is taking you to your room," Cruz explains. "That okay?"

"M-kay."

I motion for Eva to follow me, ignoring the soft coos from Consuela as I move down the hallway with my angel in my arms.

6

CRUZ'S FUTURE BRIDE

CRUZ

I awake in a cold sweat, clutching my pillow as if it's a weapon I'm ready to put to good use.

It's not real. She's gone now. La Sayona's torment robs me of proper sleep, but it's my elevated heartrate that worries me most. It feels like the beginnings of a heart attack, and I really don't have time for that.

My stomach jerks me off the bed with a growl. Even though I know I could sleep for another hour, on the second rumble, my feet find their way to the bathroom and then the dresser.

The guys sleep like babies whenever we come back to the village, so I know they're still out. Aarón cooks all our meals, Berta keeps us in clean clothes and fresh sheets, and Dad acts like everything we do is a big deal.

I don't expect to see anyone in the hallway, so I'm surprised when I nearly trip over Santos, who's camped out in front of Adelita's door in his wolf form. "What are you doing?"

He blinks himself awake and stretches out his back in a yawn. I don't know how he sleeps on the drafty floor, but he's never surly after a night spent like that, so I don't question it. There's a lot about Santos I'll never understand. But the things I admire far outweigh the nagging mystery. The second he transforms back into a person, I give him a hand up and pull him into a quick back-slapping hug.

When he steps back to lean against the door while he yawns again, he signs that he didn't want to leave her unprotected.

"In the village? There hasn't been an attack in Cáceres in years, Santos. No one can infiltrate our border walls. Do you know something I don't? Rafi did two rounds along the perimeter before turning in. Did he see anything off?"

Santos shakes his head but doesn't look like he regrets his choice.

"So you slept on the floor? You probably could've asked if she would let you sleep in the room with her, you know."

Santos looks away and rubs the nape of his neck, unable to look at me through his bashfulness. Rafi would rip into him for getting all soft for her, but I go easy on the poor guy. This is all new for him. Even though we're pretty sure Santos is my age, it helps me to imagine he's thirteen years old, and trying to figure out how to tell the girl in his grade that he thinks she's pretty.

Santos signs that he needs to shower. He wants to get ready for the day, and can I please watch her room.

I glance down the hallway, keeping my voice low. "You know she's perfectly capable of taking care of herself. I almost feel bad for the *tarado* who tries to take her down."

Santos points to his spot with a firmness to his jaw that her security will not be taken lightly.

I hold up my hands, ignoring my stomach so Santos doesn't have a heart attack. "Okay, okay. I'll stay right here until you're back. I'm here, Brother."

Santos is exhausted. He hugs me again, this time out of

sheer relief. He's not used to worry that messes with his entire body. He worries about me and Rafi, I know that much, but this is different. It's all exploding out of him in a nervous jumble. I hope it doesn't scare Adelita off. Though, she seems so out of her element still that maybe she appreciates how protective he is of her.

I dunno. I don't want anything to do with whatever it is they've got going. Too much work.

Santos shuffles into his room, and I can hear Adelita meandering around in her bedroom while he showers. I lean against her door and wonder how she'll take to staying here the next time Santos, Rafi and I have to leave. She has Eva. She should be fine.

The door pops open and I nearly fall backward, but manage to catch myself after I bump into her. "Warn a guy before you do that!"

"Before I open the door? You're some piece of work, you know that? Good morning to you, too!"

She's wearing a simpler dress this morning but it's still the strappy kind. Pink, so I know Eva chose it for her. Adelita's crown of braids is still intact, but a few curly wisps sneak down the nape of her neck.

My stomach growls, so I figure I probably don't have to stand in front of her door anymore. "Breakfast is this way."

She harrumphs, her lips pouting. "Were you seriously waiting outside my door? What for?"

"Santos wanted me to make sure you were safe. He's overreacting, but that's why."

"Well, I'm safe. I don't need you lurking, scaring the living daylights out of me for no good reason."

"How about the next time I scare you, I make sure it's for a very good reason?"

"Pass."

"Then I suppose just eating breakfast the normal way with no hijinks is how you prefer it."

She rolls her eyes at me. "Imagine that."

I don't know why I offer her my elbow. I'm even more confused when she takes it without any further antagonism. It's like we need to get the insults out of our systems before we can coexist.

We walk to the dining room together, and I nod at my sister. "Morning, Eva."

"Morning, buttface." Though Eva's a grown woman, she slaps her knee and mimes laughing because she's just that kind of a sister. "Get it? Because your face stinks like a butt."

"Hilarious." I pull out Adelita's chair because that, apparently, is the thing to do. My sister's eyebrows raise, but that seems to be the worst of it.

Eva and Adelita chatter away while I eat. Well, Eva's chattering, pausing only for Adelita to ask those infuriatingly insightful questions of hers.

I'm halfway through inhaling a plate of eggs and chorizo when Tio Bruno comes in. "Cruz, one of the men found something you should come see."

"Yes, sir." I stand without hemming and hawing, though all I want to do is eat ten pounds of the meal. I miss Aarón's cooking when I'm on the road for weeks on end. "Come on, Adelita. Santos doesn't want you unguarded, so grab something to go."

She raises her eyebrow at me, as if to silently ask why the crap I think she needs guarding, but doesn't otherwise argue.

I walk slower whenever I'm in the village, my shoulders back as I nod to a few people. They bow and greet me with deference, reminding me that I belong here, however short our stay might be.

I can't imagine that's true; I don't belong anywhere near

people. I belong on the road, so that's where I spend the bulk of my time. It's safer for everyone that way.

It's not too overcast, but a few point to the grey clouds overhead with a patronizing faux-scold. "It was sunny two days ago. I knew you were home!"

They chuckle at the town joke that I bring the rain and chase away the sun. They are not wrong, but it's not like I'm trying to make it like this. Maybe they should try being a man who is haunted by La Sayona. See how sunny their disposition is after a decade or so of that.

Of course, I don't bite back. I wave and take the chiding without a word.

Usually Tio Bruno doesn't bring the next mission to me until I've had a few days to unwind, but I don't mind the quick turnaround. As much as I like the slower pace of life here, I get itchy for adventure if I am in the village longer than a week.

Tio Bruno doesn't speak about the job out in the open. He leads the way in silence, not that anyone aside from me ever tries to engage him in conversation. Even the soldiers give him a wide, respectful berth.

"Cruz? Cruz! I heard you were home, but I had to see it to believe it. Maria, it's Cruz!"

Adelita stiffens on my arm when two, three, then a dozen, twenty, and finally three dozen people crowd us. The older villagers give me enough space, tossing weather-related comments my way every now and then. It's the people my age and younger that come right up and get in my face, acting like my life on the road is so very glamorous. They ask questions on top of each other and fight for attention.

I don't mind it. It's part of the job that comes with being the chief's son. But I can tell Adelita's spooked as more people press in around us.

She clings to my arm when one of the women reaches

out to touch the hem of her dress. People are always doing that to Eva, but Adelita is used to living alone and working in a stiff office with little or no physical contact all day long.

I know I'm not her favorite person, but right now, I'm her only person, so she grips my bicep tighter, making me wince.

Dang, she's strong.

"Ease up, Addy," I remind her through a tight smile. I hope it looks like a smile.

She remembers her strength and lightens her squeeze. "Maybe I should go back home."

"Are you living with Cruz?" someone asks.

Before I can answer, Adelita nods. I fight back a groan. If the rumors were kindled before, they'll be roaring now.

I greet a few more people and shake their hands before excusing us. "Sorry, everyone. We've got official business to see to."

"Oh, did you hear that? It's official! Cruz has found a bride, and she's still alive!"

I cringe as too many cheers rise up from the younger people, and the older ones take a wary step back. Several people try to bless her as we pass, shouting out pleas for her to be careful and never ever to sleep with me.

Feels great. Just… great.

I try to set them straight that of course Adelita isn't my girlfriend, but it's no use. A few eavesdroppers are already scattering to tell others. I know it's too late to be undone.

When cries of "La Sayona!" break up the merriment, my whole body tightens. It's not their business what haunts me. I've got it under control.

"La Sayona won't harm her. She's not my…"

"No!" Adelita tells them. "No, I'm not his bride. I'm just staying with his family." But no one is listening to her.

Now all the women step back from her, and the men look

at me like I'm the most selfish bastard in the world to claim a treasure I'm bound to destroy.

"We're not getting married," I assure them, but they move back from us as if they're afraid of being struck by lightning. They're excited I might continue the family line, but they are afraid for Adelita—this vision in a pretty dress, on the arm of a bulky lug nut.

Just like that, my good mood falls. The sliver of sun hides behind quick-moving clouds that darken quicker than I can cap my mood.

Adelita shivers and looks up in confusion, but I'm not about to explain it all to her.

Tio Bruno turns and stomps near. Just like that, the villagers scatter, though they cast Adelita looks of warning as they go.

"Let's move, Cruz." As if I'm trying to be difficult. He frowns at the people, standing a head above them all. "Leave Cruz and his bride alone. He has much work to do."

I'm sure he said it as a joke, but I narrow my eyes at him. "Not helpful."

"Sure it was. See? They're scattering from her because they are afraid La Sayona is going to fry her brain right in front of them. This way."

Adelita drops my arm, her cheeks pink. "Maybe I should go back to the house."

"Santos didn't want you left alone. This will be quick."

My legs are longer than hers, so she falls behind a few times. I have to stop and make sure she's in my eyeline. I'm frustrated at the lengths I'll go to for Santos, which normally doesn't bother me one bit.

When she falls behind again, I tuck her arm around my bicep once more, pinning her dainty hand to my ribcage.

She's silent when we reach the barracks, taking in the concrete walls and floor with wide eyes. There aren't too many men around, but the few dozen stand at attention when we move through the cold hallways that lead us at a slope down under the earth.

Tio Bruno doesn't react to the cold, but I can never suppress a shiver when I come here. Too many echoes of my own grunts and angry cries during training haunt my mind.

I'm glad to be rid of this place. I don't belong underground. I like the open road, the variety of different landscapes, and being the man who makes the judgment calls.

Tio Bruno scrapes his fingers across the underside of his angular jaw. "One of my men found something I want you to look at. It's what I wanted you to go check on, but you came here instead. I sent out a separate party to investigate, and they came back with a snakeskin you should see."

"A snakeskin?" I don't whine, but honestly, he can handle this without my help. Tio Bruno doesn't like to leave the village, so he sends me out to investigate every little thing that worries him. I never protest because he's my uncle and our commanding officer. But still, it's a snake. Pest control only falls in my domain if the pest is a member of the Kalku.

Tio Bruno fixes me with a cold glance over his shoulder. "I can hear your exasperation. Is that what you want to show your future bride? That you are disrespectful? That you are too good to protect your people?"

It's not me but Adelita who speaks up. "Knock it off. You know that's nothing like the truth."

Tio Bruno raises his brow at her sass. "What I know is that La Sayona won't care if it's not true. If you sleep with Cruz, she will come for your brain."

Adelita stops and puts her hand on her hip. That stubborn look of frustration warns me a fight is brewing that I won't be able to brush off. "Who the crap is this La Sayona, and why does she want my brain?"

I hear the heavy tread of boots gunning for us, and I couldn't be more grateful for the interruption.

I know before I turn around that I've made the wrong choice, taking Adelita with me. It only made life more complicated, explaining things to the villagers. Now the rumor mill is totally out of control. On top of that, Santos looks like he's on the verge of a heart attack as he runs toward us down the concrete decline of the barracks.

He's signing a mile a minute, angry without blaming me for any of it. *"Why did you take her out of the house? Why is she in the barracks? I took a shower and she was missing!"*

"She's not missing. I thought Eva would've told you. Tio Bruno needs me to look at something, so I took Adelita with me because I assumed that would be better than leaving her unguarded. I didn't mean to worry you, Brother."

I hug Santos, steadying him with a kiss to his cheek.

Tio Bruno isn't a fan of big, emotional displays. He looks like he's swallowed something sour when Santos moves to Adelita. He wraps her in a hug that softens her irritation at me to something sweeter.

"None of this matters," Tio Bruno comments, fanning his hand toward the three of us. "La Sayona is going to kill Adelita long before anyone else tries to get their hands on her. I see the way she clings to your arm, Cruz." When her face goes red, Tio Bruno fixes his eyes on me. "And I see the way you let her."

Santos is livid, but doesn't do more than hold tighter to Adelita. He signs in jerky motions. *"La Sayona is no fool. She knows it's not Cruz who belongs to Adelita. I do."*

I pinch the bridge of my nose. "This whole thing is my fault. I didn't think when I took her through the village. Now there's talk, and you know how that can get."

"Let them talk. It won't sway La Sayona. I don't care what they

say. I never have." Then he signs to Adelita, mouthing, "*Are you alright? I can take you home, if you'd like.*"

He is gentle with her, so soft and careful with his movements.

Tio Bruno cuts through their conversation as he throws open a door and motions for us to go inside. "La Sayona is the least of our worries, boys."

When I step into the dim room that's lit only by a blinking bare bulb dangling from the center of the ceiling, I stop short. I don't see eye-to-eye with Tio Bruno on everything, but when I take in the husk of a twenty-foot-long, five-foot thick culebrón, all other concerns run out of the room.

7

I HATE ADELITA
CRUZ

*a*delita gestures wildly with her one good arm. I can only imagine how emphatic she could be with two. "You're seriously not telling me anything about it, other than they found the husk near a curse tree? That's crap, and you know it. If I'm supposed to be going on this trek to dispose of this culebrón, I should at least know what that hairy thing can do."

Santos shakes his head in time with mine. *You're not going to chase down a culebrón. They're dangerous, Adelita.*

I'm glad we're on the same page. I sit on the edge of my bed and rub my neck. I'm stiff all over, and just want to go to sleep. Unfortunately, Adelita's been cooped up in the house all day after we deposited her home so we could further discuss things with Tio Bruno, so she's brimming with questions.

She gapes at Santos. "Are you seriously leaving me here while you go slay the dragon? Do you really think I'll stay, twiddle my thumbs and just wait around for the big men to come home? This place is not my home!"

Rafi chuckles, but then passes it off as a cough when she

glowers at him. He still hasn't seen the culebrón husk, but he doesn't need to. All he wanted to know is where it was found and when we were leaving to go hunt it down. Rafi's good like that.

Unlike Adelita, who is a fountain of unending questions.

Santos keeps his cool, and I expect him to say something like, *"I'm sorry, babe, but it's got to be done. See you in a week or so."* Instead he shocks me with a sober, *"I'll be staying here with you. Of course I won't leave you unprotected."*

It's my turn to gape at Santos, and Rafi does the same. "Are you joking?" Rafi balks, his arms crossed over his chest. He's leaning on my bedroom wall with his leg kicked up behind him, but I can see he's ready to fight this thing through, despite his attempts to look casual. "You really think we're going to up and leave you here? That's not how we work. It's always been the three of us ever since you got here."

Santos runs his hand over his face. *"What do you expect me to do? I can't leave her here unguarded, and I also can't take her with us to kill el culebrón. There's not a third option, so I'm choosing the one that will keep her safest."*

"There's no danger here!" I say a little too loudly, throwing my hands up in exasperation.

"No danger here?" By the slow way Santos turns to me, I can tell I've said the wrong thing. *"Tell me how many people still call me a savage. This village was not made for outsiders. If I am overreacting, I can live with that. What I cannot abide is abandoning her."*

"You're seriously going to leave us to go off and fight el culebrón without you?" I'm glad it's not just me who's not having this. Rafi is equally as irate.

Santos spouts back with, *"You're seriously going to save her life and then leave it unguarded? This is the right thing to do."*

I hate this whole exchange. It's *her* who's causing a rift between us. Santos never says no to me.

I kick off my boots and get up to open my door. "I'm turning in. I don't want to talk about this anymore. If Santos wants to stay, he can stay. I didn't free him so I could buy myself a new slave. He can make his own choices." When Rafi opens his mouth to argue, my tone turns more biting than I mean for it to be. "I'm tired, and we're not getting anywhere like this. Rafi, you and I will leave in the morning."

I'm keeping my cool pretty well. But when Adelita offers up a meek, "I'm sorry," to me, I snap.

My finger jabs in her face. "This is on you, I hope you know. Santos doesn't like the village. He wants to be out on the open road with us. As much as you think you care about him, you're taking him away from what he loves. You're taking him away from the people he loves. It's selfish."

She balks at me. It's clear my words have formed into an arrow and pierced straight through her. She thought I was on the side of their... love? No, that's crazy. They are still new to each other.

I hurt her on purpose, and what's worse is that the look on her face is sheer betrayal. Her eyes well up, but she holds it in, thank the clouds.

I can see all the arguments she wants to push back at me to put me in my place: She never asked Santos to stay; She wants him to be safe too; One mission isn't taking him away from us forever.

Adelita holds them all inside, and then in a purposeful move, she lowers her chin. She's got plenty to say, but she swallows it all down.

I don't need this shit.

It's a true testament to how pissed Santos is with me that he guides her out of the room and then leaves her side to march back in to give me a piece of his mind. He closes the door halfway, so he can still hear if she needs anything.

Then, as if unsure, he trots back to her room to double-check she's alright.

She doesn't need a thing, Santos, I want to shout at him. *She can bench-press you!* But I don't say it. I let him be as neurotic as he likes.

Rafi runs his hand from his hairline to his chin. "I honestly hope Santos tears you a new one. The asshole you're using now is currently clogged with too much crap."

"Shut up. Like you're okay going without him."

"I'm okay treating Santos like a man. You're the one who's determined to be his wet nurse forever."

It takes everything in me not to shove Rafi, who says and does what he likes, and always gets away with it. I say one stupid thing, and I get nailed to the wall for it.

Okay, maybe it was a few stupid things, but still.

Santos marches back in. His hands flick in angry staccato motions, with the space between his brow puckered. *"I can't believe you put that on her. She's just lost her home, her friends and her job. She's living with strangers who've hurt her, and are about to abandon her in a place where she doesn't know the lay of the land."* He pauses for my pushback but it never comes.

He's right, and I can't believe I've become so awful that I've managed to piss off Santos, who always acts like I can do no wrong.

Santos signs slower now. *"From the beginning, she said she didn't want to live in the village. She doesn't like the idea of the border walls."* He shakes his head at me. *"You don't understand what it is to be among strangers in a new place like this and pretend it's your home."*

I motion around the room. "You've been here for two years, Santos. This is your home."

He shakes his head once so angrily, I'm sure he's going to

shove me. *"No! You and Rafi are my home. Santiago was my home! You didn't let me out of your sight when you rescued me, but she gets a week or two before you let her sink or swim? I'm doing what you taught me—taking care of the Kalku's victims—and you're being terrible to her. Like it's her fault she's here in the first place."*

Then he stops and allows fresh hurt to flood his features.

I loathe that look. Santos usually doesn't let his underbelly show this much.

"Why do you hate her?"

I go still, unsure what the right answer is.

Rafi kicks his foot off the wall and moves to stand between us. He looks older in this setting, the one in charge when I'm floundering all over the place like an idiot. He cuffs one hand on the nape of my neck and one on Santos', as well. Then he leans in and brings our heads to lean in, too. It's so intimate, I stop breathing, stop arguing, stop being angry altogether.

Rafi's voice is quiet, and deflates the building tension like a slow leak in a balloon. "Santos, you're a good man for staying with Adelita. You're right. She was just uprooted and didn't want to come to Cáceres. Handing her off to people in the village to get her acclimated will be a bad idea, now that people think she's Cruz's future wife. They're afraid of La Sayona, and Adelita will be marked in their minds as her next victim. They'll spook her with all their warnings. Watch her, okay?" Rafi kisses Santos' cheek, and I can see the tenderness chasing away the tension.

Insecurity shines in Santos' eyes. *"Do you think La Sayona will go after Adelita?"*

"Nah," Rafi replies. "La Sayona is a cranky witch, but she's not stupid. Anyone who knows Adelita can see she's only got eyes for you." Then he brags about his own connection with Addy in the form of a cocky grin. "And me."

Santos' neck shrinks. I can tell he likes that very much.

I swear, these two.

Rafi squeezes our napes lightly. "If La Sayona was going to strike, she would've done so the night Adelita held his hand while La Sayona was torturing his mind when he slept. But she didn't, so Adelita is fine." Rafi turns his eyes on me, and he shifts from paternal to serious. "Gruz and I will go sort out el culebrón, and then we'll be back to spend some real time here. Then it'll be a solid week of hanging by the pool and eating paella in the village. Maybe two weeks."

Two weeks? That's not happening. I'm here for two days and I start to get itchy to leave.

Santos signs quickly but not in anger this time. *"Take a bottle of aguardiente with you. More than you think you need. You have to really douse the ground if you want the snake to let its guard down. The husk in the barracks still had its three longest hairs, so it hasn't been domesticated by a master yet. That's good. It means there haven't been regular sacrifices made to appease el culebrón."*

Dang, Santos is knowledgeable. I hate that we're leaving him behind. I was content going there to cut off the giant snake's head; I didn't think about whether or not it had a master to deal with also.

I try to erase all aggression out of my tone. "I wish you were coming, Santos. We really need you out there."

Santos tips his head up in our huddle and holds my gaze. *"You didn't answer my question. Why do you hate Adelita?"*

It's my turn to go mute. I don't want to think about that. I don't want to think about her—this woman who keeps bringing more questions and drama into our lives.

I know I should tell Tio Bruno about her strength, but she's so protective of her secret that I haven't opened my mouth about it to him yet. But he should know.

Rafi speaks, but the second his words hit the air, I wish he hadn't. "Cruz doesn't hate Adelita. Once he figures that out, I think we're going to have some real problems to deal with. Enjoy his denial while we have it, Brother." It's Rafi's knowing look that breaks me from our huddle.

Rafi's got no business giving me that look. I move toward the door and push it all the way open. "We're all fine. It's good. I'm going to bed, though. Get an early start on the morning. Everyone, get out." Stupid Rafi gives me another look after Santos exits. "What?"

Rafi is unperturbed by my grumping. He fixes me with a stare that sees straight through to things I don't want to look at myself, much less allow other people to invade and judge. "You know what. Let them be."

"You're one to talk. I saw you kiss her cheek."

Rafi rolls his shoulders back. "You're keeping tabs on who she's kissing, are you? That's not suspicious at all. Santos doesn't mind, but I see that you do."

I'm too livid to respond with anything but pure acid, so I keep my mouth shut and glower at the back of Rafi's head as he exits, leaving me with shadows marking my thoughts.

I don't want to think about her…

…yet I can't stop.

8

SLEEPING WITH SANTOS

ADELITA

It's the fourth time I've turned onto my good side but I can't get comfortable, no matter what I do. I'm tired yet wide awake. This place is too new to be familiar, and too big to be cozy. I'm not sure if that's a complaint or just my sleepy brain making excuses as to why I'm not drooling on the lace-covered pillow right now. The bed is huge, and I feel alone on it, drifting and uncertain as to how I got here, and if this is where I should be in the world.

I just caused a fight between the guys without knowing how. The weight of that sits on my chest as I try to calm my thoughts down so they don't take me over.

But it's too late. My stomach is in knots over the drama I didn't mean to start. Worst of all, my door keeps making weird noises, like someone is pushing against it, trying to get in.

Though I know I am stronger than whatever it is that's out there, I don't often use the full breadth of my muscle. I prefer talking things through instead. I'm used to believing there was a monster under my bed and making sure the closet is closed at night. Those childish fears are never gone completely, or maybe I'm still too naïve to understand that monsters are what you make of them. That's what Mama always said, anyway.

On the fourth muffled push against my door, I decide I am not going to be scared anymore. Or at the very least, I'm going to be scared while I confront whatever it is that's out there.

This is how women die. Confronting a killer while wearing nothing but a silk peach nightgown. I wince as I feed my bad arm through the matching knee-length robe, as if that'll make me less murder-able.

My fist closes around the handle and I jerk the door open, my shriek muffled behind closed lips when none other than wolf-Santos falls back and rolls over until he's on all four legs, blinking up at me. "Santos? What are you doing? You scared me half to death!"

He changes into his man form, rubbing sleep out of his eyes. I help him up and shut the door, turning on the bedside lamp so I can get a good look at him.

"*Sorry*," he signs.

That's right. I know that one now.

"Are you alright?"

He stretches out his back and rubs his neck. "*I'm fine. I was just making sure you're safe.*"

"By sitting outside my room? Hun, you have to sleep some time."

He points to the door. "*I was. If anyone wants to get at you, they would have to wake me.*"

My mouth falls open and I beeline for the door, throwing it open to see the space where Santos was just sleeping. Then I shut the door and spin around, pinching the bridge of my nose. "You were sleeping on the floor to keep me safe?"

Santos nods and runs his hand across his stomach. He's wearing jeans and the standard black t-shirt, ready to pounce whenever there's a hint of trouble. I don't understand this world, but I know enough to make out the bags under his eyes and the stiffness in his back. The bags aren't as purple as Cruz's, but any sign of wear and tear on Santos is impossible for me to ignore.

"Am I really in that much danger in this house?"

Santos shakes his head, as if sheepishly admitting that he's gone a little overboard with his quest to make sure I am alright.

"What are the chances of you sleeping in your bed tonight, instead of in the hallway in front of my door?"

Santos cuts the flat of his hand across his body, resolute that I won't be left alone.

"Did you sleep there last night, too?"

He nods, and I feel awful.

My posture softens as my heart tugs in my chest. "Oh, my heart. That's not going to work. You're going to hurt your back, laying against the door like that." I bite down on my lower lip, and before I can really think through my words, they tumble into the nighttime air without polish. "Sleep with me."

Santos' eyes go wide, and it dawns on me that I've basically propositioned this man in the middle of the night, wearing a silk robe.

"I mean just resting! If you can't sleep in your bedroom without worrying, but there's really nothing to be concerned about, then maybe you might want to…" I motion to the bed, but my face is too red to look at him.

I tuck a lock of hair behind my ear. It's crimped from taking my black waves down from the braids. I'm sure I look a complete mess right now. This is the worst.

"Never mind. I'm saying it all wrong."

Santos is frozen like a deer, as if he's waiting for me to

pull the rug out from under him at the golden offer. *"You'll let me sleep in here with you?"*

I nod slowly. "I think the bed is a better choice than the floor. You don't have to do that to yourself."

Santos moves slowly, maybe to give me time to renege on my offer. He pulls the comforter back and motions for me to get in.

Though we've slept in the same bed before, we were also with Cruz and Rafael at the time. This is different. Intimacy hangs in the air like honey, and I'm not sure how to act.

Should I be funny?

Should I try my hand at being sexy? I've never been all that great at flirting.

"Pajamas!" I work out, too nervous to go to the bed. "You can't sleep in jeans. You'll be uncomfortable all night long. Go put on pajamas, then come on in."

Santos looks down, and then quirks his eyebrow at me as if to ask what the purpose of pajamas is. But he goes, taking the sexual tension from the air with him. Now that he's gone, I can get into the tall bed ungracefully and without nerves making me giddy. Maybe this is no big deal for most people, but for me, it's enough to make me overthink every detail.

When Santos comes back in, the sight of him in grey flannel pajama pants and that same black t-shirt is too adorable for words. He steps forward but stops at the edge of the bed. I can tell he's nervous too, which for some reason puts my mind at ease.

I tap the covers on his side, and he slides in. I expect him to cling to the far edge while we get used to each other, but my spine turns to jelly when he molds his body to my side and presses a kiss to my sore shoulder.

His hands aren't used to silk. I try not to writhe with obvious lust as he runs his fingers over the sleeve of my peach robe and then sweeps them across my stomach. His arm drapes over my abdomen as his hand caresses my hip, and then the silk covering my thigh.

I feel precious to him, and breakable with beauty. It's an incredible sensation, the reverence of his hand on my body. I can't roll on my other side to face him, but he seems to understand that I want him closer than even this. Though his forehead is pressed to my temple and his arm is draped across me so his hand can covet my thigh, it's not close enough for either of us. Though I haven't even kissed the man yet, my body is completely open to him.

I lay on my back, my side warmed by his torso. My knees fall apart, so Santos can sandwich my leg between his, parting my thighs.

In that moment, I am certain I can trust him. I may not understand everything about him yet, and he might not understand everything about how the world works, but my intuition sings a peaceful lullaby when he's snuggled around me like this.

I love his scent—earth and aftershave and something that smells like a hug. That's what it is. Santos smells like the best kind of hug. The kind you can wrap yourself in after a long day and be immediately renewed.

"Santos?" I whisper.

His response is to thumb my hip.

"I don't want you to sleep on the floor anymore, okay?"

He runs his hand downward, tracing the outside of my thigh. I'm utterly wrapped in him, and I love how very safe and right it all feels.

"I like you close, just like this."

He kisses my shoulder, then my cheek, and settles in on the pillow we're sharing. It's easy to share with Santos, who requires so little. When my lashes finally flutter shut, I'm fairly certain there's never been a better night anywhere in all the world.

9

HOLDING HANDS
ADELITA

'm awoken with a jolt that I realize didn't originate from me. Santos sits up, not even taking the time to rub the sleep from his eyes before he is on his feet and beelining for the door.

"Santos?"

He turns and points to the wall that's bumped up to Cruz's bedroom. It's then that I hear the muffled shouting, but I can't make out the words. I'm out of the bed in the next breath, tiptoeing on bare feet into the hallway after Santos, who slips into Cruz's bedroom.

I'm ready to defend the household, emboldened by the fact that Santos is in the room. Whatever is amiss, I don't want it near him. But when I look around, there is no one. Cruz is fighting with himself, shouting in what sounds like fresh trauma as he writhes in the blankets.

When Santos leans over to try and shake him awake, Cruz growls in a way that worries me. Then he shoves Santos so hard, my sweet man stumbles back several feet.

Santos catches my fretful eye and motions for me to stay back. I know he's going to get his healer bag when he exits, but with the way Cruz is crying out, I don't have it in me to deny him what worked last time. Even if Cruz is a surly jackass to me, I don't care. I don't have the gumption to run away from someone who is in obvious agony.

I step closer and reach out to snatch at his hand. "Shh. It's alright."

I can tell part of him can hear my voice in his unconscious state, but there is still a war in his mind. He is in the middle of fighting it for all he's worth.

Cruz twists in the sheets. Despite the fact that he's not exactly my favorite person, my heart jerks in my chest at the sight. He looks like he is in physical pain from being stabbed in the kidney or something.

If this is how he sleeps normally, it's no wonder he always looks unrested.

I keep my fingers gentle but firm as I hold onto Cruz's hand, noting the tension in his forearm.

The longer I touch him, the more the pain seems to die from piercing agony to something more akin to an annoyance. As the seconds pass, it seems the danger in his dream is dying down.

He whines like a little boy in his sleep as his thrashing finally settles.

I sit on the edge of his bed, studying his features in the barely-there hallway light that's filtering in through the door. It casts shadows on his stern jaw, highlighting the years of nights spent much like this.

There was no one to hold his hand back then, though.

I am here now, and though I know he doesn't like me in his home, taking up space in his life, I'm grateful I am around to bring some shred of peace into anyone's world. To me, that is the best kind of connection. It reminds me that even though we are all very different, everyone is in need of gentleness. As often as we welcome it in, it comes to us, finding us even in the dark of night.

Finally, Cruz goes limp with a soft whimper. The sound is too sad for me to maintain any sort of grudge against him. I'm sure our disdain for each other will resurface in the morning, but for now, I honor the truce that has to happen if I want to respect myself. If I could've helped him but didn't because of a fight, Cruz would in some small way have power over my choices. Tonight, I choose to be myself, despite my audience. I like being helpful, and I cannot find peace for myself when there is turmoil in the next room. I work hard with my patients to get to the bottom of their frustrations. It's slow work, but when I can bring solace into their sadness, I feel like anything is possible.

Here in the dim light of the night, holding Cruz's hand gives me that same hope that I might crumble without. Maybe it's prideful, but I like being part of what makes the world a better place, even if it's a small change. It might be insignificant to others, but to me, I feel alive when I connect broken parts of someone. I feel the most myself when I get to show them how to breathe in a full breath again.

When Santos returns with his healer bag, he freezes when he comes in and sees Cruz sleeping soundly, with me hold his hand while I sit atop the large mattress.

He signs slowly, his brows furrowed in confusion. *"I don't understand."* Then he comes over and rubs some cream into Cruz's temples, releasing a menthol and eucalyptus scent into the air.

"I think he's calmed down now. Let's go back to bed. In the morning, I'm going to be obstinate until I get actual explanations on this. Don't say I didn't warn you."

Santos lowers his chin but doesn't protest. I don't need to know all of Cruz's secrets, only the ones that keep me up at night.

I yawn and pull away, but jerk back into place when a loud shout erupts from Cruz's lips, breaking the hushed mood.

It dies as soon as my hand is in his.

The whole thing would be precious if it was anyone but Cruz. Though, as his face relaxes back into his slumber, I cannot deny the note of sweet boyishness to his features.

"What should I do?" I ask Santos, willing him to tell me to go back to bed with him in the next room. I want to hear that Cruz's nightmares will go away eventually.

Santos sets down his healer bag in the corner and sighs into his palm after rubbing his face. He moves slower now, peeling back the covers on the side of the bed with the most space. When he jerks his chin toward the open spot, I wish for another answer.

"You'll stay with me?" I know it sounds weak and vulnerable, but I don't trust Cruz.

Santos nods, his golden eyes reassuring me that this is totally fine.

My evening was going great until this. But I know I don't have the heart to ignore someone in such obvious pain.

Still, this feels like a bad decision I'll regret in the morning.

I slide into the bed, careful not to drop Cruz's hand as I shift on the mattress, trying to find a comfortable spot.

My body is not as open this time, but Santos doesn't push it. Instead of sandwiching my leg between his, he changes into a wolf. It's like he knows I'm worked up and need the therapeutic calm only an animal can grant a person.

Santos presses his warm fur to my side, and a hefty dose of tension exhales out of me. He drapes his tail across my stomach so he can protect my body as best he can in slumber. He licks my cheek, and another gust of anxiety leaves my lips. I nuzzle my cheek to his, loving the feel of his breath on my face.

The evening went from wonderful to crummy, but with Santos by my side, I drift off to sleep with the promise that I just might find myself smack in the middle of the good life.

10

MORNING LIGHT

CRUZ

I feel like I've been hit by a truck. I never sleep this hard or this long. But when the birds wake me instead of the moon begging me to go back to sleep, I know it's got to be light out.

The last time I slept until it was daylight was when Addy held my hand while I slept. Before that? I can't remember that far back.

I'm having the most incredible dream. I don't want to wake from it. A woman's body against mine is just about the best fantasy a man can ask for.

I can't remember the last time I dreamt about anything pleasant.

Flowers. My dream smells like flowers. I don't know how, but this is the most potent dream any man has ever had. I can feel the heat of the woman warming me. I can smell her.

As I roll onto my side, my body curves around her, begging my brain for just a few more minutes of this most perfect of dreams. My arm slides around her waist. I love the feel of her curvy body pressed against me.

"You just about awake, Cruz?"

The voice is too familiar, too soft, too wrong.

My eyelids fly open, and when my reality crashes into my subconscious, my body goes rigid. "What the... What are you doing in my bed?" I skitter off the mattress, equal parts livid and spooked.

I glance around my bedroom.

I'm awake. This isn't a dream.

Santos picks up his head and yawns, then shifts into his man form.

Adelita sits up, her shapely legs darting out of the bed before she stands, giving me a view of her clad in only a peach silk nightgown that barely brushes the middle of her thigh.

Terror floods my system. I mutate from the most relaxed man in the world to a live ball of nerves. I charge at her, eyes wide enough to frighten even me. My hands coil around her bicep as I back her into the wall.

I mean to sound concerned, but I'm not good at that. Instead, my worry comes out in an angry shout. "Are you okay?"

Adelita flinches and actually trembles in my arms. Though we both know she could easily throw me to the ground, I am the thing that scares her. "I'm fine, Cruz."

I don't take her word for it. Instead I pry at her eyes, testing the focus in her pupils. "How old are you?"

Her face pulls. "Why do you care?"

"Do you know how old you are?" I bellow. I'm such a lunatic that Santos stands beside her, getting in my eyeline to silently ask me what on earth I think I'm doing, talking to her like this.

"I'm twenty-eight," she confesses. "Cruz, tell me what's got you upset."

But I don't care to explain myself. Instead I pepper her

with questions I'd know the answer to. Her hot chocolate recipe. The color of her hair. Her occupation.

When it doesn't seem there's any brain damage, I should be relieved. Instead, I'm irate. "Do you understand what you could have done, getting into my bed like that?"

Finally, I've pushed her too far. With embarrassing ease, Adelita removes my grip from her bicep. Then she situates the peach short robe over her disheveled nightgown. "You were having another nightmare. When we came in to see if you were alright, I held your hand. Whenever I let go, you cried out and your nightmare came back. But when I was holding onto you, the nightmare seemed to fade. Santos and I decided to bunk in your bed, so you could get a good night's sleep. You're welcome!"

I glare at Santos. "You let her sleep in my bed? At what point did you think that would be safe? You, who sleep outside her door to make sure nothing gets at her in your own home. This is infinitely more dangerous, Santos! You know to keep women away from me when I'm sleeping."

Santos signs to me with a frantic look about him, like he's terrified he frolicked into a perilous situation, mislabeling it as harmless. *She's been near you, holding your hand while you slept before, and La Sayona didn't come for her!*

"You know that's still a risk! Do you understand how horribly this could have gone? Just because La Sayona let me sleep for one night, doesn't mean she will allow it a second time."

Santos pauses, and the world begins to still. *But she did. La Sayona didn't come last night after Adelita and I got here. Adelita chased your tormentor away.*

I don't know what to say to that. I don't want to need help from anyone, least of all Addy, who knows nothing of our world. Beyond dangerous, it's embarrassing to be plagued by something as childish as nightmares.

I stumble back from the both of them. When they make to apologize, I hold up my finger.

I have to get away from them.

So I run away, quite literally fleeing out the bedroom door, so I don't have to see the agony in Adelita's eyes.

The agony I caused.

11

DRIVER OF THE YEAR

RAFAEL

I'm breathing easier already, and it's only been half a day we've been away from the village.

Though the passenger seat is so uncomfortable that my lower back keeps seizing up, there's nowhere else I'd rather be. I want to be with Adelita and the guys, hitting the open road and blazing a new trail. Tio Bruno caught wind of us leaving Santos behind, and he put his foot down that Santos needed to offer his assistance on the job. Santos knows more about el culebrón than anyone, thanks to his time with the Kalku. They loved tracking the giant snakes down and turning them submissive.

With Santos comes Adelita, since Santos wouldn't dream of leaving her behind, unprotected. I love having her around. She's sweet and funny, which is sort of the opposite of Cruz.

Our fearless leader is in a mood, which is no real surprise, but this one has lasted longer than normal. He really didn't want Adelita on the trip with us, and he hates losing an argument.

It's raining, of course. Whenever Cruz is irrationally angry, the clouds open up and unleash.

Cruz keeps jerking the steering wheel and slamming on his brakes at the last minute. I know if he keeps this up, I'm going to be sick. "Knock it off, Cruz. I don't need to see the gas station burrito in reverse."

"You got a problem with my driving all of a sudden?"

"Yeah, I guess I do. Take it out on a punching bag or something. You're going to get into an accident, and then we're all screwed." My eyes flick in the rearview mirror to Adelita, who's gaunt with worry. She doesn't look like she's going to be sick, but like she might burst into tears. She's tightly wound, clinging to the door like she's honestly afraid for her life. With the erratic way Cruz is driving, she's not far off.

Though she's buckled, Santos has his arm stretched across her midsection, like he's expecting to be her backup seatbelt. His face is taut, and I know he wants to tell Cruz to knock it off, but he won't dare cross the brooding Alpha. The scarring on the left side of his face only increases the menace in his glare.

When we hit traffic that's too thick to maneuver, Cruz punches the steering wheel and swears loud enough to made the person in the next car jump. He nearly rear-ends the pickup in front of us.

Adelita murmurs something over and over, like a mantra she's saying to herself that I cannot make out.

My foot presses to my imaginary brake pedal as I brace myself for impact that thankfully never comes. I don't mean to transform, but my scales pop out because my brain is shouting to my body that I'm in danger, and need to protect myself.

"Act or accept. Act or accept. Act or accept," Adelita says over and over, her worry filling the car.

I inhale my olive scales with gold on the tips away, trying to talk my adrenaline down so I can stay in my human form.

"Jeez, man! What is your deal? You're going to get us killed if you keep on like this."

But I don't get to hear Cruz's surly reply. There's a click of a buckle, the backdoor opens, and Adelita shouts, "I don't accept this!"

Before I can stop her, Adelita darts out of the car and threads through the bumper-to-bumper traffic in the rain.

It's my turn to cuss as Santos goes after her, his eyes wild in what looks like a crazed man trying to kidnap a fleeing woman.

"Are you happy?" I shout at Cruz, who deserves far more than that. But I don't have the time to really tell him what I think of his surly behavior that's gone off the charts.

I jump out of the car and run for the two, who are clear across the freeway and darting toward the nearest exit. It's still half a mile away, but Adelita's just scared enough to run it along the side of the road.

Santos doesn't slow her down when he catches up to her, but rather runs alongside her. Despite everything, it's a sweet sight. He's not telling her to go back to the death trap with a deranged driver; he's willing to go with her, wherever she's running.

I really like the two of them together. The sight of them running side-by-side makes me lonely for someone I can fawn over, the way Santos adores Adelita.

Adelita and Santos are quick on their feet, so I really have to up my game as I chase after them. I never like to think I'm out of shape, but I don't do much long-distance running on the regular. And never after feeling this carsick.

By the time I see Santos has coaxed her into slowing down, we're at the base of the entrance ramp. My chest is burning from the effort, and I'm a mixture of pissed at Cruz and perplexed at the idea that some people actually go running for fun.

"What was that?" I work out, my hands on my knees as I bend over to catch my breath. "You're going to get yourself killed, running into traffic like that."

Adelita's got her face buried in Santos' shoulder, her body trembling as he cups the back of her head. His fingers massage sweetness into her scalp. With her good arm, she clutches his soaked collar while the rain pelts us.

"I want to go home," she works out through hiccups and sniffling.

Santos meets my eyes as I straighten and wipe the sweat from my brow. He doesn't want to be the one to refuse her, but by this time she knows there's no way around reality.

Instead of answering, Santos kisses her hair and holds her while she cries into his shoulder. I watch him mouth promises he can't speak aloud to her, knowing she cannot hear them or draw comfort from their truth.

Santos' promises are for him alone, vows that seal him more closely to her.

Most people we rescue are glad to be rid of their old life if it means the Kalku are out of the picture. They understand the danger because oftentimes we liberate them after they've already been captured, so they know of the darkness that lurks in the caves.

Cruz's temper, it seems, is more frightening to her than the whole of the Kalku.

We haven't given Adelita a safe place. Not really.

I try to keep my voice gentle as cars roll past us. "As much as I want you to be able to go back to your life, that's a suicide mission."

"So is getting into a car with Cruz!" she counters, hitting the nail spot on the head.

I can't argue with that. My lips purse in Santos' direction. "What's crawled up his butt? He's been surly all day."

Santos keeps one arm around her and uses the other to

sign, *"La Sayona. Adelita had to hold his hand all night long. He's embarrassed."*

The revelation makes no sense, but since it's Cruz, it makes perfect sense. "Ah. So he woke up to Adelita holding his hand and he got all ornery?"

"We slept in his bed and he woke up cuddling her."

My eyes squinch shut. "So he's throwing a fit because he needed her? That sounds about right."

I close the gap between us and stroke the apple of her cheek, leaning my head on Santos' other shoulder just to give her a funny mental image to distract her. I don't care that it's raining and we're all getting soaked to the bone. I can find a smile wherever I go. Adelita's skin is soft, like it's never been touched by anything that might damage it.

Figures. Our little *viento* is nothing if not soft.

Santos brushes his fingers through my hair at the back of my head, mirroring the action of what he's doing to calm her.

"What an idiot. I'm sorry, *vientito*."

Adelita looks like she belongs with her head cradled on Santos' shoulder. Her voice is meek, trusting us with her raw spots. "I don't belong here or in the village. I'll go somewhere new and start over if I can't go back to my old life. I'm not getting back in that car!"

Santos doesn't argue or reason with her. He just keeps holding her, massaging the back of her head with a pained expression. I can't tell if he's upset that his two loves are feuding, or if the mere fact that she's upset is the worst possible conundrum for him.

Maybe it's too soon. Maybe it's unhealthy. Definitely it's weird. But I see it clear as day: if Adelita leaves, Santos will go with her.

Panic wells up in me at the prospect of losing him to

suburbia. Not that he doesn't deserve it; it's selfish that I want him in this chaotic life with me.

Before Santos, it was just Cruz and me.

As great as my best friend can be, even I get fed up with Cruz sometimes. If Santos leaves, Cruz won't be the same.

I won't be the same.

Then a scandalous thought creeps into the back of my brain.

If Adelita would let me, I wonder if I would leave the village to start a quiet life with her and Santos.

I can almost picture myself reading the paper over coffee. Smoking a pipe, like I've seen people do in old movies. I could fuss about the lawn as if something so tedious could ever truly matter.

But even in this wildest of fantasies, I cannot fathom life without Cruz. He's been my brother since I was a boy. Family means precious little without him—for better or worse.

I shake the fantasy of the three of us lounging around on a leisurely Saturday morning together in our own little home, so I can refocus on reality. "How about we dry off in that diner over there. You want a milkshake, *linda*?"

She peeks at me, and my heart breaks a little bit. She's a pretty little thing, but now her face is all red. Her eyes are puffy. She looks so pitiful that I instantly want to promise her everything will be okay, even though we both know it might not.

Her pretty lip quivers. "Why is he so mean?"

I work up a smile and point to the diner. "Not even your psychology degree could get to the bottom of that one. My advice? Milkshakes. Those can cure a myriad of problems."

She finally consents, but Santos doesn't fully pull away. He takes the position closest to the road and moves her to walk between us, protecting her even on our rain-drenched stroll.

I try to draw her into conversation, but after a few failed attempts, I let the silence do its thing. My fingers twine through hers, which settles the rapid thumps of my heart.

Santos sees our connection and doesn't look irritated. In fact, he looks relieved, like now there are two of us to keep her safe from the Kalku.

There are two exits which are easily accessible.

I hate that I size up an establishment before I can enjoy it.

The reds frames of people on the brown walls shout at me that this is a family joint, tracing back several generations.

Must be nice to be that close with your parents and grandparents.

The smell of beef permeates the air, making my mouth water for a burger. But of course, no dining experience is worth the paper napkins they give you unless it starts with milkshakes.

All the milkshakes. It's a thing I have to do at every new establishment we frequent. I order all flavors they offer so I can try each one.

When they come, I take a long pull, savoring the real ice cream I can tell they used. The milkshakes are good, which is usually the case in mom-and-pop diners. I get us all six varieties on the menu with extra cups so we can try each one.

When Santos gives a silent snort at my unending appetite, I explain. "Now that you eat sugar, I figure it's time you're thoroughly corrupted. Try this one." I pass him the butterscotch malt, but both of them are too upset to be distracted by my game.

That stinks, because Adelita's the only one I can count on to laugh at my dumb jokes.

"I like having you around," I blurt out, surprising all of us when the unvarnished truth pops out of my mouth. "Cruz is so serious, and Santos doesn't always appreciate my finer jokes. But when you're around, it's better. You don't look at Santos or me like we're monsters."

She sniffs and shakes her head. "'Monsters are what you make of them,' and I've made friends of you both. Everyone else is missing out. Plus, I know how to spot a monster easily enough. You two are nothing of the sort."

I reach across the table to thumb at her fingers. "I want you to stay with us. So does Santos."

Adelita is tucked into Santos' side in the booth but there's no note of possession to it. She looks up at him, then across the table at me. "I like being around you, too. Both of you. But I can't deal with Cruz anymore."

And there we are, left with the clear divide between what we want and what's possible.

Cruz has a problem, and we've ignored it for too long.

"I need to talk to you," comes a voice from a few feet away.

Speaking of monsters...

Adelita stiffens, and though Santos loves Cruz, his head whips to him with a firm look of a warning to back on up.

Cruz stays where he is, drawing the attention of several diners. He's too tall and bulky to escape notice. He shoves his hands into his pockets. Though he's still got a hint of aggravation to him, his shoulders are slumped in a clear show of submission.

It's about damn time.

I motion to the spot beside me, making sure to keep him away from Adelita. "Have a seat. Anything off the menu for the Driver of the Year?"

Cruz's eyes fall to his shoes. "Adelita, we have to clear the air. Guys, can you give us a minute?"

Santos is done being obedient, and I love it. He stretches

his arm out in front of her and leans forward, making it clear that Adelita is not to be alone with him.

"I guess I deserved that." Cruz takes an entire minute to sit down, moving his silverware around while he organizes his thoughts and attempts to put them into some coherent order that isn't offensive. "Adelita, I… And then you…" He shakes his head and covers his face with his hands, leaning his elbows on the table. "You guys suck that you're making me do this in front of you."

I tap a rhythm on the side of my cup with a straw. "I can live with that. And I think we all deserve to hear why you were playing it fast and loose with the laws of the road out there. Just because we're used to you doesn't mean we don't have questions."

His snarl is half exasperation, half self-loathing. "Would you shut up, Rafi? I'm trying to set things right, and you're not helping."

"Oh, you want me to make this easy for you?" I bat my hand in his direction. "Nah. How about one snide remark for every time I asked you to slow down and you ignored me. Your ears didn't seem to work then, but now you're picking up on everything I say? Curious."

"You're impossible." Cruz orders burgers for everyone when the waitress comes.

It's the first time him taking over has bothered me.

But he's always doing that, ordering for everyone. Like I don't know how to read a stinking menu.

Cruz fiddles with the plastic edges of the menu before he cuts to the heart of it. "Adelita, there's a lot going on that you don't know about. When you held my hand that first time in the night, it was a fluke that it worked to calm me down. It was a fluke you didn't end up in the hospital. Sometimes I have a hard time when I go to sleep. I hurt people without meaning to."

Santos and I freeze. Cruz never talks about this. If either of us tries to bring it up, he gets all surly and shuts it down. But now he's really stepped in it, so he has to talk about the one thing he has never dealt with.

Cruz's cagey eyes finally meet her wide stare. "Do you know the story of La Sayona?"

12

THE STORY OF LA SAYONA

CRUZ

I pause for so long, I am certain I'm going to choke on my words. I hope Santos or Rafi will jump in and explain it all to her so I don't have to, but they let my silence hang in the air, afraid to touch something so volatile.

I hate this.

"La Sayona is a woman. A spirit. A curse of sorts. She comes to me in the night and torments my mind. Only it's not just my mind she leaves marks on. She's so powerful, she's marked my body before. The battles in my nightmares sometimes leave bruises in the morning. Not every time, but often enough to be a problem."

Adelita gasps in horror, and I hate the sound of it. I don't want pity. I don't want any sort of a reaction.

The guys are frozen, which saves me from dealing with their take on the sore subject. But Addy wears her heart on her sleeve, begging me to stroke it, be gentle, when she knows damn well all I am is rough.

"Start from the beginning," Rafi coaches me when it's clear Adelita isn't understanding the whole of this. I probably sound like a lunatic.

I blow out a long gust of air, which only I can hear above the clattering of silverware and clinking of plates throughout the diner. "My grandfather, Umberto, was chief of the Cáceres tribe, as was his father before him. He was engaged to a woman named Hilaria when he was in his twenties. He had a woman on the side that everyone knew about, but he still wanted to go through with the marriage."

I can tell by Adelita's curious stare that she's at least listening to me, which I guess is the best I can hope for. She's pursing her lips, doing that therapist parsing that irritates me to no end. I know she's dissecting. I know she's digging for buried issues that somehow she's going to make me deal with.

She is the worst.

Even so, I drove like a maniac, so I owe her the truth. "The morning of his wedding, my grandfather stopped by to sleep with Juanita one last time before he tied the knot with Hilaria. Juanita didn't want him to get married to his fiancée, obviously, so she got him drunk. Stinking drunk. Bastard missed his own wedding. His fiancée was so distraught, she found his sword and ran herself through, binding herself to him for all of eternity."

I can tell by the way I'm retelling the story in the exact way my dad has isn't getting through to her. No doubt it sounds like a tragedy that happened too many years ago to be relevant today. She's reacted at all the right parts, but this isn't just an entertaining story. This is *my* story.

"What Hilaria did—using his sword to kill herself— connected her to him long after she died. She haunted him until his dying day. Every time he fell asleep next to Juanita, Hilaria's ghost—La Sayona—came to him to torment him while he slept. He lasted two years before he hanged himself to get the graphic images out of his mind. People say he was driven insane by the insomnia. Toward the end, he tried to stay away from her torment by purposefully keeping himself awake for too many days." I meet her eyes with purpose. "That's when he ordered a wall to be built around Cáceres. He had logical enough reasons at the time, but I always wondered if he would have gone that far if he was truly right in the head."

Adelita covers her mouth. I feel bad because I'm scaring her all over again. I'm only talking about this in the first place because I scared her with my angry driving.

This was a bad idea.

Adelita is secure in Santos' half-embrace. "Oh, Cruz. That's awful."

I guess I have to finish the story, now that I started it. Each word feels like puss being squeezed from an infection—painful but necessary.

"Juanita gave my grandfather two sons, my dad and Tio Bruno, who grew up without their dad. Tio Bruno is a fierce fighter. He became Commander of the Guard. My dad proved his worth to the Cáceres tribe by planning out different strategies to keep us safe, extending help to the poorer families that needed assistance, and looking out for the Cáceres tribe."

My mouth shuts on its own. I can't get through this awful story. I don't like to think about it. Dad and I never talk about it.

I grab the nearest milkshake and take a long pull. The sickening sweetness is just enough to distract me. "Ack! What is that? Is that chocolate banana? Why can't they just leave well enough alone? Fruit is fruit, dessert is dessert. Get it together, people."

Rafi won't let me off the hook that easily. He puts his knee up on the bench in the booth, turning sideways to face me. He looks so casual like that, but I know his stubborn face when I see it. "Go on with the story."

"Right." The milkshake turns hot in my throat.

A crash of thunder from outside makes a few people jump, but Santos and Rafi are used to my moods being too great to contain.

"Everyone assumed that when my grandfather died, that would be the end of the hauntings. But the first time Dad took his girlfriend to bed, La Sayona targeted him. She wasn't content driving grandfather to insanity. She had it in her mind to make Dad pay for the sins of his father. Every night that Dad slept in a bed with a woman, his mind was tormented to the point where Tio Bruno had to…" I swallow hard, hoping another way to describe this will come to me, but there's nothing except the cold, hard truth that stings my open wounds. "Tio Bruno did all he could, but it wasn't enough."

I tug at my collar. Why is it so hot in here?

"Dad fell in love with a woman after he graduated, but La Sayona was stronger now. Dad married my mom and never was unfaithful, but it wasn't enough. When Dad didn't break, La Sayona tormented Mom's mind as well as Dad's every time they slept near each other."

I hate this part. I hate this part. I can't get the words out. The silence hangs in slow drips between us. While I know Adelita deserves more, my mouth staples itself shut to keep my broken glass parts trapped inside.

Adelita's voice is gentle, as if I'm fragile, which I am not. I'm brittle and rough and I cut people for getting too near, yet she opens her mouth and asks permission to get closer. "Cruz, your voice is important. Please tell me more."

I point my finger at her. "That's therapy talk, and I don't need it."

Her lips firm up, and for a fleeting second, I can almost feel how soft that small, pink curve must be. How Santos hasn't kissed her yet is beyond me.

Adelita takes a sip of a milkshake. "Therapy talk or not, you owe me the whole story, so spill it."

And just like that, I do. "Mom gave birth to me, and made it through two more years before she gave birth to Eva. When Eva was eight days old, Mom drove a stake through her own temple because she couldn't stand it any longer. Then the nightmares stopped."

Adelita's tears are the worst because they're for me. The sight of her tender heart bleeding all over the place makes me angry. I swallow my acidity down as much as I can and remind myself my grudge isn't with her. She's just the nearest woman, so my natural bent is to take out all my angst on her in the form of yelling.

Santos knows me well enough to slide another milkshake over to me. I gnaw on the straw instead of chewing her out.

I want to finish the story because Adelita deserves that much from me. It's not everyone who will stay with a stranger who has been an utter ass to her just because he's in pain. Adelita is a good person. I owe her the whole story, so she knows who she's traveling with, but the words stick in my throat.

Rafi knows when to push me and when to pick me up off the floor. He sees that I'm just about down for the count. No one makes me talk about this in the village because it's common knowledge.

Tio Bruno and Chief José: the bastard brothers who grew up to rule the tribe. Everyone knows the hard road they've journeyed down to get to where they are, and the son who inherited the curse that should've died with Grandfather.

Rafi does me a solid and takes over so I don't have a stroke or something, trying to get the words out. "Don José raised Cruz and Eva, with Tio Bruno helping out. Then I came along, and Dad raised the three of us. If Dad went to bed alone, La Sayona stayed away. Don José stayed single for years after his wife died, thinking that would be the way to beat La Sayona at her own game. It wasn't until Cruz turned eighteen that we learned La Sayona had moved on from José to plague the next generation."

Adelita's nose crinkles. "What? Wait, I thought you said the woman haunts the men only when they're asleep with another woman."

Rafi nods. "That's right. But La Sayona got more powerful with the second generation, haunting José *and* his wife. Now that she's turned her focus to the third generation, she's even stronger. She haunts Cruz whenever she feels like it during the night. She doesn't wait for him to have a woman in bed. She's gotten so strong that the lashes she gives him while he's sleeping sometimes leave physical marks."

It's clear Adelita is caught between worrying for me and still being upset that I was reckless with the car.

I lean my elbows on the table and push the drained milkshake away. "I can tell you're feeling sad for me. Don't. I was just the guy who made you cry not fifteen minutes ago. Don't let me off the hook simply because you have a thing for wounded animals. I am not wounded. You should be mad at me for being a dummy with the car."

I think she's going to tell me off for being pushy, but instead she says, "My mama died in a bus crash. If not for Santiago pulling me from the wreckage, I might've died. I'm not getting back in the car if you're behind the wheel. End of story." Then her eyes flick to the table. "Though, I am sorry to hear about this whole mess you inherited. There's no undoing this? No magical whatnot that can get you out of this crappy situation?"

"Having a son. That seems to be what got my father out of it." I fiddle with the knife on the table. "Well, I'm not going to do that. La Sayona is going to die with me. She thinks I can be bullied into cowering? She thinks I'll end my life so she can win? I'm far more stubborn than that vindictive shrew."

Rafi gets us back on track. "Cruz is very careful now. After his first girlfriend was driven mad by La Sayona…"

Adelita's spine stiffens. "Mad? What do you mean?"

To his credit, Rafi doesn't twirl his finger next to his temple and make light of it. "Her parents took her to a mental institution after her mind broke from the stress of it all. Bella's a sweet one. She used to bake Cruz and me cupcakes. She lost her virginity to dear old Cruz, slept in his bed that night, and La Sayona unleashed. Didn't take a week before the girl wouldn't stop rocking herself in the corner."

I hate this story. I hate this story.

Adelita's hand covers her shock. "Oh, that's horrifying! That poor girl. How long ago was this? Maybe I can talk to her therapist."

"Twelve years," I croak. "They did a lot of tests. It was brain damage. La Sayona can cut my skin while I sleep if she's determined enough. She did far worse to Bella. Touched things in her brain that shouldn't be messed with. Bella died a few years after, so that's that." I grab the next milkshake and take a long pull. "Like I said, the curse dies with me this time. La Sayona can haunt me all she likes."

The silence feels like it's being shouted in my face. I fight back a wince as I endure it, trying not to bury myself in memories of Bella with her cupcakes, surprising me in the evening with something sweet just because. I don't know if I was in love with her. I was eighteen, and pretty young for that kind of thing. But I ruined her life all the same. There's not a single forgivable thing about that.

The burgers come but no one is hungry.

When Rafi speaks, I fight the urge to run clear out of the restaurant so I don't have to be present. "After Bella, Cruz has been careful. He never falls asleep in the same room as another woman, so La Sayona doesn't get it in her head to torture another girl. He deals with her on his own, while Santos and I do what we can to help him through it. Santos has herbal creams he rubs on Cruz's temples that keep her from leaving marks, but they can't chase her away. She still tortures him at night, but with the creams, she can't harm his body. Growing up, I used to wake him whenever he was having a nightmare, and then it would stop." Rafi looks down at his meal and I can tell he's lost his appetite. "But in the past year, we can't wake him. Nothing we do snaps him out of it. So we have to listen to our best friend go through the worst physical torment every single night, and there is nothing we can do about it."

The twist in the conundrum dawns on her, drawing her lips to the side in confusion. "It's just women Cruz has had sex with, right? I mean, you keep saying 'slept with him' but you mean sex."

Rafi's head moves slowly from side to side, shooting Santos furtive looks. "One time, Dad slept over at a friend's house after his wife died. Just a friend. He fell asleep on the couch with her, and she was affected." He glances up at her with guilty eyes. "So Cruz never sleeps near another woman."

Adelita's words are taut with worry. "But we shared a hotel room. We put the beds together. I held your hand while you slept! Twice! I slept in your bed last night."

Rafi translates for Santos' flicking fingers. He's been quiet long enough. "That first time was a fluke. When he started having his night terrors, you held his hand before we could stop you." He shakes his head. "We thought that was it, that La Sayona would go into your mind."

"But nothing happened to me. I didn't have weird dreams or anything."

"In the hotel room we all shared, La Sayona left when you

held his hand. So we pushed the beds together to keep her away. It's the only real break we've ever found." Rafi meets her eyes with a declaration that is weighted with importance. "You chased her away."

Adelita turns her chin from left to right and rubs her temples. "I didn't see her in my mind or feel any sort of like, presence. I don't understand."

"Neither do we," Rafi and I admit in unison. We share a smirk but it quickly dies.

Rafi pries the top bun off his burger and plucks off the pickles to give to Santos, who has an affinity for extreme sours and bitters. "Cruz has a bee up his butt today because you slept right beside him last night. His rage is his way of saying he's scared he might've been part of something that permanently damaged you."

Adelita locks her gaze on mine. "I didn't know. But Santos was with me. Maybe that's why La Sayona didn't strike."

Rafi talks with a chunk of beef in his mouth. "When you hold Cruz's hand, La Sayona leaves him completely. I wonder why that is."

Santos signs the answer, having come to the conclusion far before any of us did. He was right, but I'm still miffed that he took such a gamble.

"What?" Adelita asks, and then looks to me for an interpretation. "Why does she leave when I hold your hand?"

I don't want to say it, but I'm the only one who can, since it's my head the witch has taken up residence inside. "She's afraid of you," I explain in a quiet voice. "When you're with me, she runs away. The witch isn't afraid of me, for some reason, but when you come around, she runs away."

I know I've scared Adelita by the look on her face. But now that the cards are all on the table, a giant weight feels lifted from my chest.

When her eyes zero in on mine, I grip the table because even though I don't really know this woman, I can tell whatever she is going to say will shake my world.

She should cuss me out for not being more careful. She should run away and take Santos with her, in case La Sayona gets it in her head that she's going to torment Adelita even when we're not sleeping in the same bed. I wouldn't put anything past the witch now.

Adelita is quiet with uncertainty, opening and closing her mouth several times before she puts any volume to her words. "Then I should stay with you."

I hang my head, ashamed that the best thing I can hear is a woman dooming herself to shoulder my curse, so I don't have to carry it alone.

"Under one condition," she adds, stiffening my spine. "I'll help you out, but only if you stop assuming you're allowed to treat us however you like because you've been dealt a raw deal."

I scowl at her in response.

She gives me a look that tells me she couldn't be less concerned about my attitude. "Babies do what they want and don't care about how the world is affected. That's okay, because they're babies." Then she leans forward. "You've bullied your best friends into treating you like you're a baby —incapable of acting grown. I'm not playing that game."

My mouth goes dry, but I can't fault her for any of her accusations. I do run the show, expecting the guys will fall in line because they feel bad that I never sleep.

They've cut me too much slack…

…because I've demanded it. That truly is childish. She's right.

"Okay. That sounds fair." I lean my face in my hands. "I like protecting people; I don't want to need protection," I admit, my voice gravelly with pent-up emotion.

Adelita reaches across the table and touches the back of my rough knuckles with the smooth tip of her finger. "But you do, so I will."

13

ACIDIC KISS

CRUZ

*I*t's decided Rafi will drive until I'm out of the doghouse, which, apparently, is whenever Adelita decides.

When I protested giving up the lead position of driver when we were back at the diner, Adelita, in her quiet way, sliced through the arguments with a clean blade that cut through my protests. "My mama died in an accident, and you nearly got us all killed in the car today. You aren't getting behind the wheel until you grow up, which is whenever I decide."

She's bold, I'll give her that. It always catches me off-guard when she talks like that—putting me in my place when everyone else is perfectly content letting me do things my way.

It's a struggle to give up my keys, but eventually I do it because I have no choice.

The shift in power is palpable, and I hate it.

I hate lots of things right now.

I hate the passenger's seat but I take my punishment

without visible griping because I know I deserve it. I scared that sweet girl because I was angry at my whole life. I can't believe she forgave me. I make a promise to myself not to be such a jerk next time.

We have yet to talk about sleeping arrangements and just how this will work long-term, but she hasn't cut and run, so I count the whole thing as a win.

She's tucked into Santos' side in the backseat. The two are perpetually glued together. He strokes her hair and kisses her shoulder, as if that's the magical cure for her stab wound. It's such a syrupy gesture, but part of me wishes he actually could make it all better for her with a kiss. Mortal blades take a long time to heal, in my experience. That she doesn't have any pain there anymore is strange.

Part of me wants to take her to a doctor's office so they can draw blood and check her for radioactive superhero molecules or something.

I know I'm in the doghouse, so I play my role, giving up authority when usually everything would be my call. It sucks, and I hate it, but for the most part, I keep my mouth shut.

When the sun sets and Rafi suggests we pull over and settle in for the night, that's the only time I have an opinion. "See if you can find a decent hotel, not a motel this time."

He raises his eyebrows at me. "You always want the low-brow establishments because they don't make a big to-do if the Kalku show up and some things get broken. Why the change?"

"Yeah, I know. But the Kalku aren't exactly on our tail anymore. Plus, I was a jerk earlier, driving like that. Maybe a higher thread-count will cushion the blow."

Rafi's eyebrows dance in my direction. "Fancy. Always romance us with words like 'thread-count.' You sound positively civilized."

"Well, don't get used to it." I chuckle, which draws Adelita's gaze for some reason. Like a man's not allowed to laugh at Rafi's stupid jokes.

When we stop for the night, I grab the bags. "What?" I ask Santos when he furrows his brow at me.

He looks frustrated with the change in our usual routine. *"You don't carry the bags. I do. Give them to me."*

I work up a semi-believable smile for him. "Nah. You've got your hands full with your handful. I got this. I'll drop these off, then I'll pick up dinner."

Rafi stretches his arms over his head. "A decent guy who never drives anyone off the road would ask us what we want to eat instead of making all the decisions."

It's an effort to wrench my grinding teeth apart. "Okay. Anyone want anything specific?"

Rafi raises his hand after pocketing the keys. "I want *all* the things, unspecifically. I'll go with you after we settle in. You're still grounded from driving the car, young man."

I grumble at Rafi, but that's the worst of it. "Yeah, yeah."

When I go into the lobby to book the room, I swallow hard and try not to let my eagerness show. I'm going to have a whole evening of dreamless sleep. I had half a helping of it last night, and it was so jarring, I'm not sure what to make of it. Now that I might have a whole one? I'm practically salivating at the dangling possibility. "One room. Two queens."

The receptionist doesn't even blink at the request, but it's a bold statement. It means that we're doing this on purpose. For so long we've been resigned to there being no cure, no hope, no light at the end of the tunnel.

When the receptionist slides the keycard into my hand, it feels like the most glorious middle finger to La Sayona, and a golden ticket for me.

I'm choosy when we walk into the room on the third

floor. Normally I don't care which bed I land on, but this time it matters. Everything matters.

I select the bed furthest from the window, in case any errant light filters in and tries to rudely wake me when morning comes.

I set down my backpack and run my fingers through my hair. Every detail feels important now. The meal will be good. The white sheets under the plush matching comforter are soft. The room doesn't stink of feet and fungus, which is usually the case with the motels we frequent.

"Do you want me to pick you up anything while we're out?" I ask Adelita.

Her eyes widen, genuinely shocked by my offer. She looks at me like she's not sure if I'm going to yell at her, so I attempt a smile, which only seems to spook her more. "Um, I think I'm alright. Thank you."

Well, that sucked. How am I supposed to keep her helping me at night if she's afraid of me?

Rafi is by my side as we go down the elevator and to the car. There is no traffic this time of night, so I don't have to pick whatever restaurant is closest. I can be choosy again, which is a nice luxury.

The rain is gone, and though there are still clouds overhead, whole chunks of Twilight are slicing through, letting the world know that there might just be hope for ol' Cruz after all.

Rafi is staring at me like I've grown a second head, but I do my best to ignore it. "Stop there first," I request, grateful when he pulls the car into the first superstore I see. "I need pajamas."

"Pajamas?" he echoes, as if I told him what I actually need is a roller skating octopus. "You don't believe in pajamas when we're on the road."

I pull out my phone and search for the nearest restaurant

that doesn't have a cartoon character as its logo, and fish through the menu for online ordering. "Usually I don't. But we're not being chased right now. I don't know how long Adelita is going to tolerate sleeping in the same bed as me, so I'm making the most of what I've got. I want a solid night of sleep without La Sayona. I want actual rest."

Giddiness shoots through my thumbs as I select probably too much food for everyone. Rafi selects his own meal, since apparently he super needs his independence for whatever reason.

Then I go one farther and look through the desserts.

"Did you just order chocolate lava cake?"

I shrug. "Santos eats sugar now. Adelita likes hot chocolate. That's a win, right?"

Rafi's nose pinches in what looks like distaste. "Who are you? Since when do you care about what people like? I'm the one who brings milkshakes and sugar into the mix. You're the one who scoffs at stuff like that—niceties without functionality. Everything needs a streamlined purpose for you. We sleep in our clothes for the next day so if the Kalku attack, we're ready to fight and bolt."

I don't know what to say to that, so I brush it aside and finish placing the order.

The superstore has a decent selection of pajama pants, but I take my time stroking the softness of the fabric, not wanting to slum it with something subpar. Because I've been such a tool, and I'm sharing a bed with his girlfriend, I get Santos a pair too.

Before I know it, I'm in the women's section, petting pants to see which are the softest. I've passed the point of caring if I've lost my mind.

When I go to pay, my cash is in the wrong spot in my wallet. I know I put it in the largest opening. I rifle through the pockets and come across the stack. The bills are in the wrong order.

Rafi's looking up at the ceiling with faux innocence plastered on his face.

I hate when he messes with my stuff. He does it so seamlessly; I never catch him in the act.

I grumble in his direction, and he grins that he got one over on me.

Jerk.

By the time we get back to the hotel with the food and the clothes, it's seven o'clock, which means if we eat now, I will get a full night of sleep. Actual sleep. Dreamless sleep.

The last time I was this excited was I think when I was a little boy peeking at the presents under the tree the night before Christmas. I don't remember what the presents were, but I recall the trepidation, the excitement of something good and uncharted coming to me.

When we get to the room, my smile cracks and falters as I see worry wrinkling Adelita's forehead. She's wringing her hands like she's trying to milk her fingers, her eyes darting to the bathroom. "I couldn't call you because I don't have a phone and neither does Santos. I didn't mean to do it!"

I set down the packages on the desk in the corner, my chest puffing in preparation to deal with whatever it is she's worked up about. Things need to be perfect for tonight, and the way she's stressing isn't what I've been picturing. "What is it?"

Rafi marches toward the bathroom to investigate while I draw my knife, which only makes her jumpier. She squeaks and backs up, holding up her hand in surrender. "I didn't mean to! Please!"

I glance down at the blade with a frown. "This isn't for you; it's to deal with whatever it is you're worried about. What's going on?"

She's recoiling instead of fighting. She could easily take me out if she believed in her strength even a little bit. We'll have to work on that.

It takes her a solid five seconds to convince herself that I'm not going to gut her with my knife. I feel the weight of those seconds, each one marking the many reasons I've given her to fear me.

I pressed into her fresh wound to get her to spill her secrets.

I sparred with her before her shoulder was healed enough for such things.

I yelled at her. A lot.

Then I drove like a maniac and made her think about her dead mom.

I can feel the perfect night slipping through my fingers. "Adelita, what happened?"

She steps back, her voice quiet with fear. "I kissed his cheek! That's all I did. You have to believe me! Then Santos dropped to the floor and grabbed his face like my lips were painted in acid. I didn't know that would hurt him! I kissed his other cheek before, and it was fine. He keeps trying to sign something but I don't understand it! You have to help him!"

I put the knife back in my sheath and bolt into the bathroom to find Santos curled in a ball on his knees, fully clothed in the empty tub. He's trying to sign, but his fingers are rigid, his teeth gritted as he tries to eke out a few sentences.

Rafi is kneeling next to the tub, putting together the pieces as best he can. "Adelita kissed your cheek and now it's melting off? Santos, you have to let me look at it. If what you're saying is true, we need to take you to a hospital. Move your hand so I can see."

It's an effort, but Santos finally removes a shaking hand

from his face, revealing… I'm honestly not sure what I'm seeing. I'm bracing myself for my brother's cheek sliding off his face or something. Maybe raw sinew and holey flesh dripping blood onto the white linoleum.

"There's nothing there," I say, my head tilting in confusion. "But the skin is different. It's not melting, Santos. It's…"

Rafi straightens his spine, leaning back to rest his butt on his heels. "It's smoothing out! Santos, your scars aren't all there anymore." He looks over his shoulder to Adelita in the doorway, who, now that I'm getting a better look at her, is positively drenched in tears. Rafi motions her into the cramped bathroom, and she obeys without the many questions that would come if I did the same exact gesture. Rafi pulls her down into a one-armed hug, kissing the top of her head like they are the best of friends. "Your kiss didn't do anything bad, I don't think. I don't know how, but it looks like your kiss is the thing that's healing him. His scars from the Kalku are smoothing out, *viento*. Did you know you could do that?"

"What? That's not a thing! I kissed his other cheek yesterday, and nothing like this happened."

"Ah, but his other cheek isn't scarred. Did you kiss his scars?"

She touches her forehead like she's trying to keep up. Honestly, so am I. Rafi has always been the one with the more open mind. Maybe being rescued from the Kalku at age five does that to a guy. Makes him think anything is possible, that good things do happen on occasion, whether or not our limited brains can make sense of the why or how.

I think I lost that optimism early on, but I can see now how I've shorted myself.

Santos turns into his wolf in the tub, writhing and banging his head into the ivory surface to count out the beats of his agony.

The scars on his maw are smoothing out, too.

Adelita sobs on Rafi's shoulder.

That's trust. How on earth did Santos and Rafi form such strong bonds with her in so short a time?

Adelita's cadence is dripping with tears. "I t-touched his cheek and he told me he wished he wasn't coming to me all marked up. I said I liked every part of him, even the ones he's afraid of. Then I kissed his cheek, and he shot back from me like I'd shocked him. He told me his face is burning and melting off, and then locked himself in the bathroom!"

I fold my arms across my chest. "You didn't know this would happen? You've never kissed someone's boo-boo? I find that hard to believe. You've got that bleeding heart disposition."

She tips her chin up to scowl at me, as if I'm making fun of her.

I'm not. She does have that way about her. It's what's driving her to agree to share a bed with me.

Her tone clips with indignation. "No, I do not go around kissing people at random to test out insane theories."

Rafi, a firm believer in the ridiculous, rolls up his sleeve to show off a puckered line on the outside of his bicep near his shoulder. "Right there, *linda*. It's a scar from a run-in with the Kalku last year. If I'm wrong, the worst that'll happen is I get a kiss from a beautiful woman. If I'm right, then we'll know Santos will be okay once your kiss does what it needs to."

She casts him a dubious look through her tears but then takes another gander at Santos, who is doubled over in the tub, clawing at the air in silent agony. "It's not possible," she argues, but I can see the debate plain on her face.

"Actually, an untrained woman who can bash in the skull of a man schooled to fight from birth is impossible." Rafi's eyes lock in on hers. Her tears pause for the doting look he fixes on her. "But see, I'm not interested in a world that bends to nature. What I want to see is nature rising to the occasion when we need her most." He kisses her wet nose. "We need you, *viento*."

And that's exactly what she is. Darn him for picking the perfect nickname for her. She is the wind that's come into our lives, changing things whether we're ready or not.

Santos rolls onto his side, holding himself tight in a ball in the fetal position in the tub with his tail hooked over his face.

Adelita runs her fingers over Rafi's scar, testing the skin for who knows what reason. She moves slowly, and as much as she's dead set against the idea of her kisses holding some kind of healing power, there is great care she takes when her lips move to his arm.

"This is probably the wrong time to let loose a loud fart."

Leave it to Rafi to break the sweetness of the moment.

Adelita snorts, butting the top of her head to his arm while she giggles at his stupid joke.

Adelita strokes his arm tenderly, as if trying to sooth the cut with compassion.

I mean, honestly.

She could have made it a quick peck, but the touch of her lips on the outside of his shoulder is so intimate, I wonder if I'm supposed to look away.

Rafi lets out a soft "mm" at the contact as half a smile pulls up the corner of his mouth. "Santos and I aren't going anywhere, even when you're afraid of yourself."

Then it happens. The transition takes only the span of a gasp for Rafi to shift from sweetness to suffering.

"Ah! Oh, ow! What is that? Is it acid? Glass?" He backs away from Adelita so he can shake his arm out. Then he resorts to smacking it like he's trying to put out a fire. "Undo it! Oh, it's..." His scales pop out and his tail sprouts, swishing like a thick vine that aims to swat at his imaginary enemy.

"I'm sorry! I didn't want to do that but you told me to! Rafi, what did I do? How do I make it stop?" She fans him with her good hand, as if that will help anything.

As if anything we do might be able to help them now.

14

BURNING LOVE

CRUZ

*R*afi doesn't even have the presence of mind to fix her with a reassuring smile, which I know means he's in terrible pain. "I don't know! I didn't have a brilliant plan beyond seeing if we could recreate Santos' distress. Mission accomplished. Oh, it's getting hotter! Is my skin melting? Did your kiss to my scar burn my skin off? I'm afraid to look! Are my scales ripping off or something? Ah!"

He shows off his tensed, olive-scaled arm to us. "I don't see anything different," I say, earning a scowl of disbelief from him.

"It's burning!" Rafi jumps to his feet and turns on the faucet, angling his arm under the flow.

Santos raises his nose up in the air to tell us something incoherent, but it doesn't register in time.

Rafi's whole body shudders as he grips the side of the sink. "That's just making it worse! Oh! Out. Out, guys. If this is doing what I think it is and deep-cleaning my scar, I need some space. Santos needs some space." Rafi shoves me toward the door, allowing me just enough pause to help Adelita off the floor and yank her out of the bathroom.

She shakes off my grip and covers her mouth in an attempt to shove her sobs back down her throat. She cries to the tune of Rafi's howls, which I'm sure are a fraction of Santos' pain. Rafi's scar is one line, but Santos' entire left side of his face is ribbons of abuse stretched across the span of too many years.

Neither of us knows what to do. We can't help them in any way I can guess, but we're in agony out here, listening to Rafi wail with no solution in sight.

I can't calm Santos or Rafi, so I turn to the fire I can at least attempt to put out. Adelita is crimson from crying, her face wet with more streaks lining her cheeks to replace the ones she is trying to wipe away.

I've seen my dad offer his handkerchief to Consuela when she breaks down on occasion. Maybe that's what I'm supposed to do.

"I don't have a handkerchief," I say lamely, worried that I have no idea what to do with a crying woman. Whenever we rescue one from the Kalku, Rafi is the shoulder they cry on. I'm the muscle, and that's all I've ever needed to be. But when this heartbroken woman blinks up at me, utterly lost and afraid of her own touch, I want to be more than just muscle for her. If she is truly healing Santos in more ways than just getting him to eat at the family dinner table, then she deserves more than I can give her.

"What?" she croaks.

I'm frustrated with both of us—with her tears for being so loud, I practically flinch at the sight of them rolling down her cheeks, and with myself for being a caveman who doesn't know how to do normal things, like offer comfort.

"A handkerchief! I'm supposed to have one to give to you when you're crying. I don't have one!"

I probably shouldn't have shouted that at her.

She looks at me like I've gone insane. "I don't need a handkerchief. I hurt them!"

"You didn't mean to. I saw the whole thing."

Her sobs quiet to a handful of hiccups that make my heart stutter. Damn this woman for making me overthink things. I never cared about crap like this before. We've rescued women who have had their heads shaved, a limb missing, and I still couldn't manage more than a lame, "We'll get you help in the village," before passing the wailing woman off to Rafi.

But Rafi's not here.

I sit on the edge of the bed, leaning forward to rest my elbows on my knees. I hate the sound of pain on Rafi, and I can't stomach the look of agony on Santos. Santos has been put through too much. I'm supposed to look after him. Everything in my gut seizes up as Rafi cries out louder, which I didn't think possible. I don't do well with powerlessness.

Adelita moves to put her hand on my shoulder, which is so like her. Though she's going through a real meltdown coupled with an identity crisis, my palpable angst is more pressing to her. But before she makes contact with my shoulder, she jerks her hand away and backs up. "I'm sorry! I won't touch you."

I turn my chin to frown up at her. "What a way to kick me when I'm down."

She shakes her head, pressing her hand over her heart. "You don't like me near you. And besides that, I just took down two of your men! Rafi and Santos are incapacitated because of me!"

I don't know why her words cut me open, but there I am. In the span of three sentences, I'm split and spread for strangers to poke at, testing my innards to see how soft they are beneath the muscle that's been hard-earned, yet right now is utterly useless.

I see my life clearly. Years lived with a blind eye have been far easier for coping. This is hard.

My voice is rough when I finally speak. "The children don't touch me. Cordelia, Roberto and Mira. The younger ones sit on Eva's lap and take naps in her arms. Cordelia is always hugging her. But I scare them."

"Why do you do that?" Adelita works out, her back hugging the far wall.

Her words place the blame squarely on me, and while I want to argue, I know I can't. Mira is too little to be at fault for anything.

When denial isn't within arm's reach, I'm forced to dig deep into my disgusting habits and scrape away at the raw flesh until something real beats in my palm. "I don't know."

"I don't believe you," she whispers, and then shudders at the sound of Rafi's howl.

The monstrous beating of my heart rises to my cheeks. I am fairly certain this woman, this stranger, can see straight through me.

When I finally open up my mouth, I'm not even sure she can make out my words. I say them anyway, and let the world decide what it wants to do with me. "My grandfather died young. My mother died in her mid-twenties. I made it to thirty without driving a stake through my temple. I'm not sure how many more years I have in me to stand against La Sayona, the Kalku and all of this." I wave my hand from top to bottom over my form, letting her know that, of all my problems, even if the first two were solved, parts of me are too messed up not to be a true hindrance to anyone who dares come near. "If the kids get it in their heads that I'm here for the long haul, it's only going to mess them up. Besides, I've got a lot to do before my bell's rung. I don't want to slow down. The tribe needs me. The kids don't need me. They have Dad, Consuela and Eva."

"And who does Eva have?"

I scoff. "Eva has whatever she wants. Plus, she has Consuela and Dad."

"Do you think that's enough for her? Do you think she's okay living with this half-version of her brother? Protection isn't always about muscle and keeping the doors bolted shut." She pauses for Rafi's scream, closing her eyes through his pain. She wears his agony around her neck like a chain. "Sometimes it's about keeping your doors open."

Adelita is on the verge of saying too much, of stomping on my busted and bruised organs. I'm starting to buckle under her dainty weight that carries with it the force of an army.

"When was the last time you opened your door for Eva?"

Then everything inside me shatters. I know without a doubt that the things I was so certain of have only led me further and further toward the edge of the cliff. La Sayona has been trying to push me off it for nearly a decade and a half, and finally, here I go.

The witch got what she wanted. I am alone.

"Call her," Adelita urges, pushing my face in the mess I have created. "Call her now."

I shake my head. "Call my sister? What for? We don't talk on the phone. She's got better things to do than roll her eyes through a call from me when I've got nothing to say."

Adelita is firm in her softness. Though she doesn't raise her voice, there is a command that shoots through me like a nonnegotiable order. Her edict contains as much authority as a directive from Tio Bruno. "If the worst that's going to happen is your little sister rolling her eyes at you, then you're cowering for nothing. Call Eva. You cannot let La Sayona take you away from your sister. Then the witch wins. You're letting your demon win."

I scowl at Adelita but she doesn't wither. She holds my glare with an earnest note in her big blue eyes that pushes back against my gruff demeanor. There is strength in this gentle creature. Whether she's punching me in the face or not, I see it clearly.

Finally, I surrender to it and pull out my phone, tapping out the beginnings of a text.

"A text is not a phone call." Adelita sounds like I've pushed her to the point of aggravation now. "Stop putting buffers and distance between yourself and the people who love you, despite all this. Call her."

I want to argue because I hate being pushed around, but I keep my mouth shut and breathe through my extreme discomfort.

On the first ring, I hope Eva doesn't answer.

On the second, I *pray* she doesn't answer.

On the third, I'm relieved I might get away with leaving a message. Adelita's gaze is burning a hole in the side of my head, but she can't possibly argue with voicemail.

"Cruz? What's wrong? What's happened? Are you alright?"

"Hey, Eva. I'm fine."

"Is it Rafi? Tell me Rafael's okay!"

"Rafi's fine. Santos is fine."

"The girl? What happened to Adelita?"

"Nothing! Jeez, woman. Calm down. Nothing's wrong," I lie, grateful she probably can't make out Rafi's muffled shouts.

"Oh, thank the stars. I was worried the Kalku got her, too."

"Too? Did they abduct someone else?"

"A group from the Mendez tribe fought with the Kalku and lost. A woman was abducted by the Kalku last month.

The scouts from the Mendez tribe traced her to a cave, but when they got there, she was dead."

Another woman, sacrificed for their disgusting rituals.

I cannot stop the growl in my voice. "Let me guess, the Anzaldúa tribe did nothing, as they always do. So the Mendez tribe had to handle it on their own, which they suck at."

"You guessed it right. The Anzaldúa don't involve themselves. You know that. Though, I wish they would. They're so far ahead of us with their medicines." Her voice is thick with worry. "Keep Adelita with you. Not out of your sight."

My eyes flick to Adelita, needing visual proof that she hasn't been abducted. I the Kalku got their hands on her… "Was it anywhere near the village?' Why wasn't I told until now?"

"The fight happened in the complete opposite direction from where Tio Bruno sent you. We only just heard about it." She pauses for my cussing. "I thought you knew. Why else would you call me?"

I rub my forehead. "I called to talk to you."

There's a prolonged silence before Eva's words come out like molasses. "The last time you called me was when you freed Santos and needed me to work my magic on Dad to let him into the village."

Is that true? Have I really not called my sister in two years?

I have no idea how to talk to her. Where to even start.

My eyes flick to Adelita, who is tugging on her fingers while Rafi howls. "We used to be closer than this. We sharpened arrows for hours together so we could practice splitting apples blindfolded to scare Dad and impress Tio Bruno."

"*You* did that to impress Tio Bruno." Eva makes an effort to calm down. "I remember being young. A very long time ago. What's all this about?"

I have no idea what I'm supposed to say. An apology seems too strong. Plus, I'd have to explain what I'm sorry about, which I don't really know. Instead I stick with, "I don't know what I'm doing."

My eyes winch shut, embarrassed that something so stupid came out of my mouth.

Eva doesn't laugh at me, nor does she judge me. Instead, she opts for curiosity. Or kindness. I'm really not sure.

That's when it dawns on me that I don't know my own sister anymore.

Her voice is even but firm. "Tell me the problem and we'll sort through it together. Whatever it is, I'm sure we can figure it out. It can't possibly be harder than splitting an apple in half blindfolded, which we mastered eventually."

I snort at the memory I don't often revisit. "What cocky kids we were."

"Were? Don't disappoint me, Brother. Cockiness is a useful tool sometimes. Talk to me."

So I do. Not everything, and probably not enough, but the conundrum that's rattling around in my brain about Adelita's healing kiss presents itself as a problem Eva can help me muddle through. It's exactly that—muddling, not solving—but I'm not alone in this anymore.

I have a true asset I've been ignoring. I didn't realize Eva had my back.

I didn't realize I needed her.

It's ten minutes of guesswork with too few facts to go on, but at the end of it, I have one more person on my team that's constantly on the move. "I've got the entire library here. I'll do some digging and see if I can find precedent for something like this. It's a long shot, but it's worth trying."

"I didn't even think of that." I look up, and somewhere in the conversation with my sister, I lost tabs on Adelita. She's clear across the room on her knees as she cries silently against the bathroom door, her cheek pressed to the wood so she can wallow in their pain more effectively. "Crap. I've got to go, Eva. I'll call you after we know more of what we're dealing with."

I end the call and rush to Adelita, making to lift her up off the floor. But she shakes her head, adamant she not be parted from the guys an inch further than they insist. "I can't," she admits. "I don't care what you think of me. I can't. I hurt them!"

I have no idea what to do with this woman who feels too much, tries too hard and frankly, scares me a little.

So I sink to the floor beside her and lean against the bathroom door. I drench myself in Rafi's howls and the angst that comes from knowing Santos is stuck in silent agony.

A crack of thunder outside makes Adelita jump. I fight the urge to apologize, knowing the sudden shift in weather is my fault. There are too many of us Acalicas in the world for meteorologists to have a fighting chance at accurately predicting the weather.

It's a solid minute before my hand grows the courage to reach over and latch onto her elbow. I'm not sure why I choose that spot, which hardly seems ideal for comforting a person. But at my touch, Adelita collapses in on herself, her anxiety over setting all of this in motion finally overtaking any attempts at holding back.

I have no idea what I'm doing. Somehow her head finds its way to my shoulder. My shirt is soaked in seconds with her tears, but I find I don't mind it as much as I thought I would.

I turn a little so she can lean more comfortably against my chest. She bathes me in her tears, handing over her angst as if she trusts me to know what to do with it. Her hand rests on my heart, convincing us both that the useless organ is still in there, and that it has far more purpose than either of us could've guessed. I thumb her elbow and she sags against me, tying us together tighter than words ever could.

No one is watching, so I close my eyes and inhale, filling my nose with the flowery scent of her hair. Though there's chaos on the other side of the door, I finally let Adelita fill me with peace.

15

LOVERS DOING LOVERLY THINGS

ADELITA

It's not until midnight that Santos and Rafael finally emerge from the bathroom. I can't stop apologizing, stuck on repeat until the bags under their eyes and the war-torn looks fade away. "I didn't know. Santos, I'm so sorry. I would never hurt you like that on purpose!"

Santos manages a weary smile, forgiving me far easier than I ever will. He waves off my concern and points to the bag on the desk. Then he mimes eating.

"Oh, Cruz picked up dinner. Let me get you a plate." I want to help in any way I can, but Santos rests his hand on my arm, letting me know he doesn't want that. He wants to do it himself, and stubborn mule that he is, he reaches for two plates, as if I'll be okay with him waiting on me after the evening he's endured. "No, my heart. I can get my dinner. Please don't wait on me. This whole thing is just... Don't be nice to me. Don't forgive me." I turn from the confusion pursing his lips and face Rafael. "What do you want to eat, sweetie? Go sit on the bed. I'll get it."

Rafael doesn't have the same qualms about me waiting on him, so I fix his plate and bring it over. I fuss over him, making sure he has everything he needs before I check his arm for the scar.

"It's gone, *viento*. Completely gone. It's like new skin or something. I don't understand it. I've had that thing for a year."

I pull on my fingers as the angst in me builds. "Please forgive me, Rafi. I shouldn't have experimented on you like that."

Rafael manages a smile, as only he can do after what sounded like surgery without anesthesia. "No more apologizing. Why would I be mad at you for healing me? That's what you did, you know. I don't care if it hurt for a few hours. You healed me."

I fight the urge to tell him how sorry I am again.

Rafael tilts his head up at me, taking in my anxiety with compassion. Maybe people think Rafael is a joker, but I know a kind heart when I see it.

He jerks his chin to the spot next to him and I take it because I'm selfish. I like his arm around my shoulders and the easy way he kisses my temple, like we've known each other for years. "You're all bent out of shape, but really, we're better than we've ever been. Just tired. Tell me I look incredible with my arm all smooth like this."

Rafael pulls me closer so my forehead rests in the crook of his neck. My hand climbs up to loop around his shoulder, holding him while he holds me.

"I don't like to see you all marked up," I admit. "I don't like that anyone's ever hurt you. You are precious to me."

I can feel his jaw move as a smile takes him over. "You're my little softy. I like this—having you around." Rafi's palm moves up and down my arm a few times to soothe my nerves. That's how good a person Rafael is—even though he's been in agony, he is thinking about me. "Now get some food before Cruz inhales it all."

But Santos already has my plate ready, taking care of things before I can even consider them.

I move away from the guys and sit on the floor with my food in silence. There needs to be a healthy couple of feet of distance between us. I'm afraid to touch them now. I'm afraid of so many things. I kissed Santos' cheek and ended up hurting him. Though the scarred half of his face is smooth now, I wonder if that's what he wanted.

I'm worried about what other glitches might be lurking in my genetics that were twisted without my permission.

The food is delicious but my stomach is churning with questions, confusion and self-loathing. What other surprises are lurking in my body, just waiting for me to have a vulnerable moment to pounce on my unsuspecting victims?

"Knock it off," Cruz barks at me apropos of nothing.

My spine straightens. "What? I'm not doing anything."

Cruz leans forward from the foot of the second bed, rests his elbow on his thigh and points his plastic fork at me. "You're punishing yourself for doing something good just because a few eggs got broken along the way. That's not helpful. Stop it."

My jaw tightens at being told how to feel.

Cruz is bossy. Maybe he means well (and that's a hefty maybe), but his sharp tone is so biting, any hints of looking out for my well-being are lost to a scowl that takes over my features. "I'm allowed to be upset that I hurt the people I care about."

"You already were upset for the last few hours. Now be done."

Too many swear words are rolling around on my tongue to pick just one.

Luckily, Rafael chimes in before any of them spill out. "As important as el culebrón being spotted near a curse tree might be, I'm sleeping in tomorrow. I'm beat, and I'll be no good to anyone running on half a tank." When Santos signs something to Rafael, Rafi shakes his head. "Sharpening the weapons can wait. We're always running at things full-speed. We can deal with the knives tomorrow. In fact, everything can be dealt with later. I'm tired." He takes a bite of pasta and sighs. "I don't want my entire life spent like this—always running from one thing to the next without stopping when I'm beat. This is me throwing up a warning to the universe. I'm taking a break."

Cruz's jaw is firm with displeasure. "You can sleep in the car. I want us up and moving at six, like usual. Santos, you can sharpen the weapons that need it in the morning."

I frown at Cruz's unswerving focus. "Rafael and Santos just went through something. If they say they need time, why are you fighting it?"

Cruz's eyes narrow in on mine. "I know the danger of a culebrón on the loose far better than you do. We've got another two days in the car ahead of us. It matters if we lose el culebrón's location. The thing is dangerous, roaming around unchecked. Plus, I don't like keeping you in one place for too long. The Kalku might still be looking for you."

Rafael waves off my impending arguments, feigning ease as if him asking for a couple hours of sleep and being denied is no big deal. "It's fine, *viento*. Cruz is right; I can conk out in the car if I'm still tired in the morning. A culebrón roaming about is worse than me not getting my beauty sleep." Though I can see by the weary weight to his shoulders that he doesn't believe what he's saying.

I fight the urge to ask about the snake monster as I chew my dinner. Part of me doesn't want the gory details.

Cruz finishes his mountain of food and dumps out the contents of the untouched plastic grocery store bag onto his mattress. He doesn't look at us while he speaks. "Rafi got everyone pajamas."

Rafael's eyebrow raises. "Did I, now? That's awfully thoughtful of me." There's a tease to his tone that I don't understand, like he and Cruz are having a silent conversation that Santos and I have not been invited to.

The pajamas fit well enough, and when I slide them on after dinner, there's a softness to the fleece that feels like my legs are being hugged by a cloud. "These are so nice. Thanks, Rafi. I don't really like sleeping in my jeans. This is way better."

Rafi is putting the leftovers in the mini-fridge but I can hear the grin in his voice. "I think I deserve some sugar for being so thoughtful. I mean, I was in the store thinking of how sexy our Adelita would look in pajamas, and I couldn't help myself."

"You were not. You wanted everyone to be comfortable, is all," Cruz grouses.

"Not true. I touched at least ten pairs of pants to make sure I got you the softest ones." Rafael bats his eyes at me, and then sends a wicked grin in Cruz's direction. "I'm very romantic, but only when I'm in deep."

I cannot help but smile at Rafael. He has this teasing way about him that makes everything harrowing seem manageable, and everything serious seem light enough not to weigh you down. "Yes, you are. Thank you."

Cruz keeps running his hands over his stomach, which I'm guessing when paired with that surly expression, means he's nervous. He fiddles with the bedsheets before pushing the two queens together. Then he studies the beds and restraightens the sheets. He calls down for another comforter and then spends the next ten minutes arranging it just so. I'm not sure what his deal is, but he's got a touch of nerves tonight, that's for sure.

Rafael flops onto the far right end of the beds and spreads out his limbs, messing the meticulously lain comforter like a puppy who's begging to be put outside. "Ah, that's perfection. Come to bed, Adelita. It's been far too long since I've slept with a woman in my arms."

I cast him a dubious look. "I cannot imagine that's true." He's so handsome; it doesn't seem logical that he would often go to bed alone.

His eyebrows dance as he stretches out his arms to me. "Come on in. Santos can take your other side so he doesn't have a conniption, watching our love bloom from afar."

Santos rolls his eyes at Rafael, who chuckles. Then he grabs up his pajamas and moves into the bathroom.

"Lucky me," I drone. Rafael is such a cad.

Our fearless leader's voice raises an octave. "Wait! She's supposed to sleep next to me tonight." The second the words tumble out, Cruz's cheeks flame red and his neck shrinks.

Rafael smacks his forehead. "Ah, that's right. Cruz wanted your other side. I thought he would ask like a gentleman. Maybe he's working up to it."

Cruz glowers at me, as if any of this was my doing. He can't seem to work out a hearty "please," so he settles for pointing to the bed.

What a jerk.

Santos comes out of the bathroom in his pajamas. Just the sight of him makes my heart ache. I hurt him. I hurt Santos, who has always been sweet to me.

Santos reaches for my hand but I step away with an apologetic look. "I can't. If I hurt you again, I'll never get over it."

Santos' eyes widen, stunned at the shift neither of us can reconcile. He starts signing to me, but Cruz turns out the overhead light.

Santos is adamant I hear him, despite the obvious disconnect. He casts around for some way to be understood, and finally settles on turning on the lamp and reaching for my wrist. I don't pull away when he guides my hand to rest on his freshly healed cheek. He trills my fingertips over the new skin so I can feel my handiwork.

He looks strange like this, without his scars. It almost feels like a well-meaning lie—like his face is trying to hide the trauma he underwent while in captivity.

Though I only met the man once, Santos is now identical to Santiago.

I don't know what to do with that, so I keep tracing his cheek as long as he will let me, brushing his soft chin-length hair behind his ear. Trust is hard to come by, but Santos leans into my touch, his lashes closing with something that looks like sheer contentment.

His arms curve around my hips, bringing my stomach tight to his. I love being this close.

My abs do a dance of tightening and loosening. I'm unsure if having him pressed up to me like this is exciting or relaxing. Either way, I cannot bring myself to pull back. Scared as I am that I might accidentally hurt him again with some new twist of nature, Santos is patient with my worry. His breath on my nose makes my insides scream to draw closer. I want to kiss him so very badly, but if a peck to his cheek drove him to lock himself away for hours, I shudder to think of what damage a real kiss would do.

But I'm selfish, because I still want it.

Santos motions to his new skin, his eyebrows dancing with questions. "What do you think?" he mouths in the lamplight.

I don't know how to speak. His presence is so over-whelming that words don't feel like the right move.

Instead, I lift myself up onto my toes and brush my cheek against his, savoring the softness. His hand tightens on the small of my back.

His breath hitches while my hand climbs up to rest on his

chest. I love how muscular he is, and how wildly his heart beats when I'm near. It's a heady feeling, being close to such a stunningly beautiful enigma.

His lips move against my ear, and it's then I realize that he's confessing things to me he won't own up to. He doesn't want me to know his hidden thoughts, so he tells me everything in ways I cannot hear—admitting but not.

I don't pull away to try and make sense of his secrets; they don't belong to me yet. Not really. Instead I let him tell me everything and nothing. In exchange, he lets me indulge in the scandal of stroking his chest while it swells just for me.

Rafael starts singing some song about "lovers doing loverly things," while Cruz takes the spot furthest from him, leaving a space for Santos and me in the center. Rafael's song breaks our haze just enough to remind us there are other people in the room.

I am far more relaxed now, and don't resist when Santos turns into his wolf and peels down the covers with his teeth. He trots to the foot of the beds and motions for me to join them. He doesn't look nearly as nervous as I feel. Something about the way he invites me to bed with such certainty puts my racing thoughts at ease just enough to climb atop the mattress.

I fit perfectly in Rafael's arms as he rolls me over to spoon me. His body coils around mine in a way that makes me feel safe and protected, like I'm hemmed in from any outside threat. The weight of Rafael's arm over my ribs erases any troubling sensations. I don't want to feel like I'm floating haphazardly through life, hurting people and bumping into things at random. His body centers me, and just like that, my whole being begins to relax. Though we have plenty of space to stretch out, Rafael and I are sharing the same pillow, happiest when we are close as humanly possible.

I really love having a friend like him. A moment like this.

Santos lays on my feet, warming me and hooking his tail over Rafael's legs.

Just like that, it feels like the three of us are stitched together, breathing as one being that is only just learning how to exhale.

"Please," I hear just as my lashes flutter shut. When they open again, it's Cruz who is watching me. Just before Rafael leans over to turn off the lamp, I catch a flicker of begging mixed with fear in his eyes. Cruz doesn't want to ask me for anything, but there it is—his weakness whispered like it's a dirty secret.

Cruz is scared to sleep. He needs my help to chase away his demons. Cruz extends his hand, but leaves it an inch from mine, letting me make the choice to either rescue him or let him deal on his own.

We both know I don't have it in me to turn away someone who needs help. My bleeding heart has gotten me into trouble before, but I don't think about that when I reach out and loop my littlest finger around his. It connects us just enough so he doesn't drift out onto his ocean of pain.

Cruz's breath catches a few times, like he's on the verge of crying, but cannot bring himself to commit to the crime. "Thank you," he whispers.

Judging from the agony etched into his forehead, it's hard to say what wounds him most—the night terrors or asking for help. Either way, his body relaxes in a gust at my touch.

I run my thumb down the curve of his massive mitt, and he scoots his whole body closer.

Rafael kisses the back of my shoulder while he hums his "lovers doing loverly things" tune. My eyes drift shut once more, hoping all that I am won't break the men in my bed.

16

WANTING MORE

RAFAEL

*C*ruz is in slightly less of a mood, but there's no undoing the surly nature that's engrained in his makeup. "Don't gloat, Rafi. It's only going to get you shoved out of a moving vehicle."

I study the brown hues of the scenery as I pull onto the highway. "What is there to gloat about? I'm certainly not going to bring it to your attention that *you're* the one who overslept by four hours. I mean, what good would that do me? It's not as if you needed to sleep in. I mean, my mind is focused solely on el culebrón. I can't imagine how deep you must have slept to override that insufferable internal clock you've always bowed to."

I turn my chin to smirk at Adelita in the rearview mirror. She's got the upper half of Santos' wolf draped over her lap. It's comforting to see them so wholly fused together. He is the picture of relaxation with her hand stroking slowly from the top of his head down his spine and then back again.

She narrows one eye at me. "Don't smile at me while teasing Cruz. He's going to think I'm laughing at him too, and we'll never see another good night's sleep." She tsks my antics, but we both know she loves that I can get away with needling the all-powerful Cruz.

Though we all agreed on the trial run of Cruz holding onto Adelita's hand while he slept to chase away La Sayona, it was a shock to wake up to it. He doesn't even hold Mira unless someone forces the baby on him. Even then, he grips her like he's holding a smelly, slimy pair of old socks he can't make sense of, and hands off his half-sister as soon as he gets the opportunity.

The sight of Cruz and Adelita clinging to each other in the morning light hollowed out a portion of my chest. I haven't been able to shake just how badly I crave a connection like that. Even though Adelita was in my arms, there was no promise of more lurking in the subtext.

I don't know who I want the precious "more" with. Pining for a deeper connection does no one any good. I don't have time for that. Defending the village is a full-time gig, leaving little room for much else. I need to hook up with someone. That should shake the ache of loneliness. I've been doing that for years.

But watching the two of them hold each other this morning is pushing me closer to the edge of searching for the "more" I've been pretending I don't need.

If I hadn't seen Cruz holding Adelita's hand so sweetly with my own two eyes, I wouldn't have believed it.

But it didn't stop at hand-holding.

There in the bed this morning was Cruz, cuddled up to Adelita with his face buried in her neck. Their hands were gripped together, smooshed between their chests like a joined prayer.

When they'd gone to sleep, I'd peeked and saw them carefully linking pinkies, which was downright precious. To see their bodies gravitating together without meaning to? I'm still digesting the sight. Though I was wrapped completely around her, Adelita's chin had rested atop Cruz's hair. He looked like her child or something, nestled in with Mami and Papi when the monsters of the night grew too scary to stay confined to the closet.

He even made this pitiful humming sound that nearly came off as a whimper, which he buried into the crook of her neck.

"No sign of La Sayona?" I ask quietly. We've all been wondering, but none of us has demanded confirmation.

"I didn't dream at all," Cruz admits, his head resting lazily against the back of his seat. "It was amazing. I don't understand why it's helping, but I haven't had a night that wasn't filled with the bitter witch in years. Is this what you guys feel all the time? Because I'm actually relaxed. It's incredible."

There's not an ounce of teasing to my smile now. I can't believe he's finally found something that works. "I'm glad for you. Well done, *viento*." I point up at the sky. "See that? You even got the sun to shine. You know how long it's been since that happened? Cruz is always making it cloudy or stormy. I haven't seen the sun with my brothers in a long time."

And I mean every word of it. Everything is different with Adelita. I feel relaxed, at home on the road or in the village. She looks at me like I matter. It's not because I'm Cruz's righthand. For no good reason, she wants to be with us.

It's two more days before we get within a few miles of where el culebrón's lair was spotted, and both nights, Cruz starts out holding onto her littlest finger and wakes up with his face buried in her neck.

The sight makes me lonely. I know it shouldn't, but it does. Maybe I'm getting old.

I know better than to tease Cruz about the new home he has made in Adelita's embrace, but I'm positively brimming with jokes I'm trying to keep quiet. I don't want to break the homeostasis that seems to have leveled off Cruz's temper. I guess I grew used to it over time—my best friend's oft-swinging anger. But now that I've had three whole days of sleeping in and sunshine, I never want to go back.

When Santos is a man and not his wolf, he has to wear sunglasses, since his eyes aren't used to this much sunshine.

When we stop for gas and to prep for going in to face the giant snake, I duck around back and make a quick phone call I need to keep private.

"Do you miss us, Eva?"

The sound of her voice carries a thousand memories with it. Cruz, Eva and me racing around the house with dishrags wrapped around our foreheads, slinging pebbles at imaginary enemies. Cruz, Eva and me climbing trees. Cruz, Eva and me pretending we knew what the adults should be doing.

Well, we still do that.

Eva snorts. "Oh, yes. I've been simply crying for days."

"Knew it. You're positively boring without us. Most people just get bored, but I know it's Cruz, Santos and me who bring the fun."

"Did you call for any particular reason, or did you just want a reminder of what it sounds like when I roll my eyes over the phone?"

I chuckle. I can't help it. Eva just gets me. "I need you to do me a favor. Can you order a new bed for Cruz? We need one of those huge ones that sleeps at least three people. Whatever the next size up from a king would be."

The silence that greets me isn't all that reassuring. When Eva finally speaks, her tone is wary at best. "Um, care to elaborate?"

I keep my voice quiet as I explain the magic that has come into our lives via Adelita's calming touch. "It chased away La Sayona. I mean, completely gone, but only if Adelita is touching him. So the bed needs to be big enough to fit your brother, Adelita and Santos."

I'll miss sleeping with the three of them, if only because I miss the feel of a woman in my arms at night.

"Are you serious?"

"Seen it with my own two eyes. Do you know what's happening right now, Eva-Diva?"

"Do not call me that."

I smirk at her insistence. "The sun is shining."

"I… what? It is? It's shining where you are?"

"In the very spot where I'm standing."

I love the sound of her being caught off-guard. She enjoys being a know-it-all. I rarely ever get to surprise her with any knowledge. "I don't understand. It's working? How is Adelita keeping La Sayona away? Is Adelita haunted now? Because that's not better! Is she having dreams with that witch in them? Is she alright? Rafi, this is so dangerous. She could get touched in the head, like Bella! Like my mom!"

"She seems fine."

Eva's words come back clipped with attitude. "Did you actually ask her? I mean, would she even tell you anything like that?"

"Probably. I…" But I know Adelita wouldn't tell us a thing. She keeps her secrets tight to the vest.

"Oh, you make me crazy." It's then I catch that Eva's not entirely thrilled with how things have come about. "You realize the last woman Cruz slept near ended up with brain damage and died, right? Do you understand that's what you've asked Adelita to risk? Does she know that is what she's braving for our brother?"

I swallow hard. "I think she gets it. We explained the backstory well enough."

Eva's scoff hits my chest. "I very much doubt that. I expected this from Cruz, but you? Rafi, don't you dare smile at her while putting her life in danger. You are better than that. Or at least, I thought you were."

I go still at her scolding. Eva is right, and I hate it. "What do you want me to do? We told her about your mother and about Bella, and she didn't run screaming."

Eva lets out a "pfft" noise, and I know without a doubt that her nose is in the air. "La Sayona could have put Adelita in the hospital. Please tell me any of you grasps that. Santos was okay with this?"

I run my hand over my face. "I'll have Santos check her over before anything else happens. She seems fine, Eva. Really."

Santos has no limits when it comes to Cruz. His rescuer can do no wrong. If Cruz wants to cuddle up to his girl-friend, Santos assumes it's fine because he thinks Cruz travels with his own superhero theme song.

"Are you coming up on el culebrón soon?"

My head bobs. "About to go into the lair in a few."

"Be safe, then. Or don't be stupid. Either way, the senti-ment is the same: don't be dead."

I close my eyes and lean against the brick of the building. "Eva..." But there are too many things I cannot say.

"Rafi, what is it?"

"I..."

Santos doesn't hold back much with Adelita. He feels something, and he's acting on it. He wants to be near her, so he is. Whatever courage he's got, I decide that I'm tired of living without it.

"Do you have any girlfriends that might..." I don't even know how to finish that sentiment.

Eva's tone turns soft. "Talk to me."

"For days, I've watched Santos hold onto Adelita. He looks at her like it hurts his heart to be near someone so beautiful. I want that. Or maybe something a notch less intense than that." Then reality sets in. "But I'm still the boy who lived with the Kalku, so no women in the village will go near me. And honestly, what woman would want to be with a man who's on the road most days of the year?" I shake my head. "I don't know what I'm asking. Never mind. Forget I said anything."

I study my black military-issued boots against the gray of the cement, wondering how it took me so long to get to this point. There is nothing around me that I care about. The few trees dotting the edge of the next parking lot over hardly add a bit of cheer. No one is frequenting this gas station, no doubt because the last time anyone cleaned the outside of this building was more than a year ago.

Eva's voice brings me home. "Those are good, normal things to want, Rafael. Let me do some thinking."

"There's not much of a point, is there. No matter how well I defend the tribe, I'll always be an outsider."

The silence that hits the other end of the phone is filled with all the things I know she is too polite to say aloud.

Good. I don't want to hear them.

When Eva finally speaks, her voice is a low croak. "I'm sorry everyone is so short-sighted. It's been unfair of them to send you out on the front lines and then not treat you and Santos like the heroes you are."

I lean against the rough brick of the gas station building, frustrated that I said anything, that I didn't say everything, that I didn't say it all sooner. "It's fine. I don't know why I'm in that headspace. I'm sure it'll pass."

I curse the tears I can hear catching her voice. "I'm sorry, Rafi. I love you so much. You and Santos both." I can picture her shaking her head, her black silky waves pulled back in some sort of hairband that makes her look like royalty. "I will look through the village for a woman who is worthy of being with the great hero you've become. If I cannot find one, that's a problem with the village, not a problem with you. Understood?"

I close my eyes and answer before common sense and pride can stop me.

I swallow hard, reining in my angst to a dull roar.

Then I end the call before another of her tears smacks my ear.

I pocket my phone and round the corner, running straight into an open-mouthed Adelita.

17

───────

HEATED KISS

RAFAEL

$\mathcal{M}$y jaw stiffens when it's clear she heard enough. "Rafi, I didn't know you wanted to settle down with someone." Though she whispers the accusation, it feels like she's shouting with the flabbergast of fresh gossip.

I hold up my hands, wishing there was a way out of this that wasn't straight through the middle of the mess. "It was just a thought."

Before I can squeeze a word in, Adelita throws herself into my arms, surprising an "oof" out of me. "I love it. I love the idea of you being with someone as amazing as you deserve."

Relief washes over me, relaxing my shoulders as I gather her in my arms. "You're no doubt the only one who will think so, *viento*. But I'll take it. If your blessing is the only one I get, I'll hold it tight."

"How could anyone not fall head over heels for you?"

"It's not as easy in the village. The people of Cáceres would never allow someone like me to be with a woman there. I'm a shifter, Adelita. A shifter who was corrupted by the Kalku. I'm not like everyone else in Cáceres."

Adelita tilts her head to the side. "Is that important?"

"To Cáceres, it is." I wave off her concern. "It was a fool's hope, is all. I'm sure it'll pass."

Adelita is frowning at me but at least she's listening. I've never been able to talk with anyone about this. "I don't understand. Is the village really so stodgy that they can't accept you? You've been part of the tribe since you were five years old, right?"

When it seems my words don't register as reason enough for her, I press deeper into the wound that might never heal. "People are afraid of Santos and me. They're afraid of anyone who has managed to escape the Kalku. Afraid of shifters, even though I can't fully shift. There is no way any woman from Cáceres will want to be with me. No one will sign up to go on a date with the Dragon of the Village."

When someone rounds the corner, I stiffen, but it's just a pedestrian searching for the bathroom.

"The car," I suggest, knowing we cannot be caught having this conversation. It was embarrassing enough to tell Eva.

My arm bands around Adelita's waist while I corral her into the car. Santos and Cruz are still in the gas station, so the coast is clear for full-range vulnerability. The car door shuts, ensuring my secrets will be safe with her.

I expect her to say something as she thumbs at the leather interior, but she simply stares at me in that calm way that demands an explanation.

It's all bubbling under my skin, begging to be let out, but I'm nervous, so I clam up. The silence is so loud, I grip the steering wheel until my knuckles pale.

When she finally speaks, of course her response shocks me. "You are worth the risk of a woman stepping outside of her norm, Rafael. You're worth everything. If there is truly no one in Cáceres that sees this, then look outside the village."

My shoulders slump. "All so I can bring her into the village where she will be ostracized for being with their resident freak show?"

"You're a good man, and well worth that risk."

"I want what you and Santos have." I shake my head. "But it's not in the cards for me. That's okay. It's just a phase. It'll pass."

"No, it won't. You're too much a romantic."

The corner of my mouth pulls up. "And how would you know something like that?"

She shrugs. "I just get you, is all."

Huh. I'm not used to being understood so thoroughly.

I'm out of my seat and sliding into the back with her before I say anything else that's completely stupid.

"Thank you, *viento*. I think I just needed someone to talk to about all this, even if we haven't solved anything."

Gratitude overwhelms me when it dawns on me that, not only does Adelita understand and accept me, but I know her, as well. Maybe I don't know every detail of her backstory, but I've seen enough to understand that most of her moments are closed book. She lives with a secret Cruz couldn't torture out of her, yet she's sitting here with me, ready to wade through the muck I haven't been able to voice to anyone, aside from her and Eva.

She reaches out and holds my hand, clasping it between hers. When she kisses the tips of my fingers, the anxiety I've put into the air softens. "I think we should see who Eva comes up with. Give her some time. It's okay to ask for what you deserve."

"What I deserve?" My nose crinkles.

She smooths her thumb over my knuckles. "You deserve to be with a woman out in the open, and to be fully loved.

Someone who can't get enough of your green eye and your golden one. That's not too much to ask of the universe. In life when you're at a crossroads, you often have two choices: to act or accept. You have been accepting for too long that there is no one out there for you. Today, you acted on your desire and called Eva for help. Your world will never change if you don't act on the things that matter. I'm proud of you. That was a big step."

A shiver rolls through me at her delicate touch, and my scales accidentally come out. "I'm sorry! Hold on. I can make them go away."

"I don't mind," she promises. "It's okay to be yourself, Rafael. I like who you are."

I blink at her, savoring the words I didn't know I desperately needed to hear.

I close my eyes and lean my head back, finally allowing myself to enjoy her touch. It's humanizing, and something I never get. Sex is different than a woman stroking your skin without the possibility of more. There's appreciation in Adelita's touch, and it sinks directly into the hollowed parts of my soul that desperately need the sanity.

Santos and I are lepers in the village. No one hugs us, high-fives us. They stay away because I'm part-monster. I'm dangerous.

Yet here's my sweet friend, dancing on the edge of danger, holding my hand because she's not afraid of me.

"Come here, *viento*." I give her a little jerk of my chin. "Words that pretty deserve to be kissed."

There's nothing to the closed-mouth smooch I press to her lips, nothing but appreciation for a friendship I've been missing my whole life.

Her blush is precious, so I savor the sight because it belongs to me.

A wave of heat brushes over me, flushing my insides with something I'm unprepared for.

"Is it hot in here?"

She rolls her eyes. "'Or is it just you?' Ha-ha."

I pull my hand back from her and crack the door open. "No, I'm serious. I'm..."

Sudden heat builds in my sternum with a force so powerful, I am positive my insides are melting. Something feels strange, like tiny forks are scraping along the insides of my veins, tickling and poking as they go.

"Rafael?"

The inferno in my body begins to collect into a ball that steadily rises to greet the world. I can feel something changing on a cellular level. There's a popping and fizzing in my blood as it heats in my veins.

I let out a choked cry as the heat inside of me barrels upward with a warning that this isn't all fun and games. The forks in my veins are scratching now, stabbing instead of teasing.

"Adelita, something's happening!"

It's the only warning I work out before the heat burns at my throat so badly that I have to open my mouth to let in something fresh to cool my insides down.

"What's wrong?" she asks, like she can't see my insides burning up right in front of her.

I claw at the roof of the car, horrified when my scaled fingers mutate into claws. My suddenly olive fingernails grow so long and dangerous, they shred through the fabric as easily as if the roof was made of butter.

"Rafael, your face!"

My mouth stretches in a yawn, and suddenly I can see my own nose and mouth. It's not lips, but a scaly maw fit for a...

But I can't shapeshift. I've never been able to complete the transformation. The most I can do is cover my body in green scales with gold tips and sprout a tail.

"Adelita, run!"

My chest heaves as the furnace in my body builds, and then doubles.

She scrambles for the door, but it's too late. A shout bursts out of my diaphragm, but it's her screams that fill my ears when pure fire belts out of my mouth.

18

COLORFUL EYES

CRUZ

I hate gas station bathrooms. They are filthy, and you never feel comfortable taking your time in there. But being on the road gives a man few other options, so I take my time as much as I am able.

Of course my phone rings the one time I have a minute to myself.

"Yeah?" I greet Tio Bruno.

His voice is rushed, like he's walking while he's talking. "The girl. Your new one. She has blue eyes."

My brow raises that weird eye color is the reason he chooses to call me. "So?"

"The Mendez tribe just rescued a woman, not from the Kalku, but from Máximo himself."

That stops me from all movement. "Come again? Since when has anyone ever ventured to Máximo's island? That's suicide."

"Apparently not. The rescue team made it back, almost all of them, with the girl they set out to bring home."

"That's shocking. They made it past the Massacoora-maan? How?"

"Your girl," Tio Bruno redirects. "Adelita."

My cheeks immediately flush that anyone thinks she's mine.

"She's not my girlfriend!" I blurt out.

The silence tells me I've said something very stupid, as if I needed the confirmation. "I know that. The girl you rescued. That girl. Adelita. Take a picture of her blue eyes and send it to me. I want to compare her shade to the Mendez's rescue. I'd never seen anyone with blue eyes before. Two blue-eyed women the Kalku captured isn't a coincidence. The fact that one of them ended up on Máximo's island is troubling, to say the least. I need information about her parents."

I fight off a groan. Adelita is a pretty private person. She's not going to let me take a photo and send it to my uncle. I'll have to get one when she's not paying attention. "Any particular reason?"

There's a pause that twists my stomach. My intuition tingles that something is very, very wrong. My brain refuses to connect the pieces of information because I don't want to dive into that deeper abyss.

"Máximo is the only person I've ever heard of who has blue eyes."

Yep, that's the part I didn't want connected. Even after the words hit the air, I resist them. "It could be a coincidence."

"The rescue the Mendez warriors picked up told them she was Máximo's daughter. One of many, no doubt." Another long pause gives the rushing train in my brain time to run full force into the brick it has no business touching. "If Adelita's eyes and her story match, then we can assume…"

"Adelita is Máximo's daughter?" The words ring in the air, changing the entire world as I have been viewing it.

"I don't like that she kept a secret like that from us, Cruz. A secret kept right under your nose."

I shake my head, redirecting Tio Bruno's train before it

runs off-course. "She was raised by a single mom. Adelita didn't know a thing about our world before this. If she is a daughter of Máximo, then she has no idea. And matching blue eyes? That's not exactly a DNA test. The color could also be from her mother."

Tio Bruno pauses before he speaks. "True, but it's too big a coincidence not to dig deeper. You need to find out if her mother had blue eyes."

I hate this whole thing. "I'll get you your photo, but what she doesn't know, she doesn't know. I'm not telling her that her father is possibly Máximo—the maniac the Kalku take their orders from. She doesn't need to own that, especially when it might not be true."

I don't want to have that earthshattering conversation.

"And I gotta tell you, Tio Bruno, she doesn't like to talk about herself. I don't like the idea of getting information out of her for reasons she isn't privy to. We're traveling together."

Matters like trust have never been all that important to my uncle. "Get the information."

At that exact moment, something tugs at my gut. A danger that tells me I need to move now. My feet itch to run out of the bathroom, though my brain has no idea why.

Tio Bruno doesn't believe in intuition. He operates by the system of "always be ready," so he always is. No need for intuition. But when my chest tightens as I'm washing my hands, I can't help but think maybe Tio Bruno isn't right on this one point.

My gut screams at me to check on Adelita.

"Gotta go." I end the call quickly, unease filling my veins.

The urgency builds until it's like a punch to my insides, kicking me out the door. The urge to check on the guys and Addy is so strong, I don't bother to dry my hands. I run out of the bathroom towards the car.

Santos felt it too, I can tell, because he is running for the car for no reason that's discernable. He reaches the vehicle first and yanks open the backdoor.

I'm not sure what I expected. Maybe Addy getting all emotional or something? Maybe the Kalku somehow tracking us down?

But when a blast of fire knocks Santos on his butt, I skid to a stop with a shout. "Addy!"

My arm raises to shield my eyes just as the fire gets sucked back in. The front seats are ablaze, filling the car with black smoke that chokes me the second I try to dip my head inside.

Where the crap is Rafi? He was supposed to be watching her.

When I catch sight of Adelita's braids in the backseat, panic grips me by the throat. "Addy!"

"Take her!" I hear Rafi beg us. "I can't stop it!"

Before I can piece the puzzle together, he howls in agony.

I don't know what I'm looking at when I duck my head into the backseat. It's Rafi's olive scales, but his whole mouth is elongated like a crocodile's, and his belly is bulbing out.

Like a dragon's.

"Deep breaths, Rafael! I won't leave you!" Addy shouts.

Santos grabs Adelita from behind and rips her from the car, not caring for his own safety.

A second blast of fire hits the air straight from Rafi's mouth.

It takes a few blinks, but I finally put the image together enough for things to make a medium amount of sense in my mind.

Rafi has never even been able to blow smoke.

Santos presses Addy towards me and points to a spot far away. It's clear he needs me to take her from the scene, but it's not clear why he shuts himself in the back of the car with Rafi.

"No! Santos, you'll die!" Addy shouts through her coughing, banging on the door to warn Santos to get out. She's weak from inhaling too much smoke, so her struggle isn't all that effective as I lead her stumbling feet away from the car, to the back of the building.

Gas. We're at a gas station, and gas is many things, the most important of which is that it is flammable.

Both Rafi and Santos are locked inside of a burning car.

Rafi found his dragon. This was supposed to be a good thing. Maybe. Probably.

My legs are rubbery as I take Santos' orders like a directive. My only friends and brothers are burning together in the car, and I'm here, obeying orders like a dummy while my life goes up in flames.

I lower Addy to the ground, grimacing when I spot a ton of broken glass everywhere. She winces, and I can tell she's cut, probably sitting in a pile of tetanus waiting to happen.

A coughing fit takes over her whole body, but she's safe enough. "Stay here!" I command, and then run back toward the car.

If I don't help the guys, they *will* burn, and Addy could be consumed by even bigger flames if the gas catches.

I'm expecting it to explode at any moment, but still I run toward the danger, my boots heavy with purpose. Rafi and Santos are my whole life. Without them, it's just me going out on these stupid missions with no backup.

The best parts of my life are burning alive right now.

I don't laugh aloud at Rafi's stupid jokes, even though I think they're funny.

I don't listen to Santos enough.

I don't think it through, but yank at the door handle. Frustration grips me when I find it too hot to touch without wincing. And of course, it's locked. I bang on the window, but the tinted glass doesn't grant a smidgen of mercy. I feel my pockets for my keys, cursing aloud when I realize Rafi has them, and he's locked inside.

The sound of Adelita's heavy cough draws my eyes toward her stumbling form.

"I can't get it open!" I shout to her.

She waves for me to step aside and grips the handle. In one smooth yank, she wrenches the back door open and actually tears it off its hinges, releasing a billowing black cloud into the open. She falls back, bumping her butt on the concrete, startled at her own strength.

"I'm sorry!" she pleads, lowering the torn-off door to the ground.

My heart stutters when I see both Rafi and Santos, but no fire. It's all black smoke, but the flames are finally extinguished.

I reach in, fumble around and tug them both out, taking inventory of the burn marks, which are hard to make out under all the soot.

They are coughing, and Santos is signing with stiff fingers. *We're okay. Rafi found his dragon. I was helping him turn it off.*

Rafi is himself again, but without the laughter in his eyes, I barely recognize him. I lower his shaking form to the ground, but he doesn't register my help. He stares up at the sky, his eyes taking in the dark storm clouds that are rolling in far too quickly for nature to be solely in control. He looks lost, utterly gone from his body, peacefully checked out from the chaos he created.

His eyes match now. One was gold and the other green, but now they're both gold.

Rafael has completed his transformation. He's a full shifter now.

I kneel beside him and hold his hand, but he doesn't grip

me in return. He's limp, his eyes wide open in what must be shock.

"We're okay," I repeat, trying to convince myself that a heart attack isn't strictly necessary anymore. "We're okay."

Maybe it's a lie, but everything in me hopes that one day, it will be true.

19

INTIMATE

ADELITA

Cruz has been in a mood all day, which is really nothing new. But today, our second day on the road, it's starting to get to me. He's not aggressive, per se, but he's secretive. His eyes track me wherever I go, so I don't wander when we make the occasional stop. He's more careful of strangers, cataloging exits with his eyes and insisting we don't linger anywhere for more than twenty minutes.

Even when we stopped to get the car detailed, the door put back on, and our clothes laundered to rid us all of the soot stink, he didn't let me wander more than a few steps from his side.

Though, he's not been a total tool. He insisted on helping Santos pluck the glass shards from my elbows and the backs of my thighs, claiming they were his fault, since he didn't check the ground before he laid me on it when he pulled me from the burning vehicle.

But we all know this whole thing is my fault. I know this. No one is pointing fingers, but it's clear it's me who set everything on this off-plan trajectory. I kissed Rafael, and his dragon came to life. After getting the car detailed and making sure everyone was physically alright, we got back on the road in total silence.

Rafi and I haven't looked at each other. He's either scared of me or angry that I was the catalyst for something that changed him on a molecular level. I don't blame him one bit, but the whole thing is awful. It feels like the universe is punishing me for kissing a friend.

I address Cruz with caution. "Are we being followed or something?"

"Probably not. Stay close, though." I get no sense of comfort or safety by doing so, but I obey all the same, mostly because whatever unpleasantness lurks in the shadows, Cruz can be far more unpleasant, I'm sure, if I give him grief.

He was starting to lighten up, now that he is sleeping regularly. Waking up to his face nuzzling my neck is just about the cutest thing. His torso warms mine in the night, and I love it. This vulnerable, docile version of Cruz is a kitten no one gets to see but us. Yet today, that man is gone. He is not his old, angry self, but the sunshine overhead is obscured by the clouds, and his brows have remained knit together in worry ever since his phone rang this morning.

Cruz is a moody mess. I've come to expect that from him. But this time, I know it's because of me. I am the bomb they are all afraid to travel with now. I am the danger. Me, who recycles, knits like a dream, and feeds stray cats.

I'm careful with the guys, keeping far away from Rafael so I don't spook him or like, touch his hand and make his dragon appear again. I am positively afraid to touch Santos. He is so thoughtful and sweet to me; I know if I get within a foot of him, I will end up really kissing the beautiful man who looks at me like I matter. I don't know what might happen to a full-on shifter if I kiss one, and I don't want to experiment with someone as wonderful as Santos.

This whole snake business keeps me tossing and turning

when we stop at a hotel for our fourth night on the road. The place is clean and my pajamas are soft. We've scrubbed all traces of the soot from us, but I cannot quiet my thoughts enough for actual sleep to find me.

"Would you pick a position and lie still? You're keeping me up," Cruz grouses.

"I can't sleep." I sit up, forfeiting the fight.

Santos sits up from his spot near my feet, shaking out his fur and stretching with a wide, wolfy yawn.

Cruz throws his hands in the air in exasperation while I rub my temples.

I shuffle out of the covers. "I'm going for a walk or something. I can't turn off my brain."

Santos breathes deeply and changes back into his man form before I can move toward the edge of the bed. His legs swing off the mattress and he's on his feet, toeing on his boots. His eyes are lidded. I know he is tired, but he doesn't look like he resents me for keeping him up.

"You don't have to go with me, Santos. I'm just going for a walk around the building. Stretch my legs and clear my head."

Santos offers up a sleepy smile and waves off my unhappiness.

Great. Now I'm keeping him awake *and* fixing him with guard duty.

"You can't go anywhere alone," Cruz rules, as if he can say things like that without having to explain himself.

"Hello, I'm twenty-eight. I can do all sorts of things by myself. I'm not going far. You already said the Kalku aren't after us right now."

Cruz rolls onto his back, blinking up at the ceiling. "I got a call from Tio Bruno. A team from the Mendez tribe liberated a woman who had been taken by the Kalku."

Rafael hisses as he sits up on his elbow to gape at Cruz. "When?"

Cruz runs his hands over his face. "For the record, this is nothing like sleeping. Answering you will only result in fifteen more questions, all of which will keep us up all night long." His eyes flick to me in the darkness, which is broken up only by the sliver of moonlight peeking in from the side of the curtain. "If you think you've got trouble sleeping now, this conversation is only going to make that worse. Come back to bed, Addy."

The way he says it is intimate, like it's just our bed. His eyes widen in time with mine, but neither of us addresses the oddity of him using a nickname for me. It's strange, this balance of quasi-relationships.

I don't know how to handle any of it, so instead I stick with the elephant in the room. "Who is she?"

Rafael's questions come a hair after mine. "What state did they find her in? Is she alright? Was she in the cave? Cruz, if they found her in a cave and didn't slaughter her captors, we should go there and see what damage we can do."

Cruz runs his tongue over his top row of teeth. Santos and I are standing, Rafael is sitting up in the bed, but Cruz refuses. His spine looks fused to the bed with his stubbornness that this topic will not keep us up all night long. "They didn't find her in a cave. They found her on Máximo's island." He pauses for Santos and Rafael to let loose their gasps.

I have no idea what island they're talking about, and I'm not totally clear on who this Máximo person is.

Cruz continues. "No idea how long she'd been there. Turns out, she's Máximo's daughter."

My reaction of "huh" is underwhelming when compared to Santos and Rafael leaning in with bugged eyes. "Are you serious?"

Cruz nods, staring up at the ceiling. "Seems like it."

My mouth pulls to the side. "What I'm hearing is that the Mendez tribe stole a woman out of her own home where she was living with her father, and then called it a rescue. Is that what's going on? Because I don't like it."

Rafael takes over filling me in. "Máximo is a monster. It's good she was rescued. There is no telling what state she has been found in. She'll be better off far away from him. He only keeps people close to use and abuse them."

I do what I can to process this information, reminding myself that I know precious little about the way their world works.

Cruz harrumphs. "So you can see why I've been on edge. You really can't go anywhere unguarded, Adelita. Not even for a walk around the hotel."

I shake my head. "That's awful she had to live with the bad guy, and I'm glad she's safe now, it sounds like. But that has nothing to do with us. It's the Kalku who want me, whoever this Máximo person is doesn't want to abduct me."

Rafael pinches the bridge of his nose. I know his body is fighting sleep. "The Kalku are an extension of Máximo. Sometimes they act on their own, but they also do Máximo's bidding. He was one of them a century ago, but then he grew so powerful with his knowledge of experimental magic that he became their leader. He left the mainland and lives on his island now."

My mouth pulls to the side. "So he's like, a hundred and… how old?"

Santos begins signing, but he's going too fast for me to make sense of it.

Cruz fills me in with an evenness to his voice that draws me closer. "Máximo found the secret of immortality. It's called the Luz Mala. As long as the Luz Mala glows its green light on his island, it keeps him alive and active. Máximo and his closest friend in the Kalku are immortal. His friend, the Massacooramaan, forever guards the island, and Máximo lives there, continuing out his experiments. Frankly, I'm shocked the Mendez group of warriors was able to get onto the island. No one has ever managed it before. The Massacooramaan drowns anyone who tries." He casts Rafi a scoff. "Plus, our scouts have always been far superior to theirs, and we've never been able to get to the island."

Rafi frowns. "That is weird. You're right."

My hip cocks to the side. "Again, super upsetting, but I'm not sure what an old crazy man on an island has to do with me not being able to go for a walk unattended."

Cruz keeps his eyes on the ceiling. "Tio Bruno told me on the phone this morning that the woman they liberated has eyes just like yours."

My hands tense, and I look away, as if that will make them forget my weird eye color. "That's... I..."

"I'm not a huge believer in coincidence." Though Cruz is giving loads of information, I can tell by the guarded way about him that he is still holding something back. "It's possible Máximo is targeting women with blue eyes."

I take a step back, suddenly feeling cornered. "I'm sure it doesn't mean anything. Why would he be targeting people with a certain rare eye color?"

Cruz holds my gaze, letting me know that he's not going to allow us to brush this under the rug. "He experiments on people, pushing the boundaries of magic."

Just like that, Rafael is out of bed, shoving on his boots. "We're moving. If the Kalku are abducting women and keeping them in the cave, that's one nightmare. If Máximo himself is going to be on the rampage, targeting women who look like Adelita, we don't have a chance. Cruz, get up. We're going. Adelita will be safer in the village. Tio Bruno can send someone else to handle el culebrón."

Cruz turns his chin from left to right. "The woman was found on Máximo's island. Nowhere near us." Cruz keeps his eyes on the ceiling, like if he doesn't look at us, we won't be able to sense his growing worry.

But I feel it. I've felt it all day. I feel it in the way he watches me whenever I walk more than ten feet from him. I feel it when he meets my eyes with a million secrets, but that's the only one he spills—the fact that he has secrets.

Cruz angles his hands behind his head. I can tell he's debating between confessing the truth and telling us to shut up again. "As far as I knew, it was only the Kalku abducting women to keep for their sacrifices. Adding Máximo to the mix makes the whole thing bigger. If it's Máximo targeting Addy and not just the Kalku after her, why? What does Máximo want with her? He is more adept at mastering and manipulating magic than anyone in the world. Kidnapping a woman seems beneath someone like that."

Santos' hand touches on the small of my back.

Rafael inches toward me, as if he's worried I am currently in imminent danger. "I don't like this, Cruz. There's something you're not telling us."

Cruz punches his pillow beneath his head, avoiding Rafael's suspicions altogether. "Nothing is going to get solved tonight, guys. We can obsess about it all in the morning." He jerks his chin to the empty spot beside him. "Come back to bed, Addy."

My whole body feels cold as I obey. Now I understand why Cruz has been so wound up about my safety today.

"I need to know more about Máximo." I tell him as I lay on my side, propped up on my elbow. When Cruz doesn't answer, I rest my hand atop his broad chest.

I don't know if this touch is okay or if it's too intimate. Cruz's lashes sweep shut, so I truly have no idea if he's about to chew me a new one, or if he is gearing himself up to talk about the super old bad guy they all know about.

The room goes quiet for a few beats. Santos' gaze fixes on his feet. Rafael rubs the nape of his neck.

Cruz's voice is low when he answers, and his eyes remain closed. It's like my touch is unlocking the story, so I keep my hand atop his chest. "A very long time ago, Máximo was raised in the Kalku, much like Santos. Only Máximo wasn't a slave. He was one of their prized warriors, brought up with their traditions and education. Trouble is, they couldn't contain him. His magic is like nothing the world has ever seen. Santos can shift into a wolf, but Máximo *created* the very first shifter."

Cruz pauses to let the story settle in my brain, giving me a chance to put the pieces of the anomaly in some sort of order. I can't even fathom a person that powerful.

When I am ready for more of the story, my fingers stroke his sternum.

Cruz surprises us all by dragging me down for a… there's no other way to describe it; Cruz invites me in for a snuggle. A real one, with my head on his shoulder and my breasts tucked tight to his side. His fingers trail lightly up and down my bad arm, lulling me and possibly soothing himself with the simple, slow stroke.

My hand remains on his chest, invoking a low hum from him before he continues.

"Máximo grew tired of living in caves with his Kalku tribe, so he claimed an island for himself where he could experiment with magic on a level too dangerous for the mainland. What he does there…" Cruz holds me tighter, like he actually cares not just about a random person getting abducted, but as if his heart beats in my direction. "We don't know what he does, what he's up to, but we know how he was raised. The Kalku have to boil down the hearts of those with extraordinary abilities, and it's never actually been proven that they can access those talents. They might feel stronger, but none of them can tear the door off its hinges, like you can. If they get any enhancements, it's so watered down, I cannot imagine it's worth it. But they swear by it, so what do I know?"

I wince. "Did I apologize for that yet? For breaking the door off its hinges?"

Cruz has his arm wrapped around me. His fingers trill on my arm in a light tease. "Only a dozen times. Knock it off. You did the right thing, getting them out when I couldn't." He runs his palm over his face. "Point is, I want you with one of us at all times. If the Kalku are abducting women with physical traits similar to yours to hand over to Máximo, we don't take chances with your safety. The Kalku are sadistic, sure, but Máximo was raised by sadists and is infinitely more powerful. Once you get taken to him, I'm not sure we could get you back. The fact that the Mendez tribe was able to liberate a woman from Máximo's island?" He shakes his head. "I'm not taking that chance with you. The fact that the woman they rescued also happens to have blue eyes like yours? I'm not letting you out of my sight. Understood?"

I nod once, cozying closer. "Understood. I don't need to go for a walk tonight." My therapist brain settles over me. "Evil only needs permission to thrive. It sounds like Máximo's wickedness thrived because the Kalku revere him. Am I getting that right?"

"Perfect, as usual."

Santos starts signing to Cruz.

Cruz sits up and nods to the guys. "Santos, good call. Yes, go do a round of the hotel's perimeter. I think it'll help us all sleep better to know nothing is out there tonight. Rafi, you take the interior. Check every floor for anything suspicious. Any sign we might have been followed."

I get up. I can't help it. Santos pauses his mission only to wrap his arms around me. *I'll keep you safe,* he mouths.

I blink up at him, unable to hide how forlorn I feel about the whole thing. "But who is going to keep *you* safe?"

A wry smile tweaks the left corner of his mouth, as if I've said something cute, instead of letting loose a real worry.

Santos kisses my forehead before he releases me, reminding me to stay with Cruz.

Rafael has apparently decided he's quite comfortable with me, and doesn't mind changing out of his pajama pants and back into his jeans in the main room, where I can clearly see he wears navy boxer briefs.

He's kept a safe distance from me most of the day, but after taking in my peaking worry, he draws near to grip my fingers. "It's alright, *viento.* We won't let anyone take you."

The simple contact, the small assurance, is all it takes for me to throw myself into Rafael's arms. "I'm so sorry I hurt you in the car! I know I set everything loose and did things to your makeup you didn't want. I'm sorry, Rafael!"

He stiffens, but then softens in my grip, even going so far as to let loose a little chuckle. "Now, now. You didn't mean to. I'm adjusting, is all. I was half a monster before. Now I'm a whole one. Jury's still out on how I feel about any of it. Give it time. It'll settle where it settles."

There is pain in his golden eyes, lurking behind the tired smile he tries to conjure up for me. The whisper tumbles out of me unchecked and unbridled. "I love you, Rafael. However you come to me, I love you. Only foolish people would pass up on being near a wonderful man like you."

And it's true. Rafael is the friend I wish I'd always had. He can conjure a joke out of thin air, and change a dire situation into something manageable with a meager shrug of his shoulders.

His eyes soften as he takes in my words that are mingled

with the worry on my face. I don't expect he will ever smooch my lips again after what our kiss did to him in the car, but that's exactly what he does.

Rafael isn't afraid of anything, not even me.

"We'll be back, *viento*. Stick with Cruz." Then he releases me and claps Santos on the shoulder.

The guys trot out the door, leaving me to band my arms around my middle and stare at the door, hoping for their safe return.

2 0

—————

LIES AND LUST

ADELITA

*C*ruz scolds me without holding back, as usual. "You're going to make yourself crazy, worrying like that."

I frown at Cruz. "Isn't that what you wanted me to do— be more aware of all the bad things? You're worried this Máximo person is gunning for me. That it's not the Kalku, but him."

"I am certain it's both of them—the Kalku acting on Máximo's orders. It made no sense that the Kalku kept tracking you. That's not how they work. Then I thought it was because of your strength. That made sense. They would want you so they could tear out your heart, boil it down, drink it, and get some of the muscle that comes natural to you." Cruz doesn't even pause for my shudder. "If Máximo wants you?" His question trails off, unanswered. "But no, you don't need to worry, because you are with us."

Maybe he thinks I'm cold, because he slowly gets out of the bed and moves in my direction with the comforter in his grip, his eyes locked in on mine.

When he drapes the heavy blanket around my shoulders

167

and wraps me up in it, I'm afraid to breathe. He's so tall, so much bigger than most people. The umber of his skin on mine is a slightly different shade, and the two together look oddly pleasant. I feel small before him, and it's just now dawning on me that we are alone in the hotel room.

When Cruz tucks his finger under my chin and tips my face upward so I have no choice but to drink in the intensity of his gaze, it feels like we might be the only two people on the planet.

"I want a picture of your eyes," he says, so quiet, it's almost like a secret between us.

The request is so strange, I don't know what to make of it. I chew on my bottom lip, looking downward. "What for?"

"For me," he says, his voice turning husky. Cruz hooks his finger under my chin, raising my face up. His eyes lock in on mine with such intensity, my knees start to feel unstable. "Please?"

No one has a picture of me anymore, not since my mom passed. The debate is strong, but I manage a small nod.

Cruz pulls his phone from his puddled jeans on the floor and smiles at me—a real one with dimples and sweetness. I almost don't recognize him.

He takes the picture and presses a few more things on his phone before putting the device away. His body returns to mine, his arms encircling me. Even though the embrace is loose, I'm so turned around by it that I can hardly breathe.

"Stunning blue. Did you get the color from your mother or your father?"

His thumb drags down the slope of my throat, and my lips part, quivering with confusion.

"I... What does that matter?"

Frustration flares in his eyes, but it vanishes so quickly, I'm not sure it was ever there to begin with. "You're so guarded. I wonder why that is. So secretive." He turns his chin and circles his fingers around my right wrist. He brings my hand up to rest on the side of his face, scratching his unshaven cheek over the sensitive flesh.

"Tell me about your mother's eyes." His intensity is still boring into me, going deeper than anyone has a right to. It's intimate—whatever this is. I don't understand it. Cruz looks so strange like this. There is a note of a low command to his voice, but his touch is seductive without being outright demanding. "Addy, talk to me."

I go mute, utterly transfixed, until his lips caress the inside of my wrist and a gasp rips from my throat. He can feel each ragged heartbeat beneath his thumb. He's touching my vulnerable spot, a part of me I can't not feel. My whole arm is humming for him.

The room is suddenly far too humid, making my skin feel strange as my hips arch in his direction. My body feels possessed, acting without thought as my free hand crawls up his abdomen and rests over his thumping heart. It's so loud, so active beneath the excessive muscle, jumping harder at my touch.

When he takes my free wrist in his overlarge mitt and backs me up so he can pin it to the wall on the right side of my head, I'm utterly beside myself with... it can't be need. The comforter drops to the floor, and though I am in my clothes, I worry I'm spontaneously naked.

"Cruz, what are you..." But my words are chopped short when his lips touch on my wrist, opening an inch so he can suck on the tender flesh. "We shouldn't..."

A rough, strangled sound erupts from what feels like my toes, rippling all the way through my body until it hits the air. My head lolls back against the wall.

When his hips meld to mine, his tongue laves over the sensitive inside of my wrist just to drive me wild. This is a new side to him—unbridled and rife with lust.

He tears his mouth from my wrist but keeps my butt pinned to the wall as his lips magnetize to my earlobe. "Tell me, Addy. I want to hear about your mother's eyes."

When his hips start to move against mine, giving me just enough friction to scramble my brains, the truth belts out of me without pause. "Brown! My mom's eyes were brown."

His cheek drags upward against mine, and I can tell he's grinning. "There," he exhales, kissing my neck just to drive me crazy. "Was that so hard?"

Then he drops my arms and leaves me panting against the wall, moving clear across the room as he pulls his phone from his pocket and starts… making a call? "Tio Bruno, did you get the picture of her eyes? Good. She confirmed her mother had brown eyes, so we can assume she got her blue eyes from her father. We have to operate going forward assuming that Máximo is definitely…" Then he pauses, casting a look at me as though hemming in his words, "Máximo must be collecting women with blue eyes."

Lightning shoots through my vulnerable spots. My mouth drops open as horror dulls the lust that should never have been awakened.

What did I just do?

Cruz grunts a few times before ending the call and setting his phone on the nightstand. "Don't look at me like that," he says of my dropped-open mouth. "Santos told me I'm not allowed to hurt you when I need to interrogate you. This was the only way to get you to talk."

A wave of nausea sweeps over me, heating my cheeks and forcing regret into every part of my being.

Rafael comes back into the room but my eyes are fixed on the stern line of Cruz's jaw. "Forgot my phone," Rafael admits, grabbing his device off the nightstand.

In this moment, I wish for dragon-like qualities, so I can breathe fire on Cruz's bravado and tear his face with my talons. As I don't have any of those things, my vision narrows in as my feet carry me toward the man I loathe.

He's avoiding my gaze, which makes my hard slap across his cheek a surprise to us both. His chin jerks to the side, his eyes bugged at the force of my assault.

"Whoa!" Rafael holds his hands up. He takes a step back at the scene when he realizes this is far more complicated than he formerly understood. "What's the problem, guys?"

Cruz holds his cheek, his chin lowering in submission. "Tio Bruno says we are to assume Máximo is targeting Adelita, too. It's not just the Kalku after her." Then he looks up and meets Rafael's gaze, saying something in the subtext I don't understand. "Her mother has brown eyes, Rafi. She got her blue eyes from her father."

Rafael's jaw stiffens, understanding more to this than I do. "I see."

"I want to leave," I say to Rafael. "I don't want to be near Cruz anymore. I'm out. Out of all of this."

The color drains from Rafael's face. "Wait, what? No, *linda*. I know I spooked you when I found my dragon. You're probably scared of me lighting things on fire. But if I promise not to shift around you, will you stay?"

Cruz keeps his eye on me. "We have to take down el culebrón. We can't do anything else first."

We aren't friends. What was I thinking?

I take a step backward, shaking my head as I try to remember how I got here. Not to the hotel, but to this place in my life where I would let someone like Cruz get that near, while having just been close enough to another man to make him breathe fire.

I want to be with Santos. What am I doing? Why didn't I push Cruz away? I shake my head at the both of them. At myself. "No. This isn't my life. This isn't me. Once we deal with el culebrón, I'm out. I'll take my chances."

"Screw the snake, Cruz. What about Santos?" Rafael's eyebrows are knit together, his fists clenched in frustration. "I get that you have every right to be worried around me, and I'm sure Cruz deserved that slap, but what did Santos do to get cut off?"

My voice raises with my peaking nerves. "If our kiss made you breathe fire, what would happen if Santos and I kissed? I changed you, Rafael! That's not good! Do you think I want to hurt Santos like that?" Before Rafael can piece together his next argument, I hold up my hand. "I'm no one's prisoner, so I get to decide where I live. I can't stay near Cruz. I just can't. And I don't have it in me to break the three of you up."

I miss my mama's voice so badly, my heart aches. She would know what to do.

My lower lip trembles, and I know I have seconds before my emotions purge themselves through my tear ducts. I won't give Cruz my tears. I won't give him my anything.

"I'd like a separate room," I hear myself say.

Cruz's head snaps up, like he can't believe a woman wouldn't want to sleep with a man who manipulates her. "We have to stay together."

My temper flares without a slow build-up, lashing out at a shout. "I will never stay with you ever again!"

Cruz finds his volume and trumps mine. "Be as mad as you want, but don't be stupid. I just told you that Máximo is kidnapping women with eyes like yours. Don't put your life in danger just to prove a point."

"And what point would that be?" Rafael interjects, his arms crossed over his chest. "What did I miss?"

Both Cruz and I go mute, neither of us wanting to admit what happened between us.

What shouldn't have happened.

What, as far as I'm concerned, never happened.

I pluck a pillow from the bed and yank the comforter off the floor. "There are showers and toilets by the indoor pool area that you all can use. If I can't have my own room tonight, I'm sleeping in the bathroom here. Goodnight."

Rafael throws his hands up in exasperation. Truly, it's not his fault at all, but it is time for me to be done. I march into the bathroom and lock myself inside, slumping to the ground as my mama's song replays in my mind.

SLEEP, baby, sleep.
   Dream, baby, dream.
   Love, baby, love.
   My baby, mine.

HOW I WISH I could hear her voice. She would be ashamed of how I carried on with Cruz, who so clearly only knows how to use people.

I'm cold all over as I spread the comforter out in the tub, saying goodnight to the person I thought I knew.

21

PURPLE JEWELRY

ADELITA

When I ask Rafael if I can take the front seat the next morning after we check out, I can see the debate plain on his face. "Why? You usually take the back with Santos."

I shrug, trying to keep the devastation off my face. "It's just time."

Last night, wolf Santos clawed at the bathroom door until I explained that I was alright, but needed some space. He'd fallen asleep on the other side of the door, our bodies separated by that two inches of a barrier. If I told Santos what Cruz did, that might divide them, and it would certainly put space between the two of us. I know Santos needs Cruz more than he needs me. It would be selfish to say anything that could take him away from the man I now loathe.

Rafael bumps his butt to the passenger door, making it so I would have to shove him aside to access it, which we both know I won't do. "Explain it to Santos, then. He's a man, Adelita. Treat him like one."

I wince at the scolding, but Rafael is right. Santos isn't a puppy; he deserves at least a conversation.

I give Rafael a nod and reach for Santos' hand, though everything inside of me is hollow.

The instant we connect, I feel warmth, like life might not always feel so very cold. I lead him away from Cruz and Rafael, who aren't speaking to each other since Cruz can't bring himself to fess up to what he did, and Rafael is pissed that whatever Cruz did has pushed me clear out of everyone's arms.

I hate that I don't know enough sign to keep me from having to say my truth aloud. "Santos, I can't be with you anymore. What happened with Rafael... I didn't mean to make him breathe fire. I didn't mean to seal his transformation. He had a shot at not being a shapeshifter before I came around. I don't know what might happen if I kissed you like that. I shouldn't be with anyone."

But that's not the real reason, or not the whole reason, anyway.

Santos is signing something I don't understand, but I interrupt him, because if I'm going to be a jerk, I might as well go full force. "Santos, Cruz and I..." I don't know how to phrase any of it. "Things are getting out of hand. I don't want to be around him anymore. I like you a lot, but you should be with someone..." I can't find the right words. "You should be with someone who isn't so very wrong. I'm wrong for this life, for all three of you. I should go take my chances on a new life, and you should stay with Cruz."

Santos doesn't understand what I let happen. How could he? I barely understand it myself.

Santos sinks onto his knees, jerking my tears to the forefront. *"I want to be with you. What happened?"*

I shake my head, trying to remain stoic and failing miserably. I don't resist when he tugs me down, so I'm on my knees in front of him in the hotel parking lot. Then I'm snatched in his arms that covet the wretched person I am.

"It just has to be this way. I'm messing everything up. I did something bad. You shouldn't forgive me." When my tears wet his shirt, I pull back, my butt hitting the pavement. "You have to let me go."

Though, selfishly, no part of me wants to be separated from him.

I kiss his cheek and then stand, moving back to the car, passing Cruz's hard expression, and jerking open the passenger door. Santos is still on his knees, not understanding because I'm not explaining anything. Not really.

"Why are you doing this?" Rafael asks from the driver's seat, sounding equal parts hurt and demanding.

"What? I just want to ride shotgun for once. Is that okay?"

"You tell me. Is it okay?"

No. None of my life is okay. Being so connected to Santos kept me from that dreaded drifting feeling that's got me by the throat now. I have no home. I have no car, no job, no real friends, no family.

I belong nowhere, so here I am, smack in the middle of nowhere.

Instead of telling Rafael the truth, I fake a smile. "Let's get going."

Rafael grimaces, and then tightens his jaw, his eyes narrowing. "Never give me a smile that fake ever again. I'd rather have you spitting in my face than endure a second of superficial nothings from you. You and I are better than that. Don't cheapen us."

I swallow hard and nod, dropping any semblance that I'm okay.

Cruz insists on driving after he gets Santos into the backseat. No doubt he wants to distance himself from any kind of emotion, and silent though Santos is, I can feel his agony radiating through the car.

We are on the road for three hours without any of us

saying a word. It's nice, the silence. I don't want to talk, filling the world with words that have no chance of making sense of it all. The quiet provides the perfect backdrop for me to pull my knees up to my chest and lean against the door. My mind drifts as the browns and greens rush by, making life seem normal, even though I barely recognize it now.

Rafael's voice is quiet. "Ease up, buddy. Here, sit back."

My chair moves slightly, and I realize Santos has been resting his head on it, trying to connect us even when we couldn't be more distant. I miss him terribly, and feel foolish for it.

When the sun is low in the early-evening sky, I know we are getting close to our destination because Cruz starts opening up after tapping on his phone for a few beats at a stop sign. "El culebrón isn't going to want to be found. We have to draw him out. The giant snake creatures are obsessed with treasure, so we're stopping at a jewelry store before we get any closer. The lair isn't too far from here, where Tio Bruno's men found the husk. There's a curse tree nearby, so you'll get to see that, too."

The whole thing is gross. A snake as fat as a playscape tube slithering around was bad enough, but to add a greedy personality to it that sounds so very human is the tipping point.

Cruz turns into a strip mall a handful of minutes later and parks the car outside a jewelry store. It's twenty minutes shy of closing for the night, but that doesn't give him pause.

Cruz reaches into his wallet and hands me more bills than I know what to do with. "Go on in and get something sparkly. Nothing fake. El culebrón can sniff out the difference. Santos, can you take her in? I need to check in with Tio Bruno."

I fix Cruz with a hard stare he pretends he's too dense to

notice. He is trying to happenstance Santos and me back together, which isn't going to work. It's sweet, though, which isn't something ever thought I would say about Cruz.

Of course, the whole reason I am not going to be sticking around is because of him, so I don't let his moment of altruism stick too deep in my heart before I shake it off.

I don't fight Cruz on this, because that would involve me speaking, which I don't really feel like doing. I expect Rafael to stay with Cruz, but he exits the car with us, which makes things far less awkward from where I stand. "Let's go, *linda*." His arm finds its way around my hips, bypassing the discomfort that's been plaguing us for hours. "Buy me something pretty."

The store is one of those rich person establishments that looks down on people who don't appear well off on first glance, so the saleswoman takes her sweet time coming over to us. I don't care what we buy, since my understanding is that we will be using it as fodder for the snake.

"Anything catching your eye, *viento*?" Rafi speaks to me as if nothing at all is wrong.

Santos has posted himself at the exit, watching from afar in the silence that is slowly sinking us.

I don't bother grinning up at Rafael, since he's well-versed in faked smiles, and can spot one a mile away. "Should we get something garish and flashy to attract the most attention?"

He touches the case, dragging his finger along the glass while he studies the bracelets below. "Doesn't matter how flashy, just matters that it's real. It's the scent of the gold and gemstones el culebrón likes." Then to the saleswoman he says, "Excuse me, miss, can I get some help over here?"

The saleswoman takes her sweet time coming over to us before plastering on a syrupy grin. "What can I show you two today?"

"I need three of your flashiest bracelets for men. Nothing fake. My girlfriend here wants..." He turns his chin to me, chuckling when he gets a full blast of my wide eyes.

"Girlfriend" is a big word for me, and not one I use even in pretending, as we are now. I know it's all a show, but still, it's not something I am used to hearing.

Rafael has never been awkward a day in his life. His confidence breezes past my awkward nature. "She can have whatever she wants, even if she's not sure what that is."

There is a limited selection of bracelets for men, leaving Rafael to buy three plain gold bands and a few ruby rings with diamonds on the sides for the guys. I cannot picture something so blingy on Santos, who prefers things simple, or nothing at all.

The saleswoman guides me over to a selection of necklaces and asks for my birth month so she can find the matching stone. "This is our more affordable selection," she informs me.

Wow. Thanks. I guess the poverty I was born into never fully washes off.

Rafael sidles up beside me with a chiding tone. "I believe I said we didn't want anything that's fake. She needs to see your high-end selection."

I didn't realize any of that was fake. I can't tell the difference. I've never owned a real piece of jewelry before.

I don't belong in here. That's obvious to both me and the saleswoman. Mama and I got our jewelry at the dollar store, if we wore any at all, or we made it ourselves out of handcrafted beads. I worked hard for my money, and didn't waste it on sparkly things that don't matter.

But standing in this store, I am certain that *I* don't matter. I fight the urge to run out of the store, catch a bus home and hide under my covers.

Except I'm homeless.

"How will you be paying for all this?" the woman asks, dubious of our existence in her store. "Because there are no returns."

Jeez.

Rafael gives her a haughty, waspish chortle. "Well, I assumed I'd pay for it in condescending remarks and snide smiles, since that seems to do the job for you."

She balks at him while I swallow a laugh. "Excuse me?"

Rafael doesn't look at her another second but fixes me with his full attention. "What's your favorite color, *viento?*"

I don't know why this question matters so much to me. It's something people ask and then answer for me with a good-natured laugh. Everyone assumes it's blue because that's my odd eye color.

My emotions must be splattered across my face, because Rafael's brows knit, and he leans in.

"Was that the wrong question?" He touches my elbow, softening my entire being. I've been rigid for too long, carrying angst I never meant to pick up and claim as my own.

In the next breath, I'm in his embrace, my cheek pressed to his chest as his arms fall around me. Rafael doesn't struggle to keep up with my swinging emotions; he gets me enough to know that any small thing is just about too much to handle right now.

"Hey, it's alright." Rafael kisses the top of my head.

Finally I feel like I might not float away on a sea of nothingness. Someone will know my favorite color.

It's not everything—it's barely something.

Still, right now, it's enough.

Rafael holds me just like that, like a friend who knows enough about you not to let go when you're drifting.

"Purple," I whisper. "Any shade. I don't like blue."

"How could a girl with blue eyes not like the color?"

I swallow hard, willing myself to be brave. "Every now and then, when my mom was admiring my eyes, she got this worried look about her. Like she saw my father in me or something."

Rafael stiffens, but rubs my back all the same. "I take it she didn't care for the man?"

"Understatement."

And that's the furthest limit of what I'll let myself talk about regarding the man I never knew.

Rafael is a good friend, because he can hear me clamming up before I tell him I am done. He kisses the top of my head.

My eyes burn into his, admitting things that go far deeper than eye color. "I'm sorry I hurt you," I whisper.

He dips his head down and pecks my lips before I can flinch away. I don't want to change him, turning his dragon into... whatever else a dragon can turn into.

But nothing happens this time.

"See?" A lazy grin sweeps over his features as he rocks us both from side to side. "There's no reason you and I shouldn't make out all the time." He nuzzles my nose. "I am not afraid of you, so you don't need to be afraid of you, either."

Rafael studies the insecurities painting my features with such love and care; I wonder how I'll live without it once I leave them.

Without looking at the clerk, he says to her, "My girlfriend would like to buy every purple piece of jewelry in the store."

"We're closing in fifteen minutes."

I can tell her calling isn't this job, or anything people-related.

I don't realize Santos is by my side until I pull away from Rafael. He signs to the woman with unveiled agitation, *"Then you should hurry."* It's clear he is upset I am being treated like I'm in the lower rung of society.

I think Santos' signing and mouthing throws her off, because her attitude dissolves after that. Suddenly three cases are opened and velvet-lined trays are laid in front of me, teasing me with beautiful things I have no right to touch.

Rafael wraps Santos' arm around my shoulder, gluing us together when I've been certain the distance would take us over.

I nod at everything, since it doesn't much matter if I like it or not. It's snake bait, after all.

Rafael leans in to whisper in my ear, brushing my hair over my shoulder. "Make sure the rings fit. They make your punches that much more painful."

"Fine, but only if you pick out something for Eva, too. She let me wear all those dresses. I'd like to bring her back something nice to say thank you. I don't know her that well, though, so you should pick it out."

"On it, boss lady." Rafael rounds the corner of the case to look at the necklaces. Now he's scrutinizing every angle, studying the jewels for the absolute best one in the store. Eva will be able to spot inferior quality a mile away.

Santos runs his thumb along the amethyst stones in each ring before he tries it on me. He slides them on and off, collecting a pile of rings that fit, and pushing the ones that don't to the side.

It's messing with my head, this perfect visual. The most beautiful man is putting a ring on my finger, over and over. My insides are doing funny flips I wish I could ignore.

We keep our eyes from each other until the clerk tallies up the thousands of dollars' worth of jewelry.

Santos runs his fingers over my knuckles and mouths, *"Please, Adelita. I don't understand why you want to leave me."*

I'm so turned around, and far from my element here in

this store, surrounded by nice things. "I don't," I admit. "Cruz and I had a fight, so I pulled back. Maybe I shouldn't have pulled back from you, too. Maybe that was rash."

A hefty portion of Santos' tension deflates. He pulls me into his arms, and finally, I exhale.

No matter what feels off in my life, his embrace is where I belong right now. His body isn't confusing. The hard planes of his chest are more welcoming than a pillow, so I burrow my cheek into them. His hand sweeps slowly over my back, moving up and down because that's how sweet he is.

"I don't deserve you," I admit.

Santos' silent, unexpected laughter jostles his shoulders. When I pull back, he mouths and signs, *I was just thinking the same thing. I don't deserve you.*

"I'm sorry I'm being weird." I move my fist over my chest in the way I'm pretty sure means "sorry."

He thumps his fist to his chest in a show of loyalty to whatever it is we are to each other.

The woman packages up our things after we pay. We leave the store more united than we were when we entered.

"Put on the rings," Cruz instructs without looking at me as Santos and I slide into the back. "Did you get me something that'll leave a mark, Rafi?"

"Only the best for you."

I feel ridiculous wearing seventeen necklaces, a dozen glittering bracelets and a ring on every other finger, but I decide to trust what little information they'll give me and go for it.

No one is particularly chatty the rest of the way there. Seriousness settles inside the car as we drive down winding roads, letting me know playtime is long gone.

When we reach a field that butts up to a wooded area in the distance, Cruz pulls over and turns off the car. Bows and arrows are pulled from the trunk, but Santos jerks his head to the side for me to join him out of earshot from the other two.

"What's going on, Santos? I'm thinking this snake needs to be dealt with before Cruz loses his patience. He's doing that frustrated pacing thing he does when he doesn't get his way quick enough."

When Santos' arms coil around my hips and pull my stomach flush to his, I finally breathe again. I love the smell of him—all man and musk.

His chest quakes a few beats, like his body needed mine so badly, it's trembling now that he is getting his fix. He pulls his face back just far enough so I can read his lips. He makes the sign for Rafi, then kisses his finger before pressing the kiss to my lips with a questioning look.

"Why did Rafi kiss me?" I ask to confirm. When Santos nods, I swallow hard. "Because that's how he is. It's sweet, and doesn't mean anything other than that he's comfortable with me. Is that okay? I didn't think to ask you. Maybe I should have."

Santos tilts his head, giving me a wry grin. *If you and Rafi want to kiss, I don't care about that. Rafi's just like that. I would never take love away from my brother, or away from you.*

I swallow hard and brave through the muck. "I flirted with Cruz. I let him kiss my wrist. It got… heated." My words come out flat. I worry Santos is not absorbing the gravity of my betrayal. "It was a mistake. I'm not sure why I got caught up in it, but I'm sorry."

Santos purses his lips, as if he can't understand why my flirting with Cruz is a problem.

I really don't understand their dynamic.

"I let him kiss my wrist," I repeat, concerned Santos is not as upset as he should be with me.

"Is that not allowed?"

I splutter through my response. "I mean, usually, no. Not that way, at least."

His hand signs slowly, making sure I catch every word. *"I hold nothing back from my brothers, and nothing back from you. If you want him to kiss your wrist, that's okay. If you didn't and he did it anyway, then that's a problem I can talk to Cruz about."*

I blink at him, unsure what to make of this whole thing. "Okay. I'm sorry I ran away from you, at least. I should've told you last night the second it happened." I lower my chin. "I did want him to kiss my wrist, but it turns out he was only being flirty with me to get information about my mother. He was manipulating me. I don't like kisses that are lies."

Santos' jaw firms. *"He should not have done that. Rafi and I will set him straight."*

Then his eyes take on a note of longing that is so sincere, it breaks my heart a little bit. He points to himself, then kisses his finger again before pressing it to my lips with that same inquisitive look he gave me before.

My tongue runs across the inside of my top row of teeth. "I'm worried my kiss will hurt you. It changed Rafi's dragon. Will it do something to your wolf?"

Santos mouths and signs, *"It's worth it."* He holds onto my hand, tracing my fingernails with the pad of his thumb. *"You want to leave us."*

I lower my chin. "I flirted with Cruz, and you're being nice to me. I shouldn't be here. I need to be away. This is too confusing."

Santos doesn't conceal the hurt in his eyes, even as he brings my hand to rest on his cheek. *"Stay with me? Even when it's hard, will you stay with me?"*

He's too beautiful. Too sincere. Too perfect.

I should say no, but when I open my mouth, what tumbles out is a shaky, "Yes. I'll stay with you."

Cruz's voice breaks us apart just when we start to lean in.

"Let's go, you two. Glad you made up and all, but we've got a snake to kill."

I want to shove Cruz in his stupid face. Santos cannot disobey Cruz, though I can tell he wants nothing more than exactly that right now.

I lean up on my toes and curve my good arm around Santos' neck, awkward as I am with my sling. Instead of his lips, my kiss lands on his cheek. Then I run my nose along his jawline, inhaling his vulnerability so deeply, I swear it's the only scent in the world.

"After we defeat the snake," I tease him. "Will you kiss me then? I don't want you distracted out there. In fact, the quicker this whole battle ends, the sooner I will be kissing you."

His lashes flutter shut and his arms tighten around me. Visible waves of lust shudder through his body, which is pressed up to mine. I love seeing this side of him—vulnerable and needing me.

Cruz calls us again, this time with more bark to his tone.

Santos pulls away, drawing his short sword from the sheath he fastened on his belt. Determination takes over his face as he grabs up a bottle of liquid from the trunk, stomps past Cruz, Rafi and me, ready to get this beast killed as quick as possible.

22

CRUZ'S ALMOST-APPRENTICE
CRUZ

Santos grips the bottle of *aguardiente* and sets the pace at a run. I am too prideful to admit I have a hard time keeping up with him. He's got renewed fire lit under his feet. I have no idea where it came from, but I am grateful his head is so in the game. I thought his focus would be divided with Adelita near, but his sole goal seems to be to get this over with in record time.

Santos only stops to sniff the air like a bloodhound, leading the way when he catches the stench of decay. Who knows how many dead animal and human bodies el culebrón has been squirreling away in its underground hoard. I can only hope he's got his three long hairs still attached, otherwise we will have to deal with his master, which is never fun.

Santos slows at a clearing and dumps the bottle of *aguardiente* on the forest floor. The liquid has no smell to us, but el culebrón can sniff the stuff out from a mile away. It's an old trick of the Kalku Santos taught us. The clear liquid helps to lower el culebrón's guard so he reveals himself to us.

"Wait! Santos, hold up." I slow to a jog, holding a stitch in my side. It's humiliating that Santos doesn't look the least bit winded, and Adelita's weariness only surfaces in a quiet, "Whew!"

Rafael is leaner and lankier than I am, and doesn't look nearly as breathless. "Need a second, chief?" he teases, though I can tell he is grateful for the break.

"Shut up. I didn't know we were going to be running. I need a second to catch Adelita up on el culebrón." I double over, taking more than a few breaths to steady myself. "If he's got three long hairs on his head, then it's just him we have to worry about. He'll be drawn to the jewels, so feel free to throw a couple necklaces away from where you're standing if he's coming at you too fast. He wants the treasure, not you."

Her nose scrunches. "Three long hairs on a snake? Weird."

"Well, his whole body is hairy, so brace yourself for that. And his head looks like a cow's head."

"What?"

I don't know why that's the part that scares her, but her eyes widen and her whole body seems to tighten.

I wave off her angst. "If he doesn't have the three long hairs atop his head, then someone has taken him into captivity. The reason someone would want to capture el culebrón is so that the snake can fetch his master more gold and treasure. If that's the case, we've got two monsters to deal with. People who own culebróns generally aren't all that reputable. They are more the enslave-someone-to-prosper kinds of degenerates."

"So we're hoping it's got its three long pieces of hair?"

I nod, grateful she understands. "We're very much hoping for that because the kill will be far easier, though no piece of cake. Another thing about el culebrón is that it gravitates to great magic when there isn't treasure around. It's the next best thing to something shiny. Can you guess at what might be in the forest that holds great magic?"

Santos is restless to keep going, but it's the longest Adelita has looked directly at me since last night, so I draw out the story.

She does a one-armed shrug. "I mean, don't the Kalku do lots of magic in their caves?"

"No Kalku in these parts. The curse trees, Adelita. If there is a culebrón in these woods on his own free will, then I'm willing to bet he has set up his hoard near the curse tree that's in the forest. Play your cards right, and you just might be able to see your very first curse tree. They love those. Something about the magic draws them in."

Her mouth pops open as she factors in this new information. "Is it Santos' curse tree? Is the axe that cursed him in here?"

I shake my head. "That's clear on the other side of the country, but you might get to see other people's curse axes." I look her over, and though I know Adelita is far stronger than I am at my best, she still looks so very small. "You. How's your shoulder holding up?"

"It hasn't fallen off yet," she replies, which I know means it's still hurting her. "I'm fine, Cruz."

My eyes flick to the guys. "Santos, you take point on this. Adelita, stick close to me."

Her scowl is predictable, but I cannot help but think how cute it is. "I'm not useless, you know. You don't have to babysit me."

"Have you ever fought a regular-sized snake before?"

"No," she sulks.

"I've killed five culebróns in my life. Rafi's killed two."

Rafi stands straighter. "Hey! Don't say it like that."

I frown. "Like what?"

"Like two is no big deal."

I exhale through my nose in his direction. "As I was saying, stay with me, Addy. Not everything is about strength. Sometimes it's about knowing your enemy, which you don't."

Then, to mollify her wounded pride, I add, "But the longer you stick with us, the more trips like this we'll go on. You'll get the hang of it."

"Like an internship? Am I like your apprentice?"

I swear, something in the air clicks, and for a solid five seconds, I love her. "Yes. You can be my apprentice." That's the perfect role for her. It'll keep her close, but define our roles so much better. She's been floating around like this half-girlfriend, half-sister. This is way better. "I'll start training you as soon as we get back to the village."

All the hope on her face closes off in the next breath. "Pass. More time with you isn't what either of us need."

It's like she knocked the wind out of me, reminding me without saying as much that I sacrificed all trust between us when I seduced information from her in the hotel room.

I guess it was too much to hope she would forgive and forget. Just because she's agreed to stay with us instead of split and run doesn't mean she is staying with me. She's sticking around for Santos. For Rafi.

I am the reason she was gearing up to leave.

I decide to tread lightly. "Well, the offer stands, if you ever want to take me up on it."

Rafi sniggers. "I think I just saw your ego grow three sizes and then deflate."

Santos glowers at me and points to her wounded shoulder, laying down the law.

I backpedal, holding up my hands. "But if you let me train you, it won't be like the last time. Not where I'll hurt your shoulder too badly."

Adelita's chin firms with defiance. "I can handle it. What I can't handle is you all treating me like my strength isn't a thing. I am an asset, and I don't want to be benched."

The fight in her feels like we are finally speaking the same language. "Fair enough. Until you get the hang of things, you're with me. Take it or wait in the car."

"Fine. How many of these things have you killed, Santos?" she asks, clutching the knife I bought her in her good hand.

He shrugs, because it's so many, he's likely lost count. *"Father always had one near the caves. It was to Santiago and me to train it. I can handle the venom, but Cruz is right. Stay with him. I will handle it."*

She frowns. "Why don't you all just lock me in the car with a lollipop?"

"I didn't bring any candy," I tease. "Let's go. Santos, you lead the way." Then for Adelita's benefit, I add, "El culebrón hunts anything alive so it can drain the blood. Fresh blood is what it lives off of. It stashes the bodies in its nest, so you can find it usually by the stench of decaying bodies."

Her nose crinkles, and I can't help it. I have to ruffle her hair.

She shoves me away, which makes me chuckle for some reason.

Rafael's eyes widen. He grins at me like he has never seen me do anything so ridiculous.

She shoves at me with far more aggression than I'm expecting. "Don't mess with me. Don't touch me. I don't trust you, and you earned every bit of that slap across the face I gave you back in the hotel. There's no part of you that should be anywhere near me."

I lower my chin in submission because she is right. I hold up my hands. We cannot go into a battle like this. "You're right. I shouldn't have..." But I can't say it in front of the guys. I seduced her to get information. I think she would have preferred the torture method. "It was mean, what I did. I'm..." I lower my voice because I'm painfully aware of Rafi and Santos staring at me in fascination. "I'm sorry," I grumble.

Addy's shoulders lower. "I forgive you. But still, stay away from me."

"That's fair."

Rafi covers his snigger. "Did you just apologize? Where is my camera? Baby's first apology. Wow. Dad won't believe this."

I glower at him and jerk my chin toward the heart of the forest, where I think the hint of the stench is coming from. "Let's go."

23

EL CULEBRÓN

CRUZ

Santos takes off at a sprint, like every minute of our conversation has pulled him tighter and tighter, readying him to spring into action.

Rafael is hot on his heels, but Adelita slows her pace for me, which is equal amounts insulting and annoying. Still, I was a jerk, so I don't say anything acerbic.

We run for approximately a hundred-thousand-million miles, and by the time we reach the sound of Rafi's grunts and Santos' knife swishing through the air, most of the damage is already done.

Santos' dagger is sticking out of the poor beast's eye. Santos hops up on top of the snake and runs down the length of its back. He doesn't brace himself as he lunges for the flicking tail.

I hate that he goes for the eyes every time we kill a beast. I mean, it's practical, but it's a sign of his cruel Kalku training.

Though I thought I explained the creature well enough, Adelita is stunned into stillness, her knife useless in her hand. The cow's head on the snake body is disorienting, but the sheer size of the snake is enough to make anyone gasp.

Though I've dealt with these every now and again during my time on the field, they still spook me.

When fire erupts from el culebrón's long-toothed maw, Adelita shrieks. "You never told me it breathed fire!"

I grimace. "Did I not mention that? Oops."

"Oops? Are you freaking kidding me?" But her eyes aren't on the fire any longer; they fix themselves on Santos.

Before I can calm her down, fear rips across her face and pushes her into action. She runs at the middle of the snake's body, stabbing her knife into its side and dragging the blade to slow him down. Maybe she wants to give the snake a distraction while Santos fights with the tail, but it's a bad idea. If she would listen to me, I could tell her that stabbing through the middle does precious little, and puts you wide open for attacks from the head or the tail.

As I predicted, her assault is hardly effective, and only manages to draw the thrashing culebrón's attention to her with more fury.

My legs swallow up the distance between us. I'm sweating from the run combined with the prospect of losing a daughter of Máximo. All it would take is a blast of a beast's fiery breath. "Back up, Addy! I've got this."

But she won't be reasoned with. I'm fairly certain she's possessed or something, what with the wild, untrained way she's slicing. Poor girl is terrified, and she's mutilating at random because that is her best bet at being helpful.

I really need to train her.

At least the beast has its three hairs, so there won't be an unscrupulous master to deal with.

Just a hairy, cow-headed snake the length of several houses.

Rafael knows how better to end this, so his knife doesn't falter when he slices across the neck of the monster. It's not enough to kill, but it does the trick of slowing it down and drawing its eyes from Adelita.

This is a mess. This whole thing. If it was just the three of us, we'd be much farther along by now. But we're all trying to throw ourselves further into the danger to shield Adelita, which is distracting us from performing the kill that would end this whole fiasco far quicker.

El culebrón screeches so loudly, I wince. I forgot how loud these things are when they're enraged. The sound is high-pitched and metallic, piercing the twilight as our knives penetrate his thick skin.

Santos is sawing through its tail, which is often used as a tool for smashing its prey.

Rafi is trying to saw off its head, but he doesn't have a good grip on the thing. The snake rears, and Adelita's knife is lost, buried in the writhing scales.

Rafi shouts for backup because the snake is too wild with pain now, fighting for its life in darting attacks and squirming jerks.

I'm already clearing the gap between us to offer up some help when a blast of fire erupts, shooting at a downward angle from its craned neck.

And that's when I see it. I've been so focused on the snake itself that I forgot about the curse tree just a stone's throw away. It's a small, knotty oak, no doubt refusing to grow another inch, riddled with curses as it is. A handful of golden axes stick out at random from the trunk, announcing to the forest the horrors they've brought into the world.

Just as I'm staring at the thing, the great snake belches a wave of flames directly at it.

The curse tree catches on fire, which is a new horror all its own. We are in the middle of a forest. While there is no chance the curse axes are going anywhere, unmeltable as they are, the rest of the foliage around us could go up in flames with the slightest shift of the early evening breeze.

Adelita screams when Santos is thrown off his perch. Again, my attention is divided. Having her here is making me a terrible leader. My eyes keep tracking her movements to make sure she is safe.

No, no. Kill the snake first, put out the fire on the curse tree, then make sure Adelita is alright.

I grit my teeth as I jump up and wrap my arms around the neck in a bloody bearhug. My weight anchors el culebrón's jerking head just enough for Rafi to get back to work, sawing through its neck.

When Adelita catches my eye as she climbs overtop the snake and slides down the other side, I call out to her to fall back. I am not surprised when she doesn't listen, but I am horrified in my shock when she bolts straight for the tree that's on fire.

I barely understand what I'm seeing when my eyes fix on what can't possibly be.

Adelita reaches into the fire with a scream, nearly stopping my heart dead in its tracks. Her arm is no doubt burning as she yanks at one of the axe handles.

"You can't get it out! It's not possible!" I shout to her, pretty sure we already went over this. "Only the one who set the curse can remove it! Get back, Adelita!"

But Addy is a woman possessed as she tugs and grunts. The fire crawls toward her arm faster than I can come up with the words to convince her to stop what she is doing and run.

When Adelita's arm finally yanks backwards with a pained howl, I heave my relief that she has given up on the effort of doing the impossible. I've got my hands full, struggling with el culebrón's neck. I'm trying to pin it to the ground to give Rafi a clearer target.

It's not until I hear her shouts of effort that I understand Adelita is standing behind me on the other side of the neck from Rafi. She's hacking away at the head with a blind ferocity. She's a mixture of terrifying force and—fine, I'll say it— she's the sexiest warrior I've ever seen.

I don't understand what I'm looking at when Adelita's arm yanks backward and comes down again in a swoop that does far more damage than Rafi's sword. She's got infinitely more muscle than he does, but I swear aloud when my eyes catch on the other thing she has that we don't.

It's not possible. I don't understand it. There's no way she could have...

The golden axe glints in the moonlight, dripping with blood as Adelita hefts the tool downward with all her might. I swallow my shock as Adelita ends el culebrón's life with a final cry that releases a hiss of smoke into the night air.

She can't possibly have done it, and yet I saw her yank the axe free.

Whatever I thought we were getting ourselves into, traveling with her, I had no idea.

24

CURSE AXES

SANTOS

She is burning. Adelita's flesh is burning, I just know it. Her hand is probably branded with the etchings from the curse axe's handle. It's an effort, but I finally manage to pry it from her clutched fist. The stench of a campfire takes over my entire being as I study her palm, grateful that no, nothing burned her bad enough to leave a brand in her skin.

Still, I tear off her rings before the gold can embed itself in her flesh, then I lay her on the grass and fall to my knees beside her, desperate to make all traces of her pain go away.

Cruz is shouting out a stream of "That's impossible," followed by "How? How did you yank a curse axe from the tree? How?"

I don't care about any of it. Adelita has been burned. My heart is singed along with her soft skin. Her hand all the way to her forearm is every angry shade of pink, though there's no charred black around her fingers. Maybe she got to the axe before the fire licked her skin too many times.

The heat from the handle of the axe burned her palm a modest amount, though, so I focus my terror on that.

Her noises of distress are pinned between pursed lips. I can tell she is in agony, but she's trying to spare me the heartbreak of hearing it.

I have nothing. My healer's bag is in the trunk a couple miles away. She is in pain now, and I don't know how to heal her. If only I could speak, I could say something to soothe her. But I have nothing.

I dig furiously at the earth, knowing that might lower the burn temperature by a few degrees. I can't shovel at the dirt fast enough, muddying my fingers and clawing away at the earth as deep as I can so her arm can be buried and hopefully cooled. I just need her agony lowered enough to erase that scared look that sears my insides.

"Is it b-bad? Will it heal?"

In the back of my brain, I know she will be fine. The fire didn't have much time to damage her skin more than the inevitable few blisters.

Still, I panic. I rest her arm in the trench I dug for her and cover it. If anything might help even the smallest amount, I will make it happen.

I do my best to answer her with what I hope is a reassuring smile, but it probably looks more like unmitigated terror. *Why did you do that?* I ask her, hoping she can make out my lips in the twilight.

"What? I don't know what you're saying."

Rafael yells at Cruz to help him put out the fire on the curse tree.

Cruz snaps back to attention and runs to the danger, as is his way. They take off their shirts and slap at the fire, suffocating it as best they can so it doesn't spread to the rest of the forest. I tear my own top off and toss it toward them to use as they need it.

It takes the entire time until the curse tree's flames are

snuffed out for Adelita's whimpering to quiet into hiccupped breathing.

I want to put her mind at ease. I want to pick her up and run her clear out of this place. I want to make her whole world better. I want...

Maybe I want too much, but I can't help myself.

Adelita is scared as she looks up at me. When she finally speaks, her voice is weighted with the ripples of fear from the fight. "That snake was way bigger than I thought it would be."

I kiss her smoky forehead, vowing in my silence that I will never let something like this happen to her ever again.

When Rafi and Cruz come over after extinguishing the flames, they sit on the patchy grass beside us, their knees bent up. We all wait for Cruz to say something that might force this whole mess to make sense. Right now, I'm beside myself with the impossibilities of it all.

Adelita pulled a curse axe out of the tree.

My anxiety lessens when Cruz takes charge, as it always does. "Only the person who cast the curse can take it out of the tree." He rubs his temples. No matter how many different ways he says it, the whole thing still makes no sense. "How did you do that?"

Adelita is on her back blinking up at the moon. When she speaks, her voice quavers. "The snake monster was breathing fire and trying to hurt you guys! When I lost my knife, I couldn't just stand there and do nothing. There were axes in the tree, so I grabbed one from the tree while it caught fire and helped Rafi cut off its head."

Cruz's brows are pushed together, just like Rafi's. Just like mine. "But how? How did you get it out?"

"I just yanked it out. Was that not okay?"

Cruz clams up, so Rafael answers her growing worry. "It was brilliant. You helped slay el culebrón, plus you accidentally freed someone from their curse. We're just flummoxed because we don't know how you did it. It's not possible. You didn't craft the curse, so you shouldn't have been able to do that."

When Adelita moves to get up, I unearth her arm, my heart lurching when she hisses at the burn. "If it helps people, then I should take out all the axes, right?"

Rafael runs his hand over his face. "I mean, yeah. If it's possible, sure."

Her eyes flick to mine with sudden excitement. "After this, can you take me to the tree where your curse axe is stuck? Can I end your curse, like, tomorrow?"

A thousand thoughts race through my mind, stumping any coherent response.

Could she? Is it really that simple? Could this angel liberate me from my silence? Could she give me back my voice?

Thankfully, Cruz answers for me. "Santos' curse axe isn't in this forest, but we can take you there. It's a longer journey, but of course that will be the next stop."

She stands, but she's not all that steady on her feet. "Then let's do this." Her eyes are screaming with pain from the residual heat radiating through her arm, but she swallows down any protest and stalks over to the tree on rubbery legs.

"What do you need from us?" Rafael asks, following her so he can be part of the action.

She flexes her burned hand and whimpers through the agony of the simple movement. I hate this. I don't want her to be in pain.

She raises her arm to reach for one of the axes that have been etched with details of the curse it bears, but she recoils on first touch. "I can't grip anything. My palm is burned. Santos, can you undo my sling? I have to use my other hand."

I do my best to make it clear that moving her shoulder,

especially in a jerking motion with any kind of strain behind it, will damage the healing muscle.

She looks up at me with ash smeared on her forehead. "But they need me. They're cursed, Santos. If I can help them, I should. I don't care if it hurts, or if my shoulder takes longer to heal." Just when I think I can't love her more, she fixes me with that determined stare and says, "If this was your axe in this tree, no way would I stop now."

That tips it. I cannot wait another second.

Though I have never done this myself, I've seen others do it lots of times in the village. Rafael has even talked me through it before.

My hands are dirty, but I can't bring myself to stop what my entire being is yearning to do. I cup her flawless face in my hands and lower my lips to hers, unable to hold back a moment longer. Insecurity shoots through me like lightning, but it's quickly eclipsed by my need for her, for this, for us.

Her lips are soft, so velvety that I can feel them all over my body. She lets out this sweet noise of indulgence, as if I'm the spicy hot chocolate she's addicted to.

But it's me who is addicted. I need her smile, her scent— everything that makes her the woman I cannot get enough of.

Adelita's lips part and she tastes me, taking over when I am sure we can both tell I'm fumbling. She is too beautiful to be near someone like me—someone who is scarred and so very different from everyone in the village.

Only I'm not scarred anymore. She healed me, giving me back to myself with a simple kiss. I do what I can to give back to her the medicine she's been for my soul.

My arm winds around her waist while my other hand can't be convinced to part from her face.

She kisses me like she's tired of holding back.

She kisses me like she was built to show me this new side of life from which I've been separated.

She kisses me like she loves all the parts of me that don't make sense to anyone.

It's in this moment I understand that she will be the only woman I ever kiss. I can't fathom sharing this bliss with anyone else.

She tastes like nothing on earth—all sweetness and something entirely other. Adelita is my new favorite flavor.

I am her servant, her slave, yet she savors me like I am something special. Everything in me begs her for more, for this.

And without a word, she understands me and gives me what I need. As always, she is perfect.

It's a moan of bliss that escapes her and traps itself between our lips. We trade it back and forth because it belongs only to us.

The kiss fades in peppered sucks and pecks until her lidded eyes finally manage to open. She buries her face in my bare chest because she knows that's exactly where she belongs. Her staccato breath teases my skin, forcing my lashes to flutter.

My heart swells just so it can be nearer to her lips, those twin pillows that heal me and remind me where my home is.

I barely remember whether or not I'm supposed to untie her sling. I do it because she asks in a mousy voice that's so unassuming, I can't not give her whatever she wants.

And she wants me. Santos the Savage.

She leans up on her toes to bless my newly-healed cheek. The heat of her blush stays with me even after she walks away from my embrace and toward the tree. I never understood the expression before, but my knees are weak as the remnants of her kiss take their time washing over me.

Cruz keeps his eyes on the forest floor, his hands shoved into his pockets to avoid looking at either one of us.

Rafael whistles and claps, earning a light shove from Adelita, who is smirking at what we've just done.

Rafael signs to me bursts of excitement and pride that I have finally kissed a woman. Not just any woman, but the best one there could ever possibly be.

Cruz bumps my fist with his, but he keeps his gaze from mine, no doubt embarrassed by the notion of anything intimate.

I did it. I finally kissed Adelita. I cannot imagine anything better. Even the high of the fresh kill is nothing to the adrenaline that is spiking through my veins.

I feel like I could lift a truck, like there is no monster I cannot slay.

There's no hope for me now. I will never be able to look at another woman. As my eyes track her in the moonlight, even her shadow is somehow superior to all others.

All traces of lightness flee from Adelita's features as she eyes the few remaining golden axes sticking out of the tree.

This is too much distance between us, so I jog to her side and study the weapons with her.

Each one has a handle so ornately carved; they are all works of art. I run my fingers over the handle of the nearest one. My mouth falls open in wonder when I recall exactly who this axe is for.

No, I never met the person, but I sat with my brother while we listened to the curse being administered to the poor soul.

Cruz and Rafael are watching me, but Adelita doesn't understand why these axes are so very personal. Rafael interprets while I sign. *"We were never told by the Kalku, only that the person was very bad, and they needed to be cursed to save humanity. Santiago was always so intense whenever we learned of a new one taking place, like he was himself going through each curse. He shook, sometimes raking his fingers across the uneven cave walls until the tips bled. Every time he bled, it felt like part of his soul had been drained away. I will not forgive the Kalku for that."* I trace the handle, remembering this particular curse vividly. *"After a few years, I started to wonder just how much of my brother was left after all they'd taken. Now there is nothing at all."*

I don't allow myself to miss Santiago all too often. That sort of emotion only leads to despair, and not action. The only way to honor his memory is to take out the Kalku members when they finally venture into the world.

Santiago ached with each curse they made us watch. Then they would mock him when he wept.

Adelita finds her way into my arms because she knows enough of me to understand that I am in a constant state of breaking without my twin. We weren't meant to be apart, but now there is no other option for us.

She burrows into my chest, confirming that my heart is there. The aching proves there is a beat that's keeping me alive, however broken.

I shove away my despair and let her love fill my bruised parts. She leans up and kisses my lips just once, but it's enough to make my eyes close in reverence for the healing she continues to bring.

Her arm is stiff from disuse, so I massage the bicep, putting away the past so I can focus on the task at hand. *"Your shoulder isn't going to perform as well as you're used to, so be careful. If you injure yourself further, you're not helping anyone."*

Cruz translates that one for me, but she's getting so good at sign language that I am fairly certain she understood the entire thing.

She winces when I rotate her shoulder just a little, and I know this is too soon. She's going to get hurt. But judging by the sheer determination on her face, there is no talking her out of it.

I shake my head and step away. *"I can't watch. I'm sorry. I just can't. It's good that you are freeing these people from their curse, but anything that hurts you... I can't."*

I should be thicker skinned. I've seen far worse horrors than a woman's shoulder getting re-injured. But when I think of Adelita crying out in pain, my stomach churns.

Rafael grips the back of my neck and gives me a light-hearted shove toward the trees behind us. "Go on. I'll stay with her."

Adelita isn't waiting for anything now. She marches over and I find I can't look away. It's hard for her to raise her arm at all, but the handle is just above her head, so she has no other choice. Her bitten-off screams flood my ears. I'm practically turned into an animal who wants to run to his mate, and who also wants to run far from anything that sounds like she is in pain.

I drop to my knees because my instincts are all over the place. I'm not sure what to do or where to run. My fists grip on handfuls of my own hair, wishing I knew how to be who she needs.

Cruz takes over when I freeze up. He lifts her off the ground, holding her waist and anchoring her midsection against his chest so she can reach the handle without too much pain. I cannot look away when Adelita grabs onto the axe's handle, her mouth tightening with determination when it doesn't unwedge itself at first tug.

"Easy," Cruz coaches her. "Breathe through it."

Like everything else in life, Cruz always knows the right thing to do. He is calm when her pain spikes, talking her through it so she stays focused on the end goal, and not the distraction of agony.

All she needs is to anchor herself, which she does by bracing her feet against the trunk to get some leverage.

Rafael's hand covers his mouth when the axe wiggles. My jaw drops open, and though I know she ripped out the first axe, there is something wholly unbelievable when I watch the magic in action. Or the bucking of magic in action. I'm not sure what this is, but it is incredible.

It takes five hard yanks, but finally the axe pulls free. Rafael starts cussing in a barely coherent stream, moving towards the two, but giving the gilded axe a wide berth.

We're all reeling, but no one is more shocked than Cruz, who nearly drops her. He manages to slow her body as it slips down his front. Though she can clearly stand on her own when her feet touch on the grass, he doesn't release her.

His hand stays on her hip while they study the axe together.

Cruz is never comfortable with other people in his space. When Mira used to reach for him, he held her out from his body until the baby understood that her half-brother has no idea how to be near someone without needing to pull away.

Adelita is pure warmth. She would hug a cactus if she was convinced it was having a bad day.

But there they stand, with her in his arms, fingering the handle and marveling at the piece of magic gone wrong.

When I come near, Adelita hands over the axe to me, as if I am the keeper of all the things that shouldn't be. I wonder who this person was that this axe was made for, and if they yet realize how drastically their life has now changed.

The next three axes are harder for her to pull out because her shoulder is screaming for relief. She remains stubborn, though, pushing the pain to the backseat so she can fight for people she doesn't know, and who will most likely never have the opportunity to thank her.

She is sweating and crying silently when the final axe is

dislodged. Her face is gaunt and she looks like she is on the edge of her legs going out.

The axes are strung along my belt, and though she insists she can walk, I don't listen to her pride. I scoop her up with her knees hooked over my forearm and march out toward the car.

The guys hang back to search for any stolen treasure el culebrón has no doubt squirreled away in his nearby lair.

They can have their treasure. I have already found mine.

25

MOTHER AND SON

CRUZ

*A*delita is shaking from the pain of re-injuring her shoulder, so Santos is a nervous wreck. She resumed her spot next to him in the backseat, which is a relief for us all. I don't like when they're on the outs. I really don't enjoy having to feel the weight of someone else's relationship.

Still, my focus is half on the road and half on the medical care Santos is giving her. I've watched him work enough times to have a pretty good idea of when he's working with a clear head, and when he is panicking.

I swear aloud when Santos gives her too much sedative to numb her agony. He's not thinking clearly. I'm not sure he's capable of rational thought whenever she so much as sighs like she might be uncomfortable. She's only been biting her lip through discomfort, not outright howling.

I grip the steering wheel. "No! You know that's too much. She can handle a few aches. She doesn't need to be unconscious for who knows how long. You're not thinking things through, Santos. You cannot let her cloud your judgment like this."

But of course, Santos doesn't listen. There aren't any

other sounds in the universe when Adelita needs him. They are so intense. I don't know how I feel about any of it.

I glance to Rafi so I have someone to roll my eyes at, but he is staring straight ahead, his face pale with worry. "Hey, you holding on okay over there?"

Rafael doesn't bother with the lie of a nod. "I don't understand what just happened. It's not possible. I mean, only the Kalku can yank these curse axes free. Only the specific person who cast the curse, and we've killed a fair few of the Kalku. So those people were supposed to be doomed in their curse forever. I thought I knew what we were getting ourselves into, taking in what could very well be a daughter of Máximo, but this is something else entirely."

I shush him with a hiss. "She doesn't need to know about that yet." My eyes flick to the backseat. Adelita is clean passed out, so I address only Santos. "The woman the Mendez tribe rescued from Máximo's island has blue eyes. She's claiming to be Máximo's daughter. Addy told me her mother had brown eyes, so we can conclude she got her blue eyes from her father, whom she's never known." I give them five seconds to process all of that. "The Kalku targeted her more than just once, so I'm guessing it's not her strength they're after."

Santos grips my headrest, his gaze burning with intensity and fear.

I finish the assumption aloud, so we're all on the same page. "We don't know for sure that Máximo is after Addy, but it seems pretty likely, otherwise the Kalku would have focused on another victim by now. We also don't know for sure that Máximo is Addy's birth father, so we're not telling her anything like that. No need to mess her up more. But between the three of us and Tio Bruno, we need to operate going forward as if Máximo is after her because she is his daughter."

Utter silence sucks up the air in the car until Rafi speaks more than a minute later. "We're jerks for keeping the information from her. She deserves to know who her father is."

I keep my eyes on the road, my jaw tight. "Her father will be Don José. Her family will be the Cáceres tribe."

"Oh?" Rafi finally turns to fix me with a knowing stare he has no right doling out. "And are you her brother now?"

Now I'm choking the steering wheel because I don't like what he is implying.

Rafi gets back to his original thought, because he knows I will snap if he pushes me further on the issue. "This is bigger than we realized, Cruz. Do you think Máximo knows she can pull out axes and undo curses? Do you think that's why he's seeking out his daughters now, after all these years? I thought his plan was the normal megalomaniac mobster nonsense, but this is bigger. There's something we're not seeing, man. I can feel it."

I hate that my imagination didn't go that far. I should be the one thinking through all the possibilities to find the inevitability, but I'm distracted by the woman in the back-seat. "Santos, keep an eye on her breathing. That was too much sedative."

Santos has Adelita in his arms, draped across his lap. His cheek is pressed to hers, like he thinks actual healing power might be laced in his touch.

Too intense.

Rafi thinks through his plan aloud. "Tio Bruno knows? That's good, I guess. We have to tell Mom and Dad. They need to know. Then we need to make a trek to Santos' tree and get him good and uncursed."

The thought of that is so incredible, my mouth goes dry at the prospect. I glance in the rearview mirror. "You hear that, Santos? You might be singing us to sleep in a week."

Though I hoped for a miracle, I never expected something so amazing might actually be within arm's reach.

By the time we break for the night and find a hotel, Adelita only rouses when Santos shakes her, and even then, her eyes are lidded. He carries her to our room. I know she's out of it, because she lets him baby her without a fight.

Santos helps her to the bathroom, but those few steps are all she is capable of. After she washes the soot off of her, he helps her to the beds Rafi and I have pushed together when she is finally in her pajamas.

Santos is scared to leave her, even to take a shower. "I'll watch her," I volunteer quietly. "It's alright, Santos. She will heal. It just might take longer than you were hoping."

The moment Santos vanishes reluctantly into the bathroom, Rafi fixes me with that knowing stare again. "That's very nice of you, keeping an eye on the love of Santos' life while he steps away."

I want to argue that I'm supposed to watch out for her, since she is one of us, but I worry my words will come out sounding like denial. I won't give Rafi that satisfaction.

Instead I manage a surly, "Go to sleep, Rafi."

Adelita is completely out, breathing evenly and without pain, so I change into my pajamas in front of her. It's intimate, getting dressed while she's in bed just a couple feet away. Eva would joke that this situation fits my fears about relationships perfectly—keeping a woman close, but only when she is unaware and doesn't realize I actually enjoy sharing my space with someone else.

I don't go near Adelita's sleeping form until Santos emerges in his pajamas. Then I slide under the covers and fight the urge to pull her into my arms. I don't want to be with her in the same way Santos does; it's the closeness I find I don't mind with Adelita, which is a new thing for me.

Santos scoops her to his chest greedily, careful not to

jostle her shoulder too much. He is always so careful with her, this man everyone still thinks of as a savage. If only they could see him now, his face burrowed into her hair and his arm coiled protectively around her hip.

I hate that I am doing this to them, encroaching on their relationship, but the promise of a dreamless sleep is too enticing to turn down. Santos even goes so far as to rest her limp hand in mine, connecting us so I don't have to live through the torment of La Sayona.

After his shower, Rafi turns out the light and lies down on Addy's other side.

Now that no one can see me, I allow myself to need Adelita for the miracle she is. I don't like to think of anyone having to protect me, but she does it without question. My whole body relaxes because she is near—my guardian angel who will watch over me in the darkness.

The last face I see before I drift off to sleep is the same one I fix my gaze on when I wake, fully rested.

My first long inhale is laced with Adelita's natural scent. I love it so much, I bury my nose in the crook of her neck.

It's embarrassing, to be sure, but I'm so mellow after sleeping the night through that I can't bring myself to scowl.

Throughout the entire day as we drive toward the village, even my breathing feels different. It's like I'm inhaling deeper, really letting oxygen into my body. I've been living with La Sayona in this constant state of near-suffocation, but now that I am starting to sleep regularly, everything seems less intense.

The next night is much the same, but Rafi doesn't rib me about my inappropriate closeness to Adelita. We've fallen into a rhythm, the four of us. I earn less anger from Addy throughout the day, and in return, she doesn't mind that I cuddle too close in the night.

When we near the village, Santos makes a joke about Tio Bruno's perpetual scowl, which draws a laugh out of me.

When Rafi gapes at me like I've grown a third head, I shrug. "What?"

"Nothing. It's just that I haven't seen you smile this much in years. Not since we were kids. You laugh now." He's saying something meaningful, his eyes shining with contentment. "Good for you, Cruz."

My first instinct is to scowl at him, but I shrug it off as I pull under the thatched awning that reads, "Welcome to Cáceres."

That's an oxymoron. The only people welcome here are the ones who were born here. The people rarely ever leave. The intimidating walls are a testament to the importance placed on making newcomers feel unwelcome.

Adelita scowls at the border wall, as if it's been rude to her. "If you all want to bury your head in the sand, that's the way to do it. Keeping people out with a wall is disgusting. It's a great way to limit any sort of forward trajectory."

The corner of my mouth twitches, but Rafi is wearing a full-blown grin. "Is that so? Maybe you should tell the elders. They love hearing stuff like that."

Addy harrumphs, but doesn't push it further. I can only imagine how her education and fiery temper would go over with Dad and the others. Dad would smile and pat her on the head. Tio Bruno would think she was an idiot. The others who weigh in on policies can't be persuaded to move for any reason whatsoever.

I don't get more than half a mile in before I take a read on the place. People are gathered in pockets along the roadside, whispering excitedly about who knows what. Some have that furrowed brow headshake going on, while others are giddy with gossip.

"Looks like we missed something big," Rafi comments as I

pull into the garage, grateful to finally be home for however long we're here. I'm anxious to get Santos' curse lifted, but I doubt Dad will let me go without taking at least a day off to decompress. His words, not mine.

When we walk into the house, I expect Roberto to come bounding out from wherever he has been hiding and smash into me with a greeting, but there's nothing. The house is quiet, which is something I always wish for but never get.

"Dad?" We move through the hallways and set our backpacks down in our respective rooms, but still there is no one.

I deposit Adelita and Santos in his room and leave Rafi to his wandering while I venture into the kitchen. There I find Consuela feeding Mira something the toddler would clearly rather wear than eat. "Hey, Consuela. Is Dad around?"

She flips her long black waves over her shoulder, her eyes fixed on Mira's stubborn strained-pea-covered scowl. "He's in the barracks with Tio Bruno. Been there all day. How was your mission?"

Consuela is always trying to draw me into conversation, and I usually find a quick way out of it. But today, I indulge her, mainly because I'm not ready to go down to the barracks and get to the bottom of whatever big deal happened while I was away. I can feel it in the air that something is off. "It was good, actually. Better than we could've hoped."

Her eyebrows raise, no doubt shocked I'm capable of speaking to her in more than grunts. "Really? You didn't have any trouble killing el culebrón, then?"

"Nah. I don't think the old snake's heart was really in it. It was barely a fight," I lie.

"That *is* a good mission. The uneventful kinds are the ones I hope you always have."

I take an apple from the bowl on the counter and carve out a big bite. "Man, I'm tired of takeout and convenience store food. An apple is like, the best thing in the world right now."

It's far more than the mumbles and one-word non-conversations I usually grant my stepmother. Consuela pounces on the tidbit, gaping at me like I've told her my true passion is singing showtunes. "Let me fix you a salad, then. I can shave some apples into it, if you'd like."

She is so eager to be helpful, which is usually my cue to leave. I had a hard time accepting that this far younger woman wasn't in it for Dad's money, but even I have to admit that, from the beginning, she's been in it because she loves him. Consuela is only five years older than I am, so it's still weird, to be sure, but maybe that is something I can finally let go.

"Do we have those dried cranberries? Maybe we should make a big salad. I know Adelita and the guys are probably sick of road meals, too." I fish around in the cupboard while she scatters dry cereal on Mira's high chair tray.

With her daughter thoroughly occupied, Consuela pulls out lettuce, cilantro, tomato, blue cheese and dressing from the fridge.

"Dried cranberries are up in the top cabinet over there."

And so we make a salad together, this strange version of mother and son. I don't think I've ever spent this much time with Consuela.

"How is Santos holding up? He seemed a little different the last time you guys were home."

I pull out my dagger to cut the tomato, but Consuela puts her hand on my wrist to stave my progress.

"A kitchen knife might be best," she suggests without drawing too much attention to my idiocy. "More hygienic."

"Of course. People with kitchens don't use daggers to slice tomatoes." I cast around for a proper knife, but she's already sliding one toward me, her eyes downward like she is afraid I might snap.

Do I really do that to people? Do I put them so on edge that they are afraid of eye contact?

I clear my throat and keep my focus on the tomato while I chop it up.

This knife sucks.

"Santos is better than ever. He and Adelita are hitting a pretty heavy rhythm. It's strange to watch, to be honest. But I've never seen Santos happier. He's trying new things. She's slowly stripping away that edge that always keeps him at arm's length. He tried sugar for her."

Consuela smiles as she chops the lettuce in big chunks. "I can't wait to get to know her better. Do you think I'll get that chance before you all leave again?"

"Not sure. We're only back for a day or so."

Her shoulders fall, as if me being around is something she looks forward to. "Okay. I know Roberto will be sad to see you go so soon."

"He'll be fine. He's young."

"No, he's not."

Consuela rarely corrects me. It stops me short, giving me the opportunity to study the lines around her eyes. She looks sad, unsure of herself. Like she has been cooped up indoors for too long. "What's going on, Consuela?"

Emotion shimmers in her eyes. She knows how much I hate the sight of stuff like that, but she's so distraught that she can't hold it back for my comfort's sake. "Tio Bruno let Roberto go into the barracks with him. He's going to train him, let him see things a boy shouldn't know about. My baby used to fight shadows with wooden swords, but Tio Bruno gave him a real knife!"

My frown chases away all traces of lightness. "He's only six."

She sniffs. "He's seven."

I grimace at my idiocy. He's my half-brother, and I don't even know how old he is. That's gotta be bad.

Adelita would engage. She would get Consuela talking. I see emotion and I want to run the other way.

Instead of defaulting to my tried and true caveman ways, I press into the urge to do better—to *be* better.

I set down the kitchen knife and arrest the bowl of lettuce from Consuela's hands. "Let's get you some fresh air." When she looks resistant to the idea, I offer her my elbow. "I'll go with you."

She gapes at me like I've grown a third head. "What? You want... You want to spend time with me?"

I scratch my head. "Isn't that what we've been doing?" When she nods, still flummoxed, I grab a second apple from the bowl. "I'll go ask Rafi to keep an eye on Mira. You look like you could use a break. Dad is still at the barracks?"

She nods. "He's talking with Tio Bruno. The rescue team that liberated the woman from Máximo's island ran into some trouble."

"Oh?"

She nods. "Apparently, one of them saw something that drove him mad. The Mendez people aren't equipped to deal with that, so they sent him to us, hoping Santos might be able to help, since he used to live with the Kalku."

"Yikes. What drove him mad?"

She shrugs. "Something he saw on the island. No one has been able to get it out of him yet. That's the main thing Bruno's been dealing with."

"I'll ask Santos to take a look."

"Thanks. Your uncle is extra unpleasant lately."

"I cannot imagine him unpleasant."

We share a conspiratorial snigger, and it actually feels nice.

Consuela's shoulders relax as she fills me in on all that I've missed. "The Mendez tribe is having issues with their rescue while she's on the mend. If only the poor woman was treated how you, Rafi and Santos dote on Adelita."

I ignore that last comment because it's just not true. I mean, Adelita is down the hall in *Santos'* bedroom, not mine. I don't dote on Addy. That's ridiculous.

Yet even as I dismiss the thought, I fight the urge to go check on her.

"No wonder everyone is all pinched and excited. Is she..." I hate the question before I can finish it.

"She's badly hurt, from what I gather. Blue eyes, same as Adelita's. They're still trying to get her to talk. Apparently she's not a sharer."

I let out a one-noted humorless laugh. The sisters are similar in that area.

"Maybe you could take Adelita to the Mendez tribe so they can meet."

My jaw tightens. "This isn't the right time for us, honestly. I'm glad the Mendez tribe still has her. Adelita needs to rest. She doesn't need to be thrown into yet more drama before she's even on her feet again. Plus, we're not positive the two are related. It's a hunch, and nothing more. No use dragging her into something that might get her hopes up, only to not be true."

"I can tell you've thought about this."

I take in Consuela's knitted brows with concern tugging down the corners of my mouth. "Why? Is that not the right move?"

"It's very considerate. That's good. You're just usually more about the job than about the people. I think it's great you are considering all the angles. It's wise. Something your father would do."

"Thanks." It's weird, this moment of Consuela validating

my judgment and me accepting it for the compliment it is. "I'll go get Rafi to watch Mira for you."

I trot down the hallways and drag him out of his room. Then I gather up everyone's clothes from their packs and shove them into a hamper that I hand off to the housekeeper, with the instructions that she is to wash and return them as soon as possible, so we can head out again.

When I trot into the kitchen with Rafi, Consuela has finished assembling the salad and slides the massive bowl into the fridge.

I offer my stepmom my arm. She takes it once more with wide eyes that inform me I'm acting strange.

I don't care. Dad is always on my case to act proper when I'm out in the village. I'm just doing what he wants.

"You're calm. What happened on the mission that made you so… this?"

I'm not sure if I should take offense. Instead of letting my feathers get ruffled, I let her in on my little secret. "I'm sleeping now. La Sayona is leaving me alone."

She stops and blinks at me in confusion. "What?" Then fear flashes in her brown eyes. "Does that mean she is coming for José again?"

I shake my head. "I don't think so. It's been a week or so now, and no dreams at all." Most people beg for beautiful dreams and are crushed when they endure the occasional nightmare. For me, the best thing in the world has been to not dream at all.

Her nails dig into my arm as her mind races to factor in this new information. "A week? If she was going to move back in on your father, she would have already done it by now. La Sayona is gone? I don't understand. How can she… How did you…"

I give her a smirk and a shrug as we walk into the twilight. For some reason, I don't want to tell them it's

Adelita who chased away my demon. She's pretty private, and I'm not sure if she wants the family to know just yet.

Consuela gawks as if me smiling is a greater shock than our family's tormentor taking a hiatus. I don't answer her, but walk with her to the barracks, where Roberto's howls quicken my footsteps.

26

THINGS CHANGE

ADELITA

"*I* thought we were going to stick around for a day or two." I look out the window for anything to clue me in as to why I was hurried out in the dead of night.

Other than that, the evening air is peaceful as Cruz drives with one hand and slams coffee with the other.

"Things change."

My mouth draws to the side as I study Cruz's stiff neck and taut forearm while he turns the steering wheel. "Care to elaborate?"

"Nope. Get some shuteye back there. By morning, we'll be that much closer to Santos' curse tree." His eyes flick to Santos' in the rearview mirror. "You ready for that, man? Ready to tell me what you really think of me?"

Santos holds up his middle finger with a tired smile just to make Cruz laugh. He's got his other arm around me, which grants me a wave of peace to cancel out the side-eye I'm giving Cruz at his evasive nature.

"Consuela was crying," I comment, fishing for an explanation.

"Moms do that when their children are injured during a

sparring match. Roberto will be fine. It's a sprain, is all."
Though even as Cruz tries to make it all sound like no big
deal, I can see the tension tightening the muscles in his neck.

I decide to leave it alone.

Rafael fills in the blanks. "Whenever Cruz stands up to
Tio Bruno, we make a quick exit. Tio Bruno doesn't exactly
invite constructive criticism."

Before I can ask, Santos signs, *"Roberto is okay. I checked on
him before we left."*

I relax into Santos' side, grateful that he checked on the
little mini-Cruz.

Santos presses a kiss to my temple, and I swear I can't
remember feeling so very cherished. Maybe I wouldn't be so
okay with our public display if it weren't for the fact that we
are never alone. Thus, the guys just have to deal with the
occasional brush of affection.

Okay, our fondness is more "constant" than "occasional".

Rafael has been so quiet; I thought he'd fallen asleep a few
miles back. When he speaks, I can tell sleep is the last thing
on his mind. "Adelita, what do you know about your father?"

It's a strange question, to be sure, but Cruz is the one
most upset by it. He jerks the car into the next lane by
mistake and slowly corrects with a seethe I can feel wafting
in the air and seeping into my pores. He turns on the radio so
loud, I flinch, drowning out any attempts at an answer.

Rafael jerks the knob with a scowl he is not bothering to
conceal. "Tell me. Your mother must've mentioned him."

No matter how insistent the moon is that the world must
sleep, I am wide awake now. My shoulder is pinned in place
by Santos' sling, but my one free arm attempts a shrug as I sit
up straight. Santos' warmth has gone rigid, practically
pinging my body away from his.

Santos avoids my gaze, staring out the window as if
something fascinating lurks just outside. "I dunno, Rafi.

Women don't usually get all chatty with their daughters about the men who knock them up and leave them without so much as a phone number after a one-night stand."

He doesn't need to know that Mom was afraid of him. The guys don't need the information that we moved around so much because she didn't want him to find her.

He was a bad guy. That's all I know.

"Your birth certificate has only your mother's name on it. Can I assume you never met him?"

My mouth drops open in stunned silence. "You dug up my birth certificate?"

Cruz hisses under his breath but keeps his eyes forward. "Way to ease her into it all."

"Ease me into what?" My spine is a steel rod, unbending and stiff with a chill I cannot shake. I study Rafael's taut jaw, Cruz's grip of the steering wheel and Santos' avoidance.

They know something. They are keeping information from me that I should have. They know more about me than I do.

Vomit churns in my gut.

My fingernails ache to be bitten, so I chew on the end of my thumbnail. Maybe if it stays in my mouth, I won't say all the things that are burning inside of me. The questions I asked Mama that she either couldn't answer—or worse— wouldn't.

Rafael turns in his seat, gripping the headrest as he faces me with a hard edge to him. His eyes are much better put to use with laughter. "Have you ever met your father?"

It's such a horribly personal question for him to ask me. I've only known Rafi a short time. Yet here he is, demanding to know something I only ever ask myself after I've had two glasses of wine on an empty stomach.

I turn my chin from left to right, unable to say the words that should not affect me at all in my twenties.

But they do. Maybe they always will.

"Leave it alone," Cruz orders Rafael. It's a clear command to fall in line, which Rafi flicks aside like a bothersome fly.

"Why would you ask me that?" I manage to say, my voice barely above a whisper.

When Rafael turns back around in his seat, my gaze bounces to Santos, who is hugging his side and looking away from my confusion as if it's a creature that is going to unleash on him.

"Santos?" I'm worried now, scared that something might be bigger than even my freaky strength can handle.

Santos glares at the back of Rafael's head, but the harsh expression fades to worry when his gaze pings to me and then darts away like a penitent puppy.

"Will someone tell me what's going on?"

Cruz cusses loudly and pulls over on the side of the free-way. He shoves Rafael and scowls at me, as if I am the prob-lem. "Let's go for a walk."

My palms are damp with nerves when I pop open the door and follow Cruz out into the night. Santos and Rafael remain in the car like misbehaving children who don't want to be scolded.

"Cruz, what? I don't understand. Why does Rafi care about who my dad is?"

Cruz shoves his hands in his pockets, setting a slow pace away from the car. I feel like we are marching to my death, or something ominous from which I will never recover.

Cruz exhales loudly. "For the record, I wasn't going to tell you any of this until we were more settled. You just learned about the Kalku and the tribe and all of it. The rest of it is a story for another day."

"Now seems like as good a time as any." There aren't any vehicles driving by at this time of night. The headlights from his car cast illumination on our shoes, but keep the rest of our sins in the dark.

I can see half of Cruz's face—enough to tell that he's spooked and he needs a shave.

"I'm bad at this, but you're my apprentice now and Rafi has a big stinking mouth, so here I am." Cruz runs his hand over his face. I can tell the coffee hasn't been doing its due diligence in keeping him caffeinated. He is exhausted, but still muscling through his obvious discomfort to tell me what I have every right to know. "The Kalku factions are run by a man named Máximo."

"Right. The man on the island who's crazy powerful."

"Máximo is a ruthless monster, always picking and choosing who gets to live, and who gets sacrificed for not performing to their best ability. Even among the people who serve him faithfully. He only cares about his own immortality and stretching the boundaries of magic."

"And... what? What does this have to do with me? Why did we have to leave the village only a couple hours after we got there?" I want to shake Cruz, demand he spit it out, whatever it is.

He rubs the nape of his neck. "Máximo was cursed, like, a century ago when he was barely an adult. Probably before the immortality thing. One of the elders in his cave saw what a tyrant he was and cursed him."

"What's the curse?"

"That whatever he most desires will always be just out of his reach."

I wince. "Yikes. That's a bad one."

Cruz's head bobs. "So when you start pulling out axes, make sure it's not his, first off. That one's kind of important. Some curses are for the good of the world. While what Máximo wanted most was to be able to break his own curse, it's remained just out of his reach."

"That's intense. Quite the crafty curse to give a wicked bad guy."

"It's fitting." Cruz clears his throat. "Máximo wanted to be able to undo his curse, but of course, the only person who could undo it was the man who put it into play." Cruz closes his eyes. "The elder who cursed him didn't know what he was getting into. Máximo tracked him down and tortured him until he cracked. The elder who cursed him finally broke down and blessed Máximo's bloodline."

My throat is dry. "What was the blessing?"

"That one of Máximo's heirs would be able to break his curse."

A ringing starts in my ears and bile begins to churn in my stomach once more.

Cruz's next words come out slow. "According to Kalku rumor, Máximo most wanted a son, so it stands to reason that if he ever did procreate, he would only be able to have daughters."

"Because anything he truly wants is kept just out of reach. That makes sense." My next words come out as a dismal grumble. "He's a jerk if he couldn't be happy with a baby girl."

Cruz laughs through his nose. "I'm sure 'jerk' is the tamest thing Máximo has ever been called."

"Cruz…"

I don't want him to continue. This is already on the edge of too much. My brain is refusing to connect the dots, dipping deeper into denial rather than dig for the truth.

"How many people have you ever met who have eyes like yours?"

No one.

But I don't want to admit that aloud. "I don't know."

Even as I step away from Cruz, he tells me things I don't want to hear. "Máximo was the only person I've ever heard of with blue eyes… until you."

I want to vomit. I want to run. I want…

I want my mama.

"You are that woman in the blessing, Addy. I'm certain of it. You can break his curse by pulling out his curse axe. I know you won't, obviously, so that's good. But it also means that you're…" He swallows hard.

Though I know the trajectory this is hurtling toward, I need him to say it out loud.

I also need to never hear it.

I stumble backward, but the words smack the air too clearly for me to pretend I can't hear them.

Cruz leaves no room for my denial, which I desperately need right now. "Adelita, your father is Máximo."

My knees are weak with regret of a life lived in the dark. I always wanted to know who my dad was, but it was impossible. A one-night stand where Mama didn't get his number and never saw him again? That kept me from looking for him my entire life. There was no point in a quest that broad. Plus, she was clearly afraid of him, moving us from town to town, always looking over her shoulder.

Did Mama know about this other world? About magic? Did she know she was hooking up with an evil immortal, not just a wicked man?

My body feels cold and my vision goes in and out of focus. I want to get out of here and go… anywhere else.

"How long have you known?" It's not the most pertinent question, but it's the only one that comes out when I open my mouth.

He licks his lower hip. "That night when I took things too far. When I pinned you to the wall and… Tio Bruno needed that information. He wanted confirmation that you are a daughter of Máximo. That your blue eyes didn't come from your mother, but from him."

I balk at him, betrayal ripping through me. "You've

known who my father is for this long, and you're just now telling me? Did the others know? Santos? Rafael?"

Cruz doesn't defend himself, but rather shoves his hands in the pockets of his jeans as his head bobs.

My world goes very still as my thoughts tunnel. "You're using me. Just like Máximo wants to do. You want me to break people's curses, like he does."

Cruz's mouth pops open. "What? No!" Then he grimaces. "I mean, I guess that's a little true, but we didn't..."

I don't want to be around Cruz, who picks and chooses what I should know about myself. I really don't want to be around Rafael, who half-tells me things, only to clam up when I need the truth.

Yet even through this, I love the three of them. Rafael, Santos, and even Cruz have wedged their way into my heart, making it so that breathing is far easier with them than without.

My voice comes out in a croak. "If I am Máximo's daughter, the Kalku aren't going to stop searching for me. Probably not ever."

Cruz's jaw firms. "I wish I could lie and tell you that's not going to happen."

"If I'm hunted, and you're with me, then the three of you are in constant danger." I close my eyes as true grief smacks my chest, making it hard to draw in a full breath.

If Cruz's stern voice is capable of sounding compassionate, that is the cadence he carries now. "Addy, that's not something for you to worry about. I always look after the guys. Haven't I kept us safe?"

"This is different. It's... If I'm with you, you'll be targeted, too."

The silence fills the space between us. Though there is nothing but fresh air, I worry I will suffocate if I look at Cruz and see the acceptance of my words splattered across his face.

I cannot bring myself to look in the direction of the car, because I know Santos is still looking away from my pain, doing as Cruz says and keeping me in the dark because Cruz will always be right, even when he is so very wrong about this.

Act or accept. Act or accept. Act or accept.

I cannot accept this. I can barely get my brain to touch it. The information is like a hot potato that burns me whenever I get too close.

Act. I'm going to act. Rationally or irrationally—it doesn't matter at this point.

I'm getting out of here. I have to protect them, and that means getting as far away from the guys as possible.

"My purse," I work out, banding my arms around my stomach. "I need my purse."

Cruz opens his mouth to protest, but it's a wasted effort. He knows he shouldn't have kept something so enormous from me. I can tell he was anticipating a fit from my end, but I don't have the wherewithal to deflect my rage onto him. Not really.

It's this Máximo person I am truly mad at. My father.

No wonder my mom was always making us move just when we would get settled at a new place.

"Your purse? Okay. I can get it."

We've wandered a fair bit away from the car, so I use the first few steps he takes away from me to step out of the headlights' range. I'm drowning in a sea of far too much, but one thing is crystal clear—I don't want to be near these guys anymore. They knew all this time, and they said nothing.

Now I wonder if they planned the mission to the culebrón, which just so happened to be near a curse tree, to test if

I am the daughter who can break the curse my father's been living with since before I was born.

I wince, not wanting to go there in my mind. I don't want to believe that could be true.

I love them.

The moment the thought ripples through my mind, I know what I need to do: I have to keep them safe.

To do that, I need to get out of here.

My feet feel like lead, but they are surprisingly silent as I hop over the railing and skitter down the grassy slope toward the main road below. Once I'm far enough away, I break into a run, ignoring the car doors slamming in the distance behind me.

I don't answer when they call my name in a panic. Minutes ago it would have tugged at my heart. Now I feel nothing.

I don't go back. Instead, I run along the road and flag down the first driver compassionate enough to stop for a crazed woman fleeing three grown men in the dead of night.

"You alright, Miss?" the mid-forties woman asks, taking in my tremulous state with a wary gaze.

"Better now. Thank you. Can you take me away from here?"

She glances over my shoulder and frowns. "I think I'd better. Get on in."

She drives off with me in the passenger's seat, my heart still thudding. I flinch when I hear the sound of my name bellowed through the dark. I don't know if they see me, but I am certain I don't want them to catch me.

The woman is silent for several beats after we lose the guys. "Where do you want me to drop you?"

"Anywhere that's not here. Please, take me wherever you're going, and I can run on foot from there."

Her black hair is tied in a tight stern librarian bun, but

there is an understanding in her eyes that assures me every-thing will somehow be okay. "It's not safe where you came from?"

I shake my head. I don't know much, but I am certain about that. They knew about my father being Máximo for who knows how long, and they kept it from me, as if my own family is privileged information I don't need to know.

And yet I'm still compelled to protect them. "Just anywhere far from here. I would really appreciate it."

She reaches over and places her hand atop mine, giving me a slight squeeze of solidarity. "Alright, then. Buckle up, sweetie. Looks like you've had a long night, and it's not halfway over. I'm Fernanda. You got a name?"

I shake my head with my best representation of an apolo-getic smile. "My name won't do you any good to know it." When my seatbelt clicks into place, I let out a quiet sob of relief.

She pulls onto the freeway, and I swear, a mountain of stress leaves me. The more miles put between me and the guys, the more I don't have to think about my absentee father who apparently only conceived me so he could undo a curse it sounds like he well-deserved.

I don't have to deal with Santos kissing me and keeping huge secrets from me that are every bit my business.

I don't have to laugh at Rafael's jokes when I know now they only exist to distract me from finding out the truth about my own life.

I don't have to think about Cruz, whose sleepless nights will no doubt match my own. I don't wish mental torture on him, but I cannot stay with them anymore. I don't want the Kalku, the tribe or any of it.

I want my Mama, who would never have lied to me about something like this.

Would she?

Fernanda's voice is quiet. "I'm heading to Baez. Does that suit you?"

"How far is that from here?"

"About twenty miles."

"That's wonderful. Thank you."

She turns on the heat when she catches my shiver. "There's a police station not too far from my place. How about I go with you in there? We can file a report on whoever you're running from."

I shake my head. "No, thanks. It's not that kind of situation. Just one I needed to get out of quickly. Thank you for this. I promise I'm not a criminal."

She chuckles softly, as if that thought never crossed her mind. "Well, I'm glad to hear that. Would you like me to take you to a motel?"

"No." My reply cracks out harsher than I mean for it to. "No, thank you. I don't have my purse on me anyway."

"So, what's your plan?"

I give her half a shrug. "I'm not sure. I'll figure something out. Just the ride is all I need right now."

"And twenty miles from now?"

Another shrug, though Fernanda deserves better. The truth is, I don't have any answers to give her. I only have an abyss of questions.

She seems to sense this, and keeps her eyes on the road. "I have a spare bedroom that's doing nothing but collecting dust these days. Maybe you can stay there until you figure out the basics, like your name."

I blink at her, in awe of humanity, and that the basic tenants of life haven't failed me thus far. No matter how cruel, life will always find a way to be kind. "Are you serious?"

Fernanda smiles at me. "Well, you already promised me you aren't a criminal. Why not?"

She offers kindness like the world is filled with buckets of the stuff to pass around at random. She spills the sweetness onto me when I need it most, and for the life of me, I'm so lost that I can't hold my tears back another second.

I barely work out a nod of gratitude before the droplets stream down my cheeks, leaving hot lines that announce my sadness to the world. "Thank you. I'll get myself together. But right now, I really need a place to fall apart."

Fernanda hugs my hand with hers, and then reaches past me into the glovebox for a wad of napkins to stem the flow of my agony. "Now, now. I'm sure we all do sometimes. Deep breaths, sweetie. Deep breaths."

I listen to her, lost as I am, and inhale the possibility of a life lived without the Kalku, without secrets and without the guys. I exhale the ache of a father I never knew, and inhale a numbness I decide will be my new best friend.

My head leans against the window, and though I don't have a plan or even a true friend, I have direction.

The road I'm aiming for is anywhere that is far away from where I've been.

Love the book? Leave a review.
Otherwise, I'll be sure Adelita
falls in love with Tio Bruno.

TWISTED HEARTS

Enjoy a free preview of *Twisted Hearts*,
book three in the "Savage Hearts" series.

HIDDEN

$\mathcal{H}$idden

Adelita

WHEN I STRETCH my arms over my head, I'm careful not to bump my hands to the ceiling. The bed I've been given is tucked into the corner of the attic in the bungalow, so I have to watch myself to make sure I don't bash my head or hands on the ceiling every morning.

You only learn that lesson the hard way once (I hope).

It has been a week since Fernanda brought me into her home. It's not every stranger who sees a woman on the verge of a nervous breakdown, being chased by three men, and drives her off to her home, no questions asked.

Fernanda lives far away from Cáceres, which is just about the best gift in the world.

Actually, a better one would be for me not to be in this

mess in the first place. That would mean I'm not Máximo's daughter—a man who is bent on gleaning power at all costs. That would also mean the Kalku aren't hunting me. The savage miscreants are trying to find me, either to bring me to Máximo, or because they want to tear my heart out of my chest, boil it down and drink the broth so they can gain my superhuman strength.

Whatever their motivation, I am glad I'm off their radar, tucked away in Fernanda's home as I am.

If I wasn't in this mess, though, I wouldn't have met the guys. I miss them terribly, but it is better this way. I'm not used to people this entwined in my life. Santos, Cruz and Rafael lodged themselves in my heart, so I knew I had to get out of there. Moving around all the time growing up made me hardwired for flight, rather than fight.

When it became clear that the Kalku will never stop coming after me, I decided it was time to cut and run. It's the only way to keep the Kalku from taking the guys down in their attempt to capture me.

I just didn't expect it to hurt this much.

It's good that I'm away from them, painful as it is. I don't want to be the one to invite danger into their lives. The Kalku are after me, and they are not going to stop. I am Máximo's daughter. The more I distance myself from them, the safer they will be.

I wonder if Rafael is back at the village, or if he is out in the world, trying to find a real girlfriend who will love him for the amazing goofball he is.

I wonder if Cruz thinks I'm angry with him, or if he even cares. I very much doubt my opinion of him registers in the slightest. He should have told me sooner about my parentage, yes, but I don't hate him for it. There are many reasons to loathe Cruz, but right now, none of them seem all that important.

Everything is secondary to the heartbreak that is finding out my father is the king of all the bad guys, and third to the pain of missing the guys.

I try not to wonder about Santos. I touch my lips and still recall the taste of his kiss as I stare at the unpainted wooden walls of the bungalow.

I shouldn't have run out on him with no explanation. Of all of them, he's the one I should have stayed for.

But I didn't. I ran away.

It's for the best. If I had stayed, that would be selfish. I would be leading the Kalku straight for the guys. I am too infatuated with Santos to let him come to harm.

When faced with the impossibility of my parentage, I had two choices: act or accept. I didn't know what to do, so I ran from the whole thing, hiding out here, where nothing and no one can chase me down.

I can sink quite nicely into my denial out here, where Fernanda knows nothing of the demons that haunt me.

I shake my head at myself and stand from the bed.

Santos will move on, and so will I.

Even if this is the seventh day in a row I tell myself this mantra, one day, it will be true. As it stands right now, I miss Santos horribly.

I flit down the steps, doing my best not to make the wood creak. I don't like waking up Fernanda, but it's hard to tell when she's home and when she's not. Being a nurse, her hours are sometimes graveyard and sometimes during the day. It's cruel, switching a person's schedule so drastically all the time like that.

We drank tea together yesterday and had a good gripe about the system that undervalues her, when she is clearly amazing.

Taking in a stranger without hesitation puts Fernanda on the shortlist for sainthood in my book. She hasn't pressed me to spill more information than I am ready to divulge, and in return, I have been looking for work in her area, so I'm not a burden.

Fernanda insists that she has been looking for a roommate, but I'm certain she was envisioning a roommate who could chip in for rent.

After a shower and a quick breakfast, I head out down the street and make my way into town. Sure, there's a bus that could take me, but I have a thing about busses.

After watching my mama die in the bus crash I narrowly escaped from, I'm okay with being a little superstitious and taking the long road.

Fernanda loaned me some of her clothes she doesn't wear anymore, so I have three whole outfits. I like to think the baby blue t-shirt and the slightly loose jeans are the business suit I would normally wear when applying for jobs. But as I am applying for things outside of my normal field, the pretending might not be necessary.

If the Kalku or Máximo are still hunting for me, they might look for me in mental health facilities, where I could use my hard-won degree.

I can still listen to people and build them up while bagging their groceries. I'm sure I can make that happen. I need to connect with people that I can also keep at a distance. Connect and release, connect and release.

That was the problem, living with the guys: each time there was a connection, they stuck deeper in the unfeeling crevices of my heart. I couldn't release them as easily.

I fill out an application at the first grocery store I come to, giving them a fake name, Fernanda's phone number and address. I make it to four stores before I realize I've wandered perhaps too far from Fernanda's home, so I turn back around.

It's hard to keep my mind from wandering back to the

guys. It doesn't matter how much I miss them, or even if I regret leaving. I couldn't find them if I tried. I vaguely know where the Cáceres tribe was located. I never drove there myself, and the details are lost in the fuzziness of an endless series of road trips, where all the streets sort of blend together in your mind.

My chest aches to be near Santos.

No. This is better. I shouldn't be with them. The Kalku are trying to find me. Máximo wants me brought to his island. I'm... it's safer for them to be away from me. I love them enough to distance myself so they don't live a life hunted.

My footsteps quicken. Even though it's barely noon, and the small town streets are not at all sketchy, anxiety has been bred into me over these past several weeks. The phantom feeling of being watched creeps up my spine. Though my head darts around, confirming no one cares that I'm here, I still feel the danger.

By the time I reach Fernanda's home, I'm out of breath and scared of my own shadow. I lock the door behind me, leaning against it as my chest heaves.

This didn't used to be me.

I'm a therapist who likes to knit. I live alone and feed stray cats that wander into the alley.

After a few beats, I gather enough of my bearings to breathe without panic.

I can still be me. I can still do the things I love.

Fernanda left her laptop for me, in case I wanted to apply for things online. I was wary to leave any sort of digital footprint at first, but the more I think about it, the less concerned I am with someone tracking me down online. The Kalku live in caves and Máximo lives on an island. The only thing I've seen the guys use their phones for is actual phone calls and texting.

A niggling thought itches the back of my brain: the Kalku put a tracker in my phone once, so they're more computer adept than your average caveman.

I ignore the hesitation in my gut and assume I can apply for jobs online without anyone tracking me down.

And I know exactly where I want to apply.

Therapy online isn't the same as meeting with someone in person, but it fulfills that need inside of me to listen to a person's journey and help them figure out which foot they want to put down in the sand to start out on a new direction. It makes me come alive to help a person find their path.

My smile comes naturally as I fill out applications to a few different online therapy support sites. I even counsel a few of their dummy patients, so they can see what sort of life advice I give in order to further vet my skills.

The three-day wait time is apparently just a formality, because the very next day, I have a job offer that I happily accept.

"I've never seen someone so happy to get a job before. Good for you, girl!" Fernanda applauds me as she finishes her coffee, her umber skin beautiful when framed by the light coming in from the kitchen window. Her home is bright, just like her personality. The cheery buttercup yellow walls add to my happiness.

I try to keep my tears demure, but they come in spluttery gusts because I am so relieved to be back in my element. "Thanks. Feels like a weight has been lifted off my shoulders."

Fernanda tilts her head to the side, her black hair pulled in a bun to reveal a slight smile. "It's a whole new life, Adelita." She rinses out her coffee mug and sets it in the sink, blowing me a kiss before she leaves. "Working a double today, but fair warning: I'm waking you up when I get home so I can hear all about your first day on the job."

"Deal." After Fernanda leaves, I scrub the tears from my

face as best I can. My work day starts in half an hour, and I'd like to get all the chores done first. I start with the dishes, then I shine the sink. Even though I've vacuumed every day I've been here, I figure another time is just good practice. I don't mind dusting again, either, since Fernanda goes wild when things are perfectly cleaned. It's the little things I try to do to pay her back for her kindness.

When it's time to meet my first patient, I couldn't be more excited. I bounce in my seat as I turn on the laptop and sign in to the portal, trying to look professional and not overly giddy at being back at work, however remotely. My long inky hair is swept into a bun, and I smooth out any wrinkles from my black t-shirt. Fernanda let me borrow a scarf of hers, which I think makes the whole getup look stylishly casual instead of just casual. I want my patients to know I'm showing up for them. I care about them. I showered for them.

They matter.

The countdown starts, and I straighten my posture.

When the feed connects, my very first patient comes into view.

Her shoulder-length curls spills down on the left side of her visage, giving me a blast of her high cheekbones and quizzical face.

My stomach hollows out as my eyes widen. I grip the sides of the laptop with sudden angst. "Eva?"

Cruz's sister, the eldest daughter of the chief of the Cáceres tribe, looks at me with worry lining her pretty eyes. "Adelita, thank goodness. I've been searching for you for a week!"

Continue the journey and read *Twisted Hearts* today!

ABOUT THE AUTHOR

USA Today bestselling author Mary E. Twomey lives in Michigan with her three adorable children. She enjoys reading, writing, vegetarian cooking, and telling her children fantastic stories about wombats.

While she loves writing fantasy, dystopian, and paranormal tales for her readers, Mary also writes romance under the name Tuesday Embers.

Visit her online at www.maryetwomey.com, and sign up for her newsletter, so you never miss a new release.

9 781088 177600